THE *Erotic* REVIEW

BEDSIDE COMPANION

The right of the contributors to be identified as the Authors of this
Work has been asserted by them in accordance with the Copyright, Designs
and Patents Act 1988.

First published in 2000
by HEADLINE BOOK PUBLISHING

2 4 6 8 10 9 7 5 3 1

British Library Cataloguing in Publication Data

Erotic review beside companion
1. Erotica – Literary collections 2. Erotic stories
I. Pelling, Rowan
808.8'03538

ISBN 0 7472 3597 X

Designed by Essential Books

Printed and bound by
Mackays of Chatham plc, Chatham, Kent

HEADLINE BOOK PUBLISHING
A division of Hodder Headline
338 Euston Road
London NW1 3BH

www.headline.co.uk
www.hodderheadline.com

THE *Erotic* REVIEW

BEDSIDE COMPANION

Edited with an introduction by
Rowan Pelling

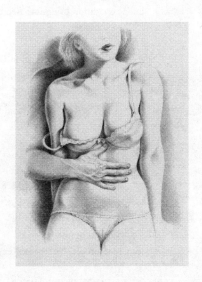

HEADLINE

ACKNOWLEDGEMENTS

It would be remiss of me not to thank some of the people who have strayed beyond the bounds of public decency in their support for the *Erotic Review*. Without them, the magazine would have shot its bolt and wilted into obscurity. So, special thanks to Auberon Waugh, Andrew Edmunds and Mandana Ruane for the nurture we have found at the Academy Club, to my publishers, James Maclean and Tim Hobart, for letting me put out a magazine which looked at times as if it might land them in the dock of the Old Bailey, to the many writers who have received no payment other than the odd filthy print and the occasional dirty lunch, and to my staff, who never tire of asking me as I sit at my desk, 'Mind if I rummage through your drawers?'

R.P.

CONTENTS

INTRODUCTION

*T*he *Erotic Review* was established as a literary magazine for unreconstructed pleasure-seekers. It will appeal to anyone who wishes with all their heart that the vast breast-like structure in Greenwich had been built by Kubla Khan as a stately pleasure dome.

The following legend adorned the front cover of the *Erotic Review*'s launch edition: 'The erotic is what you do with a feather; the perverse involves the whole bird.'

It has since become the office motto for the magazine's staff. As with any good aphorism, there is a world of meaning behind its *bijou* packaging of words. It reminds us that the erotic, at its finest exposition, is a tease, that the tickling of a feather can keep a victim in a frenzy of anticipation without ever releasing the prisoner to the blessed relief of orgasm. The evanescence of a feather evokes the subtle nature of eroticism, with its instant appeal to the mind before it triggers a response in the groin (unlike the hardcore stuff, where the appeal to the groin is instantaneous). And the fact that feathers are used to induce laughter is a timely reminder that the British have always liked their sexual inclinations to be tinged with humour. The French may have given the world de Sade and S&M, but the British have always excelled at the art of bawdiness. There's a fine tradition of laughing at the idiots sex makes of us all that runs from Chaucer's *Canterbury Tales*, through Fielding's *Tom Jones*, to *Carry On* films and West End bedroom farce. And it's a fact that of all the lonely hearts ever placed in *Private Eye*'s small ads, the one that received the most responses described its lady petitioner as 'a woman who likes laughing in bed'.

Laughing at the comedy of sexual manners is a tradition that the *Erotic Review* has been happy to run with: a hefty sprinkling of stories and articles in this compendium are humorous. Toby Litt's story, 'DaDa', about a Scandinavian pop band's frenzied night of wife-swapping will do nothing for the dirty mac brigade but may well erode your funny bone, while Barry Humphries's kind loan of an extract from Sir Les Patterson's journals is more scabrous than sensual. But that is not to say that there's not plenty here to get your vital juices flowing. Christine Pountney's tale of a teenage girl who deploys her naked body as a sushi bar for Japanese businessmen, Alan Jenkins's poem of overripe fruits and sexual appetites and Christopher Hart's priapic tale of a sage's pilgrimage to the Aphrodisia at Paphos are just three stories which reduced the magazine's sub-editors to sweat-drenched, cross-legged wretches.

Working on the *Erotic Review* is something of a health hazard. Our daily post-bag is stuffed full of the most febrile outpourings of our readers', writers' and illustrators' imaginations. It seems as though almost everyone has something to hide in their sock drawer. Sometimes the material is sublime, and sometimes it's utterly ridiculous ('Roland eased his space-ship into earth orbit and relaxed', springs to mind); occasionally it makes our eyeballs swivel. And if someone else were editing the magazine, they would, no doubt, reverse some of my judgements. But that's the whole point about the erotic: one person's wet dream is another's dry-thighed nightmare. I can only say that the stories in this volume did it for me and my editorial staff, and we're a pretty diverse lot, ranging from an ex-RAF pilot turned arts editor and film critic, to Dorian Gray's doppelganger, to an Art History graduate who used to manage a lingerie shop.

In fact, it's true to say that no one on the *Erotic Review* (myself included) began with any qualifications for their job, since the magazine wasn't initially conceived as a commercial enterprise. The *Review*'s roots are in an eight-page foolscap journal set up as a newsletter for members of the Erotic Print Society, an enterprise that sells fine-art erotic prints and books. The editor of this fledgling magazine, James Maclean, handed over the reins to me when he lured me into joining his erotic empire. I was amazed at how keen a response there was to such a slim, esoteric and downright filthy publication. The post brought ever increasing amounts of unsolicited manuscripts and poems; more surprisingly it also bought unsolicited cheques from readers, worried that we couldn't sustain the magazine without charging for it.

This extraordinary response made me wonder if there was a wider readership for our own particular brand of literate smut. I suspected that the mad tumble of rival 'lifestyle' magazines' attempts to increase circulation by suggesting sex was a sport for which you could train, and even win, left many people cold. There was agony and ecstasy long before there was Dr Ruth, so it seemed logical to conclude that there were rafts of people able to have highly charged erotic liaisons without the aid of an instruction manual. Perhaps such seasoned lovers would prefer a flight of the imagination from time to time? The *Erotic Review* seemed the perfect vehicle for their fantasies.

I rooted all over for new writers and found them in the most unexpected quarters: a barrister amused by court cases involving exotic sexual practice; a Cambridge classics tutor entranced by the excesses of the Roman emperors;

an art-gallery owner from Norwich with a talent for conjuring up the sex lives of dead writers; a doctor in the West Country who collects chastity belts. And then there were established writers like Michael Bywater, Stephen Bayley and Jonathon Green, who wrote for the sheer hell of it, for the chance to go off-leash and say whatever they damn well pleased.

These roués were accompanied, as roués so frequently are, by a flood of talented women; Lizzie Speller, Clare Naylor, Angelica Jacob and Lilian Pizzichini became *Review* regulars. And then there was the writer whose name we never knew: the hilarious, elegant and depraved letters we titled 'Misdirected Male' were signed with an oblique 'R.H.'. When we wrote to the address R.H. had given, the letter was returned marked 'no such address'.

When, in December 1997, we launched the magazine in its new incarnation – sixteen pages on glossy white paper, available via mail order or selected branches of Waterstones, price £1 – it was successful beyond our wildest imaginings. Our first print run sold out. We printed again, and our circulation leapt from 4,000 to 20,000 overnight. In the three years since then it has continued to grow in size and frequency (we now sell 30,000 copies), and it has become as appreciated for the skill of its erotic illustrations as for its writing: Martin Rowson, Stephen Appleby, Michael Heath and Sylvie Jones are all regular contributors. The *Review* has even boasted sketches of enormous depravity from the pads of the artist Damien Hirst and the non-artist and putative Tory MP Boris Johnson.

Recent issues of the *Erotic Review* may be more sophisticated than its earliest incarnation, but the magazine remains unchanged in its motivating spirit: it is a romp through some of the chambers, both homely and baroque, that make human sexuality so endlessly fascinating – and if it occasionally flies off at a tangent (an article on the erotic appeal of quality stationery springs to mind), so much the better. It never pays to be prescriptive about sex. But if you are still unclear about the character of the *Erotic Review*, here are the thoughts of a gentleman from *The Times* (April 2000) who spent several days in the office while researching an article: 'The flavour of the magazine is wistful, retro and elitist (none of which I regard as a dirty word) without descending to moralising, reaction or snobbery . . .'

This volume presents, for the first time, some of the finest writing of the *Erotic Review* to a wider audience, and includes a raft of new work commissioned specially for the book. I hope that it gives you some idea of the pleasure we've had in putting the magazine together. I also hope it makes you moist as a sea-sponge and steamy as a Turkish bath. Failing that, I hope it makes you laugh until you come.

Rowan Pelling
August 2000

PART 1

At First Sight

SETTING OUT

Anna Chancellor

*T*he strain of urban life, parking and talking endless rubbish has become too much. Peace is required, and solitude in equal measure. I board a train, enter my personal couchette and travel in an exhausted, dreamlike haze through cities of smog and noise, through black nights, with only the mechanical noises of the train for company. The morning breaks, with views of soft valleys and liquid light; the train ploughs on up hills,regardless of the heavy storm which now breaks; rain thunders on the window obscuring the view. Only heavy ancient trees are visible. As the night again descends, I reach my destination.

I have decided to spend my days in a monastic retreat – medieval, cloistered and severe. Through the relentlessly pouring rain, I am led, soaking, to an ancient fortress built on huge boulders, by a nun of the strictest order. Inside the huge oak door, bolted and locked behind me, I am relieved of all my clothes and possessions; young novices hand me a white linen sheath dress and rope shoes, and tie back my hair. With no food or water, I am led through candlelit corridors up a worn stone staircase and into a cell, cold and lonely and starving. The Mother Superior tells me prayers will be at 5.30 a.m. With no mention of food, she locks the door behind her. I lie on my bed, deafened by the rumbling of my stomach. I can see the moon glinting through the rain. Through the sound of my hunger and the torrential water, I hear the accordion drifting up from the valley below. I open the windows and I hear not only music but screaming laughter. I stand on the window-sill, glance back at the bolted door and jump. Clambering through vines and branches, I land on the rocks, falling on to the path below. Then I start running towards the lights, galumphing down the road in my sodden rope shoes and torn dress.

I reach the source of the music, which is coming from a small inn. I carefully open the door. Everything stops except the roaring fire in the grate. A sea of faces stare back at mine. I recognise the novices but they are now beautiful French girls, with slicked hair and painted glittered faces. There are men of all ages, dogs lolling by the fire and, at the centre of it all, Jean Gabin is playing the piano. When he sees me, he roars with delight, leaps on the piano and shouts, 'She's arrived.' The accordion starts again; the French beauties drag me to a piano, bringing plates of steaming, delicious food and hot wine. Then Gabin and I start playing and singing together beautiful French songs in total unison. I cast a shy glance at Gabin, a small, stocky man who takes up my entire vision. I laugh – the sort of laugh that contorts my face, pulling it in all directions; Gabin raises a masculine eyebrow and plunges deeper into the music.

The girls dance. We stand on the piano, playing it with our feet. The mood changes as Gabin lifts me off the piano with his huge hands. His wonderful face holds my gaze as we dance slowly round the room, the girls sing and the accordion plays.

'The Journey Has Just Begun.'

And he whispers to me. 'It's time to catch the train again . . .'

But, this time, the couchette will be a double.

GAT-TOOTHED WAS SHE

Alain de Botton

*L*overs in the early throes of passion are occasionally tempted to play a dangerous game. In the dead of night, with their heads resting close together on the same pillow, one of them may whisper to the other playfully, 'Why do you find me attractive?'

The answer is likely to be surprising, even appalling for a woman, for if a male lover is being honest, she risks discovering that what he finds sexually attractive is far from the psychological and physical qualities she most values in herself. Indeed, she could be shocked to discover that the real reason her lover finds her adorable and arousing is because she has a little mole on her chin, or because she can't quite pronounce her S's properly, because she's incurably shy when talking to sales assistants in shops, because she owns an ugly pair of pyjamas with an elephant pattern on them which she wears when she's feeling ill, or because she's always afraid that the aeroplane she's flying in will not make it to the ground in one piece.

Are these not peculiar reasons for one person to lust after another? One would expect that physical deformities, ugly clothes and unfortunate traits would be tolerated, but for these to form the basis of one person's enthusiasm for another appears to belong to the realms of psychopathology.

And yet, if one looks into the reasons why men love women, one will always find – at the kernel of the passion – a collection of these most peculiar details and irregularities. For the woman proud of her intelligence, perfect skin, confidence or psychological health, here is another painful lesson in the perversities of men. But for the woman ashamed of her mole, pyjamas, shyness and phobias, it is simultaneously a reason for extraordinary relief and comfort.

My love for Claire began on a train between Edinburgh and London, though she could not at first have known the turmoil she'd inspired. She sat with her legs crossed on the opposite bench, flipping through a company report, occasionally entering digits into a pocket calculator, unaware of a peculiar-looking character pretending to read a copy of *Vogue* (abandoned by a passenger who had alighted in Newcastle) and staring at her with a stunned, almost imbecilic expression of boundless longing. Short brown hair, wonky teeth, pale skin, blue-grey eyes, glasses, a cashmere cardigan with a small stain of what might have been lunch's macaroni. Somewhere south of Manchester, in a narrow valley filled with sheep, the angel was stirred from her work by a drinks trolley, navigated by a man identified by his name-tag as Roger, from whom she courteously bought a carton of apple juice, having initially requested orange but been told it had run out in Yorkshire. Already the prying maniac had thought of marriage, a house in a cherry tree-lined street, Sunday evenings where he would take off her glasses, she would lay her head beside his and he would comb her chestnut strands and at long last know contentment. In light of this project, it was perhaps fortunate that the angel's straw refused to follow its designer's intentions, and that after three unsuccessful stabs at the foil, the young woman leant across and said, 'Oh fuck, can you have a go?' handing over the apple carton with the most enchanting smile the tongue-tied suitor felt he had ever seen.

What was most striking about the birth of my desire for Claire was that it focused at once on the imperfections: the glasses, the crooked teeth, the stained cardigan – and these details continued to play a central part in my enthusiasm for her, even after I had been introduced to her other qualities.

Of course, as far as Claire was concerned, the gap between her teeth was the cause of much embarrassment and restrained smiles, and she repeatedly spoke of paying a good orthodontist to correct this damaging imperfection. But the paradox for those who believe that desire must immediately and necessarily collect around great beauty, character or intelligence, was that such irregularities provided the anchor of my sexual feelings for her. My desire stubbornly decided to collect there rather than around her warm smile, perfect figure or intelligent conversation. I didn't see the gap as an offensive deviation from an ideal arrangement, but as an original and most love-worthy redefinition of dental perfection. When I discussed my attraction with friends, I naturally mentioned the more respectable reasons – but to myself at least, I could not disguise that I had fallen in lust with nothing less than a gap between two front teeth.

Why do men often find something attractive in the awkward features of a woman's body or psychology, in precisely those areas where the woman herself would never expect to be appreciated and might even be embarrassed? One explanation is that men desire intimacy with the women they are attracted to, and that an indispensable part of being intimate is for a woman to reveal her vulnerabilities. And it is because these small irregularities in a woman are a sign of her vulnerability and therefore a promise of intimacy that they become attractive and are so highly valued. The gappy teeth, moles, scars, strange mispronunciations or ugly pyjamas are gateways to a more private person; they are the unusual but indispensable gateways to a woman's soul.

THE GREEK GIRL

Christine Pountney

*E*very night at half past midnight, Ariadne's father would leave her to lock up the restaurant. Just before he'd leave, however, he'd take out the bottle of four-star Metaxa he kept hidden behind the bar and pour himself a shot. Then he'd invariably remind his daughter to lay a clean dishtowel over the salted slices of aubergine and weigh them down with a small barrel of olives.

'I know, I know, baba,' she'd say, ruffling his hair. Then he'd reach up and pull her head towards him, kiss her sweet-smelling forehead and sigh at how much she reminded him of her mother.

'The most beautiful woman on the island of Paros,' he'd say and sigh as he flipped the OPEN sign to CLOSED and ambled out the door and down the hill towards the small apartment that he and his daughter had shared since his wife died seven years ago. Although Ariadne had indeed begun to blossom into a beautiful young woman, she lived in the shadow of her mother's reputed beauty. She was oppressed by her father's constant comparisons and felt somehow that she fell short of her mother's mark. Ariadne was in that paradoxical position of possessing an indisputable amount of beauty, so indisputable that nobody felt the need to tell her because of how apparent it was.

It was as a result of this accidental silence on the part of others that she doubted herself, and craved to be told she was beautiful by somebody other than her father. Not yet nineteen, the boys she knew, the ones who weren't intimidated by her looks, only wanted to stick their tongues in her ear during the slow dances at school, but never once did any of them whisper how beautiful she was. If only they knew how slavishly she would abandon herself to the first man who told her.

Ariadne went into the kitchen and began clearing up. She stood at the sink and ran the hot water. For some time now, a man had been appearing in the alley, standing in the doorway of the building across the way, smoking cigarettes and watching her through the kitchen window. If she looked directly at him for long enough, he would leave. He was always gone when it became time for her to lock up, and she never saw him arrive; it was as if he appeared out of thin air. But because of the oddly respectful distance he kept while spying on her, she didn't feel threatened but instead rather intrigued.

After a few weeks, she grew accustomed to his presence at night and felt strangely comforted by it, as if they were engaged in some kind of silent complicity. And yet, if Ariadne even gestured for him to come in, he would leave. It was when she ignored him that he seemed to move closer to the window. She realised that she knew nothing about him, but she liked his private manner, his timid voyeurism, and decided to trust him.

On one particularly chilly night, she placed a steaming cup of coffee on the back stoop and when she wasn't looking, he took it. When she finished her chores and opened the back door to put out the garbage, the empty cup was there and the man was gone. The following evening, she put out a plate of warm moussaka. This time the man left the plate on the window-sill, licked clean.

Ariadne started to long for the man when he wasn't around. She felt lonely when he wasn't there. She pined for him and her heart leapt when she saw the flare of his lighter and the dark outline of his shoulders. She grew so accustomed to his gaze that she invented games to play with him. She mimicked her own death by strangulation, using her own arm, half hidden behind the vertical edge of the window. She stabbed herself several times and died long, stretched-out deaths, bleeding into the kitchen sink. Sometimes she would put the radio on and dance herself into a sweaty frenzy, helping herself to her father's Greek brandy along the way. Giddy and dizzy, she'd stop when she was out of breath, put a hand to her neck and feel surprised to find herself alone, to find that the man wasn't actually there in the kitchen with her.

The closer she felt to him, the more curious she became. She wondered what he was waiting for, and the more she toyed with the possibility that he wanted her for sex, the more arousing his presence became, until the mere thought of him standing out there alone in the dark alleyway, watching her move around the kitchen, made her faint with desire. She seemed suspended in a perpetual state of sexual arousal.

She became distracted, almost clumsy in the kitchen, and one night she tripped while carrying one of the large flat trays of baklava out of the pantry. Half the pastry landed on the floor and the other half was strewn across the large oak chopping block that stood in the centre of the kitchen. She looked down at the gooey mess, took off her shoes and socks and tucked her skirt into the hem of her underwear, then got down on her hands and knees and started scraping the sticky pastry off the floor with a rubber spatula. She giggled when the honey, dripping off the chopping block, got into her hair.

The window was slightly open. Ariadne had got into the habit of leaving it open, and while she was kneeling on the floor, she could sense the man coming closer. She heard the window rattle as he nudged it open a little wider, she traced her fingers in the honey and tasted it. Suddenly she had the impulse to spread the honey on her face, her neck and chest. She covered her hands in the golden syrup, rubbing the honey on her thighs and stomach, spreading her legs and leaning forward. With both hands she pushed her hair back and held her breath, then strained to listen. She could hear him exhale. She hesitated for a moment, then swung around, determined to face him. But when she did, he was gone. She rushed to the window and looked out. The alley was empty, but he had left the smouldering end of a cigarette on the sill. Although she didn't smoke, she brought it to her lips and took a drag.

One night Ariadne decided it was time they went on a date. She brought a change of clothes to work and, after her father had left and her chores had been hastily finished, she started to undress at the kitchen sink. She removed her apron, took off her white blouse and black skirt, and adjusted the taps so she had a good stream of warm water. She took a sponge out of her bag and a bar of rosemary-scented soap. She opened the window wide and stood exposed to the cool night air. She could see the dark shape of her man skulking in the shadows. She unhooked her bra and pulled her underwear down and began to wash herself slowly, letting the soapy rivulets trickle over her breasts and down her legs, then pool around her feet. She bent forward and poured water on to the back of her neck, letting it race forward, tracing the contours of her face. When she was done, she dried herself with a towel which she had brought from home.

She turned her back to the window and took some fresh clothes out of her bag, then placed them on the oak table. She pulled on a black silk garter belt, then slipped her arms through the straps of a black lace bra and fastened it at the back. Raising a foot and balancing her toes on the edge of the chopping block, she unravelled a silk stocking along the whole length of her slender leg and snapped it into the clasps of her suspender belt. She pulled the other one on, then slipped into a brand-new pair of black silk panties. She opened a pocket mirror and traced her lips with a blood-red pencil, then filled them in with scarlet lipstick; she brushed out her long jet-black hair, then stepped into a black silk evening dress, struggling slightly to zip it up on her own. She went to the cupboard and took out some candles, lit them, and turned out the lights.

She took a bottle of wine out of the cupboard and put two glasses on the table. She poured the wine and took a long sip. Keeping her back to the window, she waited. After a while she said, 'I know you're there. Tell me your name.'

There was long pause. Then she heard the man whisper in a throaty voice, 'My God, you are so beautiful.'

'Do you really think so?' she asked

'The most beautiful woman I have ever seen.'

This made her flush and she wanted to swing around, but she didn't want to scare him off. Her sex was burning with heat, slippery and moist, ready to receive him. She had never been with a man before, but she was sure of this; she wanted him to deflower her. She stood with her back to him.

'I can feel it when you're near me,' she said. 'I don't need to see you. I won't turn around. I won't force you. I just want to feel you. Will you take me, please? I want you so badly. The door's unlocked. Please come in.'

Ariadne stood frozen to the spot. She was breathing fast, her heart pounding in her chest. She heard the door open and almost moaned in anticipation. She gripped the edge of the table when she sensed him enter the room. He came up behind her and ran his hands slowly from her shoulders down to her elbows. He was trembling too, but his grip was firm. His hands were warm and soft. He nuzzled his face into her hair and breathed in the scent of it, then drew it aside and kissed her neck. Then he unzipped her dress and let it fall to the floor. He unclipped her bra and Ariadne quickly pulled her arms through it. He pulled her panties down and ran his hands up her legs and hips.

'*Beautiful,*' he kept saying, over and over. Ariadne arched her back and pushed herself into him. In unison, their bodies pressed against each other, and they both bent forward. He wrapped one arm around her waist and ran his hand across her pubic hair, sending shockwaves through her body. Her knees felt weak and she swayed uncontrollably. He kissed the nape of her neck, then traced each shoulder blade with his tongue. She felt the moisture of his lips, his hot saliva, more of it, dripping on her and then she realised that he was crying. His tears were hitting her skin like diamonds, little chips of crystal.

'What's wrong, my love?'

'I can't,' he said.

'Why not?

'I'm impotent,' he said. 'I'm so sorry.' He took a step back and dropped his hands to his sides.

Ariadne didn't care. There was so much more they could do. She was a virgin, she could remain a virgin for years and still they'd make love. They would make love all over the city. She didn't care. She was consumed with a perfect love for this stranger. She had no doubt. She knew what to do. She leant forward for a moment against the chopping block, took a deep breath, straightened up and turned around. But it was too late; he was already gone.

FIRST BASE

India Knight

*O*ne of the joys of hurtling towards one's sexual prime with barely contained anticipation – it happens at thirty-six for women, I'm told – is that, by this ripeish age, one has tried most things one wants to try. Unless you're very timid or very sheltered, there is none of that frenzy of curiosity that comes with being, say, twenty-three. It's a relief, because the feeling that you simply have to experiment in case you're missing out on something quite fabulous can be exhausting, not to mention time-consuming: if you're spending half your waking hours wondering whether you are sexually naïve, and are forever seeking opportunities to have a threesome/wear rubber underwear/do it on a train/get spanked, just in case you like it, the greater picture gets somewhat obscured.

There are no such constraints as one grows older. The pursuit of the above, rather puerile, notions of sexual sophistication (my girlfriends and I used to compile great long lists and tick things off with a triumphant, grotesquely competitive 'Done that') that hung, albatross-like, around one's neck for decades on end is over. You can concentrate on the important things, the things that make life worth living, the things you'd pretty much die for. Like kissing.

What really astonishes me, what I can barely believe, in fact, is that I never really cottoned on to kissing until recently. I was kissed, of course, and did some comprehensive kissing myself, but the act was never much more than a prelude: an evocative foretaste of what was to come, but never a violent pleasure in its own right. It was nice, and I liked it, but I never did it for much more than about ten minutes at a time – fifteen at a push – and it never made me think I was going to faint. Kissing was what you did before you went to bed with someone.

(None the less, when I was studying Dante at university, I'd ignore Paradise and Purgatory and came back compulsively to half a dozen lines in Hell, to the hypnotic bit about Paolo and Francesca: she is telling her story, which climaxes with the line '*La bocca mi baccio, tutto tremante*' ('He kissed me on the mouth, all a-tremble'). Well versed, by this stage, in the Nancy Friday oeuvre, not to mention a then boyfriend's obsession with pornography, the line made me die every time I read it.

Kissing is the sexiest thing in the world; one immaculate, stellar kiss is worth a dozen fucks. What were my friends and I thinking of, with our lists, and scalp-collecting, and ideas, that swoon-inducing kissing was a figment of Messrs Mills and Boon's hackneyed imaginations?

And why, more to the point, have I only just realised this? Why have I spent decades – decades! – of my life being kissed by people who were such atrocious kissers? The thrusty in-out of drink-slackened tongues at teenage parties and, tragically, well beyond; the face-rubbing; the self-consciously 'good' kissers with their panoply of risible tricks, contorting mouths and tongues into, variously, impressions of butterflies and battering rams while wearing a look that managed to combine intense concentration with deep smugness . . . I mean, Jesus. What was that all about, and why did I never laugh out loud?

I don't think I was particularly unlucky, or that – horrors! – appalling kissers somehow made a beeline for me in the irritating way that stray dogs and tramps do. But kissing gets forgotten in the stampede southwards, particularly in youth. Men who pride themselves on their foreplay technique, for example, are, more often than not, crap kissers that remind you vaguely of amphibians. Men who are good in bed are often very mediocre kissers. People think they know how to kiss, that it's like talking or eating. It isn't.

We tolerate an absurd amount of bad kissing, settling for the averagely competent form – oh, here comes the tongue, hello, probe probe – when we should be demanding the kind that feels like an opiate. But real kissing, proper kissing, is the kind that makes you blush and then fall over in the street when you remember it ten minutes later. Kissing should be taught in schools, actually. It's so sweet, and so dirty, and so violently erotic. It's amazing that mouths can do that, I always think: the endless variations, and the fact that a mouth which kisses a child goodnight can behave so wildly, freakishly differently minutes later. This is not true of breasts, or genitals, unless you count peeing (fwoar!) or breastfeeding, which I don't. No other organ is so endlessly, shockingly versatile, so public, so literally in your face.

I shan't embarrass the person who enlightened me on this whole subject. Suffice it to say that, when we first met, we kissed for four hours, fully clothed, on some steps, and that I thought my heart would stop every time we drew breath. I have shocking thoughts when I think of him, but more shocking ones still when I look at his mouth. Which I do, obviously, all the time. The state into which I am thrown might, perhaps, be described as 'sweet torture' by Barbara Cartland. And she might, perhaps, have a point.

THE SWEET CHEAT GONE

Christopher Peachment

I always know when I am being watched. How this should be so, I do not know. But I am always acutely aware of anyone who is behind me and is watching me. You never have to look into another's eyes to know whether their gaze is trained upon you. But someone behind you is a different matter altogether. I wish I could say that the hairs on the back of my neck stood on end. That at least would suggest I was in touch with that internal caveman which can still tell when there is a tiger lurking in the grass. But that is not what happens. What happens is not easily described. All I can say is that I feel a slight change of temper.

It was ten years ago on a Sunday afternoon in early summer when I was idly wandering through the lower rooms of Chiswick House. I was living alone at the time, and working hard in my profession, which was as an architectural draughtsman and historian. Weekends were therefore something of a torture. When I woke on Saturday it was always with a headache, which I put down to the stress of the week's work finally catching up with me. What I realise now is that it was more a sense of foreboding at the yawning gap of emptiness which was all that the next two days had to offer.

And so I filled my time by visiting the buildings I loved the best and those which had inspired me to become what I was. Of these, Chiswick House is my favourite. I was in one of the lower chambers, admiring a scale elevation of the southern façade by Colen Campbell. I now realise that I had heard light footsteps down the stone spiral staircase and the tiniest change in the atmospheric pressure as someone wafted in the room. There were shufflings of feet, the faint susurrations of someone breathing uneasily, and pauses between movement as they too studied the drawings. And from time to time, the distinct feeling that I was being glanced at.

Then finally a firm intake of breath, a more determined scuffle of feet, and the person left the room. The rattling clack of high heels on the stone flags told me that it was a woman. I moved through the door and caught a glimpse of someone disappearing down the corridor and into another room. Shoulder-length hair, which was medium brown but with a dusting of blonde in it. Definitely a woman. Then I thought no more about her.

Except that there was her perfume. It was no scent that I recognised, but carried the possibility that she might be foreign. Italian or French perhaps, for the smell was not so much of a perfume as of a warm woman. Only continental women know how to choose a scent which will complement their own natural smell. That is one reason why I no longer sleep with English women.

I wandered through the rest of the house, which was deserted. And in the distance, I saw a swirling hem of a skirt disappear through a door frame. I was beginning to take notice. More rooms, more glimpses, but it was not until an hour later, when I was walking through the grounds, that I saw her full-on for the first time. I was standing on the ornamental bridge, snapping a small twig into pieces and dropping them into the unruffled water of the lake below, when she suddenly swung into view around the end of the tree-lined path. She was tall, perhaps five foot ten in her heels, and carried herself well. Her skin was dark, and she had a Roman nose that sloped from her forehead with no bridge. Then I saw what she was wearing and my heart sank. She had on a blue, striped man's shirt, with the top button done up and the collar turned up, in the manner that was then fashionable among Sloane women.

I hate and despise Sloanes. Their whinnying laugh, their unconsidered cries of 'OK, yah' and their low sexual temperature. I quite liked the way they always gave a squeal when they came, but afterwards they would always go to the bathroom for an elaborate wash. Then they would prop up their teddy bear again, from where they had turned him to the wall so he wouldn't see what we were up to. And say, 'Gurr, you won't tell Mummy, will you? She'd go absolutely bonkers. Ooh, I could murder a cocoa.'

The woman walked behind me, her heels crunching the gravel. Then she was gone again, down through the gap in a tall hedgerow. She had not glanced back, she had not needed to, since she had seen enough of me on the bridge. I was faintly annoyed, but also relieved that she was one of the hated tribe. At least I could now ignore her and return to my weekend of boredom. I continued to wander the grounds and still caught glimpses of her in the distance. And slowly I was forced to admit to myself that I was still intrigued, and could not put her from my mind. This will go nowhere, I remember saying aloud to myself, yet still I wondered how to approach her. I went to the café in the grounds, but she was not there. I walked once, twice the full length of the formal grounds, but still she was not there. I even went around the house again, but no sign of her.

Good, I thought, at least I am spared the banalities of the chase. Her ridiculous opinions, her suspicious friends, her jealous brothers. The two weekends in Petersfield with her stockbroker father and her idle snob of a mother before I can decently break it off. She was nowhere to be seen and I was a fool for thinking that she had been looking at me. When I pushed the exit gate open and stepped on to the pavement, she was there.

I wish I could say that she was waiting for me, but her back was turned to me, and she was leaning on a metal guard fence, gazing across the road.

'Can I give you a lift back into town?' I said. If I had thought about speaking to her for more than about half a second I would never have done it, but seeing her there had surprised me. She straightened up to her full height and only then turned toward me, as if she could not move in more than one plane at a time. Her gaze was steady and cool, her response unflustered, and it was then that I knew that my first instincts had been right. She was definitely foreign.

'Dat would be very kind,' she said. From the accent, she was clearly Italian. And from her colouring, northern Italian. She looked at my car and said that it looked 'like a teapot'. And she laughed gently and said sorry, perhaps she had that wrong, it was really a very nice car.

'It's an old car, and so it has curves,' I said. 'They don't make them with curves any more.' This was at the time when all cars were composed of straight lines.

'Anything old is always better than anything new,' she said, and I nodded and knew immediately that we were on the same wavelength. On the way back into town we learnt about each other. Her name was Federica Zanco.

'You must be Venetian,' I said.

'Yes,' she said. 'You can tell from the zed in my name.'

She was an architecture student, which explained her presence at Chiswick House, but she had forgotten to bring her sketching equipment. We spent the journey discussing the baroque architecture of Venice, which I dislike although I did not tell her that. I dropped her off in St John's Wood, and, no, I couldn't come in, her temporary digs were too squalid, and yes, we could meet again for dinner next week.

Over dinner she showed me photos of her flat in Venice, of her grey-bearded father, who was a professor of architecture in Rome, and whom she adored, and of St Mary Woolnoth church in the City, which she was planning to study in detail. And the last photo in the pack was one of her naked, although she was sitting on the bed with her legs drawn up in front of her breasts and her arms hugging her knees. I turned it towards her, and she didn't smile or laugh or giggle or blush or any of the silly things that an English woman would have done. 'Ah,' she said. 'Me, naked.'

And then she simply took the photos from me and put them back in their envelope and got on with her Dover sole and I with my skate *au beurre noir*, and all I could think of for the rest of the evening was: Who took the photo?

'An Italian man would have asked who took that photo,' she said to me later outside her door.

'But I am English,' I said.

'Very,' she said, and leant over and kissed me. She tasted slightly bitter and smoky, and I couldn't breathe and felt I was drowning.

'Italian men are a joke,' I said.

'They are,' she said.

And, no, I still couldn't come in, the bed-sit was just too 'horrible'. It was my first inkling that something was wrong here, but I could not put my finger on it. So I rang an old girlfriend that I had been keeping on the backburner and went round to her place and, when I gave her a kiss in the hallway, I stroked my hand across her hip and she wasn't wearing any knickers, so I lifted up her skirt and I fucked her in the hallway, up against the hatstand, then pushed her gently towards the stairs and she nodded happily, and I stopped her on the bottom step and fucked her there, then she moved all the way up and I caught her ankle and fucked her on the very top step, then I wheeled her round the corner and bent her over the banister and fucked her like that for a bit, then hoicked one of her legs over the balustrade and fucked her from behind, and then we stopped and headed for her bedroom and I held her against the door jamb and kissed her hard and gripped her by the waist and fucked her there for a while, then we went in and she sat down on her low chair over by the window, and I came over and spread her legs and lifted them up so that they rested over the arms of the chair and I fucked her in that position, then she turned over and knelt on all fours on the chair and I fucked her like that, and then she complained her knees were giving out, so she lay back on the bed and I fucked her like that, then she had to break off to go the loo, so I followed her into the bathroom, and after she got up from the loo, she held on to the towel rail to steady herself and lifted one leg to rest on the loo seat, and I fucked her like that, then we climbed in the shower and got a bit soapy and I fucked her in there, then we climbed out and didn't bother to use towels because it was hot and so I fucked her while we were still wet, and then we went back to the bedroom, her towing me by my dick, me with my hand jammed up her bum, and she bent over the bed-end rail and I fucked her like that, then she said she was a bit fucking sore, so I fucked her in the bum for a while, then went for a wash because of germs and all that, came back in and fucked her in the mouth, then she pushed her breasts together and I fucked them, and then we tried her armpits but they were all stubbly from a recent shave and it was like doing sandpaper, so we went back to fucking doggy fashion, until she came for the third time, and try as I might, I could not come, so I faked it, and as we lay there afterwards, her genitals looking bruised, and me with a hard-on still that the cat could use as a scratching post, I said, 'While I was doing you doggy fashion there, who were you thinking of?'

'Elvis,' she said. 'And you?'

'Federica,' I said.

'Mmm, you have got it bad,' she said, and put her hand between her legs. 'Dry,' she said. 'You haven't come yet. Care for round two?' So we did that.

Federica rang me the following day. She had to go back to Venice unexpectedly. 'What about St Mary Woolnoth?' I said, although the unspoken question was: What about me? 'I will come back, sometime soon,' she said. And she gave me her phone number in Venice and said, 'Call me tomorrow.' She had already written her address down for me on a piece of paper; a number 96, in a *calle* on the Giudecca.

I rang the number the following day several times, but all I got was a pre-recorded message of an Italian operator telling me, with a hollow echo that spoke of the tomb, that I had misdialled, and to try again. I tried variations of the number that I had scribbled on an envelope, trying out different combinations in the belief that I might have taken it down wrongly.

The next day I went out to Heathrow, showed my credit card at the Alitalia desk, and only had to wait four hours for a flight to Venice. I took the *vaporetto* to the stop at San Giorgio Maggiore and walked the length of the Giudecca. It was pouring with rain and I had not brought my raincoat or umbrella. Eventually I found the right *calle*. The house numbers stopped at 75.

It was five years before I saw her again.

PART 2

Heavenly Bodies

A POEM INSPIRED BY A PAINTER

Ranjit Bolt

THE TURKISH BATH BY INGRES

This great *morass* of buttocks, breasts and thighs,
This cornucopia of female flesh,
Of lolling odalisques with almond eyes
Whose torpid, golden bodies intermesh

In one, ostensibly alluring mass
Induces in me a strange weariness
As if the sheer, ridiculous excess
Of nubile forms brought lust to an impasse.

Never before or since can such a sense
Of flagrantly erotic indolence
Have been conveyed in art. Having said that
One or two ladies seem a *tad* too fat

The keynotes of the canvas being, I guess,
Feminine *languor* and *voluptuousness*,
The risk is of our surfeiting on sex
But there lies Ingres' genius – he checks

His own, instinctive urge to titillate
And the result is something more tranquil –
He had been threatening to agitate
The viewer, whom he leaves, instead, quite still

And unperturbed the itch already gone
Without being scratched, and troublesome desires
Induced to quell themselves, like forest fires
We're briefly filled with lust, then left with none

And feeling, in the clear, calm aftermath,
That we could be there in that Turkish bath,
Buttock to buttock with them, thigh to thigh,
And not so much as blink a beady eye.

FULL

Anouchka Grose-Forester

I'll start with the belly just because it's so big, curving right out from under her tits and tucking neatly back in at the pelvis. The skin is smooth and tight, the tummy button flattened. From the side she looks like a big S. Her bottom is full and marshmallowy, just right for sinking the teeth into. (I have to be careful what I say here because she's a bit sensitive about being fat.) I reach for a handful at the top of her thighs and gently squeeze, admiring the flesh between my fingers, the silvery streams of stretched skin and fine golden hairs. And you should see her tits! The areolae dark brown, with nipples the size of hazelnuts, a complex system of bluish veins lurking below the surface. She wraps her arms around me and tries to hold me close but, frankly, the bump gets in the way. Either we kiss, and our hips are angled far apart, or we put our nethers together and stare from opposite ends of the pillow. It's a bit like being on a seesaw.

I ease her over on to her back, but on the way something twangs and she yelps. It takes minutes of gentle coaxing and rubbing the right spots to persuade her to like me again. I realise I'll have to start being more careful – one false move and she'll probably flatten me.

I explore the great dome, with its mysterious lumps and twitches, before sliding my hand between her legs, pausing to focus on the silky patch of skin at the tops of her inner thighs, the softest part of her body. She begins to stroke my hair, combing her nails over my scalp, down my neck and across my shoulders. I copy her, running my fingers through her springy fur and into her warm, damp crevice. The lips feel so tender and big I want to see them. I crawl down the mattress and, as she lifts and parts her knees, I watch the labia splay out like the end of a trumpet. It's easy to forget what it looks like down there when you haven't seen it for a while – so dark at the edges and so pink and fresh inside. I get lost in the details, the miniature frills, folds and crumples, the origami shapes interlocking and overlapping, the tiny opening on to blackness at the centre.

'What are you doing?' she asks, sounding genuinely puzzled. I realise that, from the other side of her stomach, she can't see me at all.

'Just looking,' I tell her.

I slip my finger into the little hole, feeling her muscles tighten as she pulls me in further. I wrap my thumb over her pubic bone and rock my hand backwards and forwards until her breathing changes and she lets out a sigh. I wonder whether it's time to risk another roll. I pull up alongside and help to lever her over. Everything goes smoothly and I mould myself in behind, her cushiony bottom squashed against my hips, my chest pressed into her back, my hand returning to where it was before.

I bite the back of her neck and feel her go limp like a kitten being carried. Soon she starts meowing and howling, and we both start sweating, our skins slithering together. She reaches back, grabs hold of a bunch of my hair and pulls. Her other nails dig hard into the front of my thigh. I'm afraid I might come before she does but she wails one last time and her body begins to convulse, sinking further and further back into mine with each spasm. Thought slips away and all I know is that I'm here, now, with her. Our bodies relax and she lifts my hand from between her legs and sticks the thumb into her mouth. Almost unconsciously she arranges the pillows to suit her new shape – one between the knees, the other wedged under the protrusion – and, still intertwined, we fall into a deep sleep.

MISHA

Angelica Jacob

*I*f I had to describe her, I would liken her to a body of water. Something that can be contained, but more often than not slips through your fingers, something in which you can float, but in which you can also drown.

It's late afternoon. The sun is setting and I can hear the distant hum of a motorboat crossing the harbour. Light swills through the window, then Misha opens the door and dumps her bag next to my desk. She walks to the bathroom. I anticipate the sound of the shower, glimpse her undressing as she pads backwards and forwards. She peels off her jumper, lets her skirt drift to the floor.

She tells me that it's been a long day, her shoulders are aching. She stands to the side of my desk, wraps her arms round my waist and kisses my neck. She's had to take a group of tourists to the hot-water springs on the west side of the island. Her skin smells of her work. It's a heavenly mixture of hot salt and sulphur. I smell this scent everywhere; on her clothes, inside our bed, on the cushions that lie scattered over the floor. No bottled perfume smells this sweet or this good, though for some reason, I like it better when she is bleeding. There's something incredibly sexy about the undertow of her body. Her smell changes texture. It's thicker, rougher; a rich compound of seaweed and blood.

Misha twists me round in the chair. She licks her lips, then makes me stand up and unbuckles my belt. The metal rattles and the leather uncurls like a snake. She throws the belt to the floor. I take the hint and we move through to the bathroom.

The mirror is misted and the air wet with steam. Misha steps into the shower and unravels her hair. When we first met, I told her how her hair reminded me of a river. It turned me on in ways I didn't quite understand. For instance, the way in which it hung down and brushed the small of her back. It had a tendency to flow and to stream. Small curls would unspool like thin rivulets and when she swam under water her hair would spread out like a red velvet cloak. It was both soft and alive. I liked to lie on my stomach while she dragged it over my shoulders and whipped me with it, over and over.

I rub Misha's back and lather up some soap. Her skin is hot and slippery. I think of the veins that run up her arms, the way they spread out at the wrist. They're like a river's vast estuary. If I were a boat I would want to sail in these waters. I would pack a compass and map, a supply of fast food, a thermos of whisky, then start by exploring the distant archipelagos and far-flung islands and atolls. I would float down each finger, chug through the aqueous halls of her brain, sail through the aortic channel, discover the caverns inside her heart. The ebb and the flow of each thunderous blood-pulse would push me deeper and deeper inside her. I would cross to the other side of her world, dive into the Dead Sea of her tears, lie on my back and later, much later, take shelter inside her lachrymal bones.

Misha turns round. The shower continues to pummel and pound. She lifts a bottle of oil off the ledge and pours a few drops into her hand. The oil slickens her skin. It's so soft and supple, and I think of a seal pup. She nudges her head against my neck, nuzzles my dry, slightly chapped lips. Her face is calm, almost sleepy. When I kiss her, I taste the remains of the salt. In winter they spread it over the roads. It's supposed to melt down the ice and turn it to slush. One kiss from Misha and my whole body pools over the tiles.

She lifts her leg and wraps it around the top of my thigh. She's a winter landscape. I press my head to her chest, listen to her slow groans that sound as though ice were cracking inside her. Her back is curved and white, granular as sugar, like the sweep of a wind as it blows over the Arctic. She curls her arms and bends further towards me. She knows that I want to make love, but instead sits on the lip of the tub and demands that I start washing her feet.

Misha's toes are ticklish. With their bright silver nails they remind me of minnows. I hook one and Misha squeals with delight. I nibble another and each toe squirms in my lap. When we emerge from the shower, Misha wraps a towel round me and leads me through to the bedroom. We pour two glasses of wine and slip under the cool linen sheets.

Her eyes flicker, her nostrils flare. The air she breathes out is the air I inhale. I run my hands down her sides and we lie face-to-face. Downstairs I can hear the drip of the shower and outside it has started to rain. Our bodies and the sound of the water mix and then merge. A dim half-light leaks through the window, tattooing wet shadows over her spine. Misha whispers strange things into my ear.

Her mouth is a storybook. She tells me tales of fantastic sea-creatures who live twenty leagues under the ocean. She tells me of sailors who murder their loved ones, then cut out their hearts and carry them wherever they go. On an island in the far north, the people use feathers as currency (or so Misha says), while another story involves a man who makes shoes out of the throats of black-headed seagulls.

I turn her on to her belly and trace some words over her skin with my tongue. I write the word 'love'. I write the word 'fuck', then lift my wine from the table and make a lake in the small of her back. I would like to skim stones over the surface. I would like to watch them as they skipped and then sank. Instead, I bend down and brew up a storm. I blow on the wine and it trickles between Misha's buttocks while she squirms with delight. I lap the wine up, and think of a dog crouching down over a puddle, slaking its thirst.

Misha flips over and straddles my belly. She arches her back and all of a sudden I see a salmon leaping into the air. Sunlight flashes over her shoulders. Her body is packed with steel; the shave of her collarbone is silvered and bright. She opens her legs and lets a small sigh escape from her mouth while my eyes slide down her belly and nestle in the friendly cave of her cunt.

Inside Misha is moist. She smells of rock pools and crystallised brine, and I have an overwhelming desire to lean down and kiss her, to feel her lips slowly part. They're soft as anemones, pinker than clams and I want to wade thigh-deep into that water, skinny-dip in the suck of those tides. Misha goes quiet. She's staring at me and I know it's a cliché, but her eyes *do* look like lakes. Imagine a blue stretching into infinity. Imagine a chiffony, sub-aqueous turquoise. Now imagine plunging into that water, the clean cut of the deeps, the glittering spray, the joy of moving in rhythm to the beat of those waves.

I flex my muscles and try to sit up, but instead Misha pushes a finger inside my mouth. She presses the nail into the gum-flesh and I feel like a fish that's been hooked and reeled in. No matter how hard I struggle, no matter which way I twist, I cannot break free. Her arm is a rod; she switches it this way and that. Misha is teasing me and though I hate to admit it, I enjoy being caught.

'I want to make love to you.'

'I know,' she says, then she blinks and rests her head on the pillow. She licks the tips of my fingers and round each of my wrists. She tucks her knees to her chest and curls up like a shrimp.

'Later?' I ask.

'Later,' she echoes.

Sleep is deep. We both drift off quickly. I only wish I could link her dreams to mine. As it is, I wander around like a soul in search of salvation. Nothing inside my dreams compares to her mystery, nothing contains her breadth or capacity. I watch a blue fish eating a cat. I notice an egg swallow a snake. A desert unravels before me; each grain of sand is cut like a diamond. They unfold as I walk over bright yellow dunes. Streams of it blow into my eyes. The sand catches my lashes and all of a sudden I stumble and fall. The sun beats down on my neck and I can feel my skin beginning to burn.

When I wake, it's pitch black, but I can feel Misha's breath on my cheek. Her eyes are rimmed with the richness of sleep. They're swimming with dreams and somewhere within them I see an oasis. It's a lush, green, fertile place and I want to kneel down and drink all of her in. I need to assuage my thirst, to take deep long gulps of her, feel her body slip down my throat. Instead, Misha stands up and begins to get dressed.

We're taking a walk by the harbour. It's eight o'clock and Misha has booked us a table at an exclusive hotel. She strides ahead while I look out towards the long wooden jetty. I stare at the waves, the bright coloured lights that jangle and sway in the breeze. Some water swills over my shoes and there's a tide-line of weed ruffled with seashells. After ten minutes Misha stops and slips her hand into mine. There's an old man sitting outside the Fish House, scaling cod and rock salmon with a broad silver knife. Misha exchanges small pleasantries. They talk about quotas, about the best way to skin herring and sea bream. A few of the scales catch on her dress and glitter like sequins. Then she tells me that the sand feels thicker than fudge. It's wormed its way into the dips of her knees; it's grinding down the soles of her feet, scratching her ankles and buffing her toenails. The sea flings itself against the high harbour wall and quickly we make our way to the hotel.

Inside, the restaurant is hushed. Waiters glide to and fro. There's the chink of cutlery, the tinkle of cut-crystal glassware and when we order our drinks Misha starts talking about something I mentioned two weeks ago. Her mind recalls everything: the gifts I have given her, the trips we have taken, our promises, even our arguments. She's like a reservoir, damming up every last word in case of emergencies; storing up names, places and dates. Nothing is ever wasted on Misha.

She says, 'Remember how you wanted to do something exciting?'

'I think so,' I say.

'Because I've got an idea.' She dives under the table to retrieve her napkin and when she bobs up again I ask what it is.

'Not yet,' she says.

'But soon?'

She smiles. 'You'll have to wait. But I promise it won't be that long.'

Seconds later our waiter returns and we order our food: moules marinière for Misha, seared fillet steak for me. I watch as she drinks, watch as she sips the sparkling water, the deep, blood-red wine. Sometimes I think her throat is a wishing-well. It's so long and deep. I've picked cherries and dropped them into her mouth, wishing to kiss her. I've fed her truffles and oysters, omelettes and sweetmeats, wishing to touch her. The food slips down her throat with the satisfying ease of a coin. In this way Misha is richer than oil. She fizzes like silver.

Our food arrives and with a decorous flick of the wrist Misha scoops the mussels out of their shells, then slips the soft, fishy flesh into her mouth. Her swallow is smooth and sleek. Think of a swan, think of the fish that slip down its throat. She dabs up the juice with a thick sponge of bread and all of a sudden I feel a strong stab of jealousy. *I* want to be the food that she eats. *I* want to mop up the juices and be chewed and consumed.

For dessert we both need something cold.

'Ice cream?' she whispers.

'Ice-cream,' I echo.

She dips her wafer into the bowl, paddles in the shallows with the tip of her spoon. By the time she's finished her lips are coated in a thick layer of chocolate. I imagine kissing her, the glorious mixture of saliva and sugar, her tongue furred over with cream.

'Let's get out of this place,' she says. 'We'll take a car to our next destination.'

Or to be more precise, we take *Misha's* car. After all, this is her surprise, her way, she says, of showing how much she loves me. I wind down the window and let the air wash over my face. Stars crackle. The sky is a sheet of black metal. The road is studded with cat's-eyes.

'Where are we going?' I say.

'Somewhere exciting. Trust me.' She turns on the radio and for a time we drive to the sound of light-hearted pop songs and jingles. The night flashes past. The clock on the dashboard clicks and then whirrs. We pass a gas station and the occasional farmhouse. We pass a forest of stubbly pine trees. The air grows colder.

Finally, she stops the car and I step out. The first thing I notice is the smell of sulphur. She's brought me up to the pools. I can hear them gurgling, see the mist spiralling out of control. This is prehistory; a snowscape, a land of shimmering glaciers, lava and rock. There are patches of ice, dazzling flashes of steam. It's a world reduced to mineral crystal. Misha stares up and I follow her gaze. Above us the moon hangs like an icicle. Snowflakes glide through the air and catch on her eyelids. Her breath blooms out like a flower.

Misha grins and takes hold of my hand. She leads me around the edge of the pools. There are hundreds and hundreds of these deep, bubbling fissures and we walk for what seems like hours enshrouded in mist. My shirt sticks to the back of my neck. My hair drips with sweat, then Misha steps slightly ahead of me and disappears into the haze.

I can hear her voice, hear her singing. My lover as Siren, luring me towards rocks. 'Over here,' she calls, and I stumble towards the thin, reedy voice. Something warm brushes my hand. It's the foam from the pools. Then Misha calls out again and the echo swirls round and round in the mist. 'Here,' she says. 'Over here.'

When I finally find her, Misha has stripped. She's lying face-up on a slab of lava, her eyes are trained on the stars. She begins to undress me and, button by button, I unfold in her arms. My nerve endings prickle. Her eyes glisten, then she opens her legs and begins to rub herself with her finger. It's a slow movement, calm and deliberate, and my body aches with guilt and desire. Beads of sweat run down my forehead. I watch her hand, watch her finger as it strokes and caresses her flesh and after she comes, she draws this pale, oystery digit over my belly and into my mouth. I envy her hands and she knows it.

'Jealous?' she says.

'Very.'

'Exciting enough?'

I nod.

She cradles my head and embraces me with the longest and deepest of kisses. This time her eyes resemble glass-bottomed boats. Beneath the surface I see whole shoals of emotion: love, passion, desire, death. I run my hand down her back, down the ridges of her coralline spine. Her hair sparkles and the steam spits.

Misha motions towards the dark water.

'Come on,' she says. 'Let's go for a swim.'

'Isn't it dangerous? Without any light?'

'It's fine,' she says.

I watch as she dives into the pool and woozily slide in behind her. The warmth is voluptuous. She locks her arms round my waist; the water smells of steam and pure sex. It's pungent. There's the undertow of thick sulphur and the slowly fermenting aroma of mud. Our feet squelch near the sides, but the further we swim, the deeper it is. We cling to each other. We're two lobsters inside a pot. The water is boiling and our skin is bright pink. She digs her fingers into my back. I run my tongue along the line of her breasts. I can feel the rise of each cone-shaped nipple, the golden hoops of her areolae. I push her legs as wide apart as I can; I want her spread-eagled. Only then can I slide into the depths of my fantasies.

'Beyond this point, there be dragons,' she says. The quote is familiar, but I am being swept into uncharted territory. That's what she's saying. This is the end of the world.

Misha grabs hold of my hair, then pulls back on my head so hard that I gasp. I dive deeper. I ride down the waves of her body. My head slips under, my lungs tighten. It's black down here, black with a silty, sub-aqueous silence. Black with sludge and curious soft-bodied creatures. I try to speak, but each word that escapes from my mouth forms a bubble. Another wave, only this time it drags me further away. I bang my head on her shoulder. I flex my muscles, struggle to find a good footing, but the grab of the water is too overpowering. It's sucking me down – wave after glorious wave, and suddenly I know that I'm going to drown.

Misha's eyes are lighter than driftwood.

I call out her name and finally, finally, sink into the depths.

IT'S BEHIND YOU

Lilian Pizzichini

*T*he pear-shaped figure is something that is peculiar to Englishmen. A cousin on my mother's side is representative of this tragic flaw. As a boy, he was pale and winsome, with delicate features and a narrow, lithe frame. As a thirty-five-year-old man, his features have coarsened, his narrow shoulders flare out into child-bearing hips with tree-trunk legs, and his cords sag in all the wrong places. Worse, his bottom – once pert – is flabby. Pretty boys usually come to this pass, I find. The stages of their decline can be gauged from the state of their behinds. If, in his mid- to late twenties, you detect in your lover a slight blurring around the edges of what should be a razor-sharp silhouette, think carefully about the future of your relationship.

Luckily, as my father is Italian, I was exposed from an early age (nine years old, to be precise) to the tight, rounded buttocks of my Zio Sisto (Uncle Sixtus – not just popes are called 'Sixtus' – my uncle was his parents' sixth child). He was well into his forties, but his bottom was proudly encased in well-fitting trousers that were belted at the waist and tapered down to his elegant ankles.

On our holidays in Ancona – the most boring city in Italy – I would chase Zio Sisto around his well-appointed *appartamento*, skidding on the marble floors, greedily grabbing his lovely, juicy bottom; 'twixt finger and thumb. He would jut it out provocatively, urging me on . . . and on. We would pass whole mornings in this fashion. (I told you Ancona was boring.) Thus was born my fascination with men's bottoms.

Some people may think this strange, but the rest of my family didn't bat an eyelid. Our surname isn't Pizzichini for nothing. For Italians, it is a comical name (an English equivalent might be Ramsbottom or Blinkhorn), and it means 'little pinches', so I certainly wasn't labouring under a misnomer. Incidentally, I once met a man sitting under a fountain in a Tuscan piazza whose surname was Pizziccone, which means 'big pinches', but that's another story.

Even now, on occasion (and it's usually a drunken one), I find myself, before I've realised what I've done, with a chunk of male flesh in my grip. But, on the whole, I'm fussy. I like them slightly elongated, lightly dusted with fluff and with well-defined contours. Egon Schiele's depiction of a bottom in his 1913 *Semi-Nude Torsos* is my ideal. He raises the male model's shirt flap to expose a decadently rouged *derrière*, poignant in its leanness. I once knew a man with such a bottom. Sadly, his cheeks were all too often clenched with an anguish that none of my attentions could alleviate.

In a happier vein, my present boyfriend's bottom is more robust, jaunty even, with dark fuzz and adorable dimples. I like to trace his cleavage with my fingertips all the way down and round to be met with a substantial handful of flesh, muscle and bristling hair underneath. The contrast between sweet, plump innocence and that unholy conflation is intoxicating.

For, without doubt, bottoms are the most spiritually loaded body-part. If, as Vasari said, 'Michelangelo considered the male nude divine,' just think of David's colossal *culo* (It. arse: hence the brusque injunction, '*Vaffanculo*', 'Go fuck an arse' – Italians love *coitus a retro*). Its deep-grooved cleft sweeps up his back, dividing the trunk in two until it dissolves in the nape of his neck. The power of that miraculous backside resides in its ability to unite body and mind. It is the true focal point of the statue, and the greatest backside in the history of Western art.

On a more frivolous note, 'cheeky' just wouldn't have the same saucy or disingenuous resonance if it didn't conjure up the image of a bare-faced arse. And, besides this suggestive quality, our rear end has that astonishing other-worldly resemblance that rugby players capitalise on in their infamous art of 'mooning'. As for the sense of virility and power that a bottom can convey, I think the most telling observation Ruby Wax ever made was concerning Mel Gibson's divinely wrought posterior. Apparently, the redoubtable Ruby was once dining in a restaurant in Los Angeles when the Hollywood hunk stood up from his table to leave the room. The eyes of every woman in the room were riveted on his ass (as she would say) as he made his exit. A communal sigh of longing was emitted as soon as he'd passed out of view.

If only I had been there, I would have made my uncle proud that I am a Pizzichini. Because, it has to be said, a truly splendid backside is hard to find. With all that sitting around that men do, it's little wonder that they sag so. And if they are lean and fit, you can bet your bottom dollar that their honed and buffed rump will already be spoken for. In compensation, Nature has been generous with our allotted allowance of protuberant globes. Clearly, she knows a good thing when she sees one. According to Desmond Morris, who has pondered more bottoms than I have dreamt of pinching, the shape of breasts is closely modelled on that of the buttocks in order to encourage sexual intercourse among humans. Rear entry is *de rigueur* in the animal kingdom, of course, but humans are encouraged to mate on both sides of the fence, so to speak, by the presence of an imitation bottom signalling its readiness from up front. Which is all well and good for men, but we women are forced to skulk about, sneaking discreet glimpses of men's determinedly concealed fundaments. It is most definitely a man's world.

A WINTER'S TALE

Luke Jennings

*I*n my defence, Tovarich, I would state merely that the year was 1975, that the winter was an exceptionally long and cold one, and that things were different then. As you are probably aware, I was contacted eighteen months ago by researchers from the institute at Perm, who had heard rumours about the work we were engaged in at that time, but beyond confirming that I had briefly been posted to the Semipalatinsk facility (which is a matter of public record), I told them nothing. The political situation in our country may have changed, but I still consider myself bound by the oaths that I swore in the second secretary's presence at the Academy.

Today, as you will observe, very little remains of the facility. A single rusted chain secures the main gate, the guardroom windows are boarded, the doors of the huts swing from their hinges. Back then, however, security was intense, and on the February afternoon in question I was in Hut Five, transcribing data. I had managed to get the place quite warm with the help of a paraffin heater, and I was not best pleased when one of the guards presented himself at the door with orders that I should report to Elvira Filipova's office. It was snowing heavily, and the block in which she had installed herself was at the far end of the complex.

We were all curious about Elvira Nikolaevna Filipova. She had arrived a week earlier from Alma Ata, but no one was certain of her function. She wore civilian clothes of Muscovite quality, which suggested seniority, but she had yet to issue a directive. Her age we guessed to be about thirty. She was not conventionally beautiful – her eyes were small, her moustache was generous and her blurring jawline bespoke a fondness for oiled potato and tinned Danube carp – but there was a languor about her that compelled the eye, especially in that bleak place. As she crossed the canteen at meal times, not a man present failed to note the heavy sway of her breasts behind her laden tray. For her part, she seemed indifferent to us all.

No one answered my knock, so, stamping the snow from my boots, I pushed open the office door. For a moment I stood still, uncertain whether to advance or withdraw. Beneath the standard-issue portrait of the first secretary, Elvira Filipova lay snoring in her chair. Her head lolled open-mouthed against her shoulder, and a river of drool glistened at her chin and darkened the grey wool of her sweater. Given that the office door had been open to all-comers, her posture was quite extraordinarily indiscreet. One booted leg extended before her on the grey steel desk, the other trailed on the floor. Beside it lay a glass tumbler and a half-empty bottle of red-pepper vodka – an export-quality brand, I noted, rather than the local stuff.

But I am skirting the issue. I am failing to explain why, rather than returning to Hut Five, my immediate reaction to the tableau before me was to ensure that Elvira Filipova and I were alone in the block, and then to lock myself into the small, windowless office with her. The fact is, Tovarich, that Filipova's indiscretion exceeded mere drunkenness. For reasons I can only guess at, Comrade Filipova had dragged her skirt almost to her waist, and in so doing had exposed to my disbelieving gaze a pair of imported white cotton knickers.

Now, I would not wish you to think that I am unfamiliar with women's underwear – I am not. The examples that I had encountered up to that moment, however, had been more redolent of the weightlifter's locker room than of the boudoir. Grimly functional affairs, and none too clean. You will understand, then, that to see that snowy dune nestling between the truculent mass of Elvira Filipova's thighs was nothing short of miraculous. Today, of course, such garments are everywhere, and every street-corner vampire parcels her slot in spandex and Bruges lace. But to a child of the Five Year Plan, Tovarich, that taut little nexus of bleached cotton, scalloped elastic and deferred promise was a marvel that, for all our science, we could never hope to duplicate.

On the night of our graduation from the Academy, Major Dolgushin had taken our entire cadre out to get drunk. At midnight, after several bottles in the Rossiya Hotel, we went to watch the fur-coated tourists leaving the Bolshoi Theatre (there was a rumour, almost certainly without foundation, that adventurous American widows liked to solicit the services of uniformed officers).

'Tell me the truth, Nikonov,' the Major slurred, throwing a heavy arm around my shoulders. 'Are you a breast man, an arse man or a leg man?' The others fell silent and I looked Dolgushin in the eye. 'To tell the truth, Major,' I said, swaying slightly, 'I'm a cunt man.'

The quote followed me from posting to posting, but it's true; I was, am and probably will die a cunt man, and I could not lift my eyes from the fat little scoop of vanilla revealed by Elvira Filipova's raised dress. After five minutes, looking was not enough. Checking that she was still unconscious, I warmed a pair of scissors from her desk in my hands. With extreme care, holding my breath, I then cut the taut elastic at her hips. A pennant of brushed cotton fell forward between her legs. Comrade Filipova snored on.

The mound thus revealed was as darkly compelling as a forest against snow. Slowly the thick growth reasserted itself, and I could not resist drawing a finger up its parting. You would have done the same, Tovarich, believe me, and like me you would have enjoyed the faint resultant odour of Astrakhan sturgeon. Perhaps, I thought, I should return to Hut Five for one of the cameras, in order that I could revisit this scene in the long nights that lay ahead. But where, I wondered, would I get such material processed?

Returning to Filipova, I drew a second questing finger up her dark seam, and felt the soft flesh part to meet me. Resting my hand against her, I felt a suction, a gentle but urgent in-drawing, and to my surprise saw my finger disappear inside her. In response, her buttocks clenched, her jaws rolled and she emitted a loud, peppery belch. Gently, I attempted to withdraw my hand. To my horror, I was not only unable to move it, but saw two more of my fingers drawn inside. Was this how all women functioned? There hadn't been any of this weird hydraulic business with the girls from the Krasnopresninskaya bus garage. Taking a deep breath, I gave a long, steady pull, only to see the best part of my hand smoothly consumed.

A moment later, I became aware of a stabbing sensation in my wrist. Kneeling, I saw that it was held by a circlet of tiny hooks, which had somehow been extruded by Elvira Filipova's cunt. Like rose thorns, these pointed inwards, agonisingly resisting any attempt at escape. Unlike rose thorns, however, they appeared to be alive – withdrawing from my arm every few seconds and lashing the air, before once again plunging into my flesh. The pain was excruciating but so was the fear of discovery, and to my horror I saw that Filipova was stirring. Composing myself as best I could, I awaited her screams, her denunciations and her fury. Mentally, I prepared myself for Siberia.

Filipova awoke, and regarded me in sleepy silence. With one hand, she removed the remains of the imported knickers from beneath her bottom, frowned and dropped them to the floor. Crouched at her side, I said nothing, and attempted not to cry out as the tiny flagellae renewed their assault. Eventually the pain became unbearable and I was forced to rest my head on her rucked-up skirt and support my half-enclosed arm on her thigh. Ignoring me, Filipova reached for a file on her desk and began to read.

Minutes passed before she returned the file to her desk. Then, bowing over

my captive arm, she parted herself with her fingers and detachedly examined her thorned interior, now spotted like a tiger lily with my blood. Nodding to herself, wiping sturgeon-scented fingers on her skirt, she turned to me.

'I understand, Captain Nikonov, that you describe yourself as a cunt man.'

I closed my eyes, felt her broad thigh against my cheek.

'Yes, Elvira Nikolaevna,' I replied. 'That is correct.'

She smiled at the use of her patronymic, and with her smile the thorns retracted. Slowly, and with infinite gratitude, I began to withdraw my arm. When I reached the broad part of my hand, however, she reactivated the thorns. One pierced a vein, causing a tiny jet of blood to leap into her skirt.

'Are you sure that you are such a man, Captain Nikonov?' she asked quietly. I looked up at her. The pain had vanished. How splendidly, I thought, how magisterially she embodies our struggle.

'Yes, Elvira Nikolaevna,' I whispered. 'I am sure.'

THE MEMBER FOR KILBURN

Lauren Henderson

Gina came out of Threshers, plastic bag clinking by her side (Budvar for herself, Kahlua for her sister), and saw it almost immediately: a jet of water, clear and powerful, spraying out into the street from a disused shop entrance. Why would someone hose down the pavement? And why – she was getting closer now – was there a canvas holdall in the middle of the pavement, the water falling just short of it? The shoppers on Kilburn High Road on a Saturday morning were a notoriously tough crowd to impress, let alone to shock, but even the most hard-bitten people approaching Gina looked incredulous. As she reached the shop front, she saw why.

It wasn't a hose-pipe. It was a penis. A man was standing in the recess, his dick in his hand, hosing out a stream of surprisingly colourless piss. So far, so Kilburn. But this was a big, good-looking man, probably a bodybuilder, about thirty, not the usual sad old drunk. He was planted solidly, soberly, his feet wide apart for balance, one hand hanging by his side, the other holding in a silver-ringed clasp a very large, thick, rosy penis with an equally large silver ring set into its tip. It looked swollen and full enough to continue pissing indefinitely.

That was the thing. It looked – well, frankly, it looked more than good. That was why everyone was so taken aback. That image – the juicy, bluish-pink cock in the proportionately wide-fingered hand, whose silver rings echoed the Prince Albert in the tip – could have been a Robert Mapplethorpe photograph. Even for a girl who had never had a watersports fantasy in her life, it was strangely erotic. Gina wanted to stop and stare but she was too much of a coward even to break stride. Just as she passed – there was a build-up of human traffic, as everyone was skirting the canvas bag on the side without the piss, and some people were walking in the road – the gusher stopped. The guy tapped his dick, shook it and put it back in his tracksuit bottoms. Strolling over to the holdall, he slung it over his shoulder and headed off along the street.

'Fucking unbelievable!' muttered a young man next to Gina. 'Just when you think you've seen it all, eh?'

'Filthy cunt,' agreed a woman.

There was a general murmur of agreement. Gina kept walking, skirting the stretch of erupted paving stones outside Ryan's Diner with the familiarity of long habit. She didn't even see them; she was too occupied with formulating the story for her sister.

'And the worst thing was,' she would say, uncapping a beer, 'that it was a fucking gorgeous dick. Quite possibly the best dick, not to mention the Prince Albert, that I'll ever see. On some psycho exhibitionist, weeing on to the pavement outside Penny Wise. Is that sad or what?'

The thought was so depressing that she crossed the road without looking and nearly got knocked down by a 98 bus.

PART 3

Mind Games

TRUST ME, I'M A DOCTOR

Christopher Hart

*S*he is lying back on the sofa wearing only her 'patient's gown' – a short, plain white dress. He is perched on a chair at her feet. He instructs her to keep her eyes fixed on the ceiling. Then he begins.

Just a minute, just a minute, she interrupts him. A bit of scene setting, puhl-ease. That's the trouble with men's fantasies. They're so basic. No characterisation, no plot. It's all so dull, like some schlocky porn film.

There is a plot he says, a little hurt. It's the 'doctor and patient' plot.

Well, the lighting's all wrong for a start, she says. She slides to her feet and moves around the room, turning off the overhead light, putting on a sidelight and a table lamp and then, after a little pause for aesthetic reflection, laying it on its side. Then she strains upwards on the balls of her feet – thrillingly aware that he is watching every movement of her body, the taut, slim muscles of her calves – and lifts down the big gilt mirror and props it on top of the bookcase. There, she says, standing back. That's a bit better. She comes back and sits on the edge of the sofa. OK then, he says, getting more into the spirit of it. Let's have proper names.

After some argument, he is allowed to be Dr Nostrum, even though she thinks this is a silly name. And then – Miss Havisham? Miss Honeychurch? Lady de la Touche? – she finally settles on Miss Cavendish. Sort of Regency, she says vaguely. I like it, he says. Hardcore Georgette Heyer. Now then: is this your first visit to the doctor?

She lies back and then sits up again. You must wear your glasses on the end of your nose, she says. He does so. And look at me over the top of them when you speak. With your eyebrows raised . . . What's the word? Quizzically. He does as instructed, and with a little shiver of delight she lies back down again.

You find the weirdest things a turn-on, he murmurs.

Now now, she says. In character, if you please, doctor.

He coughs and then commences. Almost unconsciously he finds himself affecting a kind of mitteleuropean accent. He taps the end of his nose with his retractable pencil and says, So then, Miss, ah . . . Cavendish. You say that you have for some time been experiencing a very low level of satisfaction both prior to and during acts of, ah . . . coition?

She nods shyly. Yes, doctor, she whispers.

And for how long have you been experiencing this lack of satisfaction?

She considers. A few months, I suppose.

A few munz, you suppose. Hm, good. He pretends to make some notes. Then he looks up again. And yet you are not married?

Miss Cavendish blushes, or at least tries to. No, doctor, she says softly.

There is an awkward silence while Dr Nostrum waits for an explanation.

I . . . I just can't help myself, doctor! bursts out Miss Cavendish passionately, running her fingers through her hair and twisting tormentedly on the couch. I am so subject to the irresistible demands of my lascivious nature, so fond of the . . . the act of love! Why, only this morning I tumbled the new stable lad, and last night at Lady Mountley's ball, I extended my favours to two men simultaneously in the gazebo!

He has to start talking rapidly in order not to burst out giggling and so spoil the whole effect. And yet you say that you do not actually seem to feel very much, is that correct?

Miss Cavendish nods. Not as much as I believe I ought to, doctor, pleasant though it is. Hm, says Dr Nostrum ruminatively, half to himself. Perhaps some kind of atrophy of the generative organs, through prolonged misuse . . . (He doesn't have a clue what he is talking about, obviously, but he is thrilled to find himself practising what he terms the eroticisation of scientific language.) Perhaps with some link to a psychosomatic anaesthesia? Aphasia? Hm. He taps his nose again and speaks more briskly.

But you do, as you admit, enjoy the act of coition, Miss Cavendish – as well as the peripheral acts of stimulus, oral, digital and so forth?

Yes, doctor. She smiles ceilingwards. Very much.

Hm. Hm. Dr Nostrum pauses for thought and then says, I wonder if I may, wiz your permission of course, Miss Cavendish, perform a little experiment upon your person? Merely to ascertain the extent of your erogenetic anaesthesia?

Miss Cavendish nods demurely. Very well, Dr Nostrum. I commit myself into your hands, in the full expectation of professional conduct on your part.

Dr Nostrum nods gravely. Naturally. I do not wish for there to be any embarrassment at my actions, or indeed at your own responses. But it is important for me to understand the extent of your affliction. Of course, if it troubles you, then you only have to say . . .

Miss Cavendish murmurs that she wishes him to proceed.

Then let us commence, he says.

Taking her right foot gently in his hands, he cradles it in his lap. My word, he says, your toes are a leedle cold, Miss Cavendish. She giggles. He is starting to sound like Inspector Clouseau. I do apologise, she says. No, not at all, he says. Only, we may need to warm them up a little. He begins to knead them gently between his fingers and then to rub the whole of the sole of her foot with circular motions of his open palm. Do you feel anything? he inquires after a while.

Mm, yes, says Miss Cavendish. It feels very nice.

Hm, good. Dr Nostrum pauses to make a note.

Oh do go on, pleads Miss Cavendish. It feels so nice.

Dr Nostrum smiles benevolently at her over the top of his spectacles (at which Miss Cavendish gives another, deeper shiver of excitement) and says, Very well, Miss Cavendish. Then I shall, he chuckles to himself, proceed a leedle further, with your consent. He begins to run his fingers up and down the thin bones in her feet and over her ankles and to tickle her. She squirms on the bed in slow motion, sighing deeply.

I take it that that is a sensory reaction to the stimulus I am administering to you?

Miss Cavendish decides to play dumb at this point. For her, very incorrectly, dumb = passive = pleasurable; while being passive means not having to take responsibility for the illicit pleasures that she is experiencing. There are times – not always, but there are times – when Miss Cavendish loves nothing more than to be a dumb sex object. When she dreams of being used.

So she fails to understand clever Dr Nostrum and his long scientific words. Well, she giggles girlishly, it feels nice, if that's what you mean.

It feels nice? repeats Dr Nostrum, not unkindly. Hm. Good. Good. He begins to run his fingers gently up her calves, tickling and kneading her as he makes his shameful progress. And this – does this feel nice too, Miss Cavendish?

Oh, it does, Dr Nostrum, it does.

Hm. Evidently, no psychosomatic anaesthesia there, then.

None at all, doctor, breathes Miss Cavendish.

Good, good. Dr Nostrum summons up all his manly courage and then, assuring himself that it is all quite in accordance with the Hippocratic oath, he asks softly, and now I wonder, Miss Cavendish, if I might ask you to move your shift just a little bit higher so that I can continue with my examination? It is very important for me to ascertain precisely the point at which you begin to experience a loss of sensation.

After a little shyness, Miss Cavendish demurs, and Dr Nostrum glides his hand up under the hem of his compliant patient's gown and eases it a little higher. Miss Cavendish raises her legs an inch or two to make it easier for him, and Dr Nostrum settles the hem of her gown so that it lies in neat folds half-way down her honey-coloured thighs. Then he begins to caress her knees and the sensitive popliteal regions beneath, before running the pad of his index finger in exploratory little forays up the inside of her thighs.

Now then, how does that feel?

I'm . . . I'm not quite sure, says Miss Cavendish, sounding somewhat flustered. I think I can feel well enough, but . . .

Very well, says Dr Nostrum. Then if you will permit me – now, do stop me if you are unhappy with my actions in any way, Miss Cavendish, but I would like, if I may, to ease your gown just a . . . leedle . . . higher . . . like so. There now, can you feel this?

Shivering under his (doubtless strictly Hippocratic) ministrations, Miss Cavendish shakes her head sadly. Not at all, she whispers.

Moving his hand now in teasing circular motions, Dr Nostrum eyes her over the top of his glasses. And how about this?

I . . . I . . . says Miss Cavendish, seemingly in some distress, struggling to find the right words. I think I can feel something.

Something? Hm . . . He pauses to write 'something' in his invisible notebook, and immediately Miss Cavendish begins to stammer, Oh do go on, Doctor, please, do go on.

Dr Nostrum regards her sternly over the top of his glasses (which only makes the lubricious and deceitful Miss Cavendish wriggle all the more) and says, Now then, young lady, we are not performing this experiment simply for your pleasure, you know.

Oh no, of course not, sighs Miss Cavendish.

This is a strictly diagnostic process. However, he adds, relenting a little – since it seems that we are indeed on the very verge of establishing the precise nature of your erogenetic anaesthesia, I must ask you to permit me to proceed a leedle further in my explorations. He becomes stern and masterful again. Now then, if we just hitch up your shift like so – and then just part your thighs a little more, like so . . . How does that feel to you?

Unfortunately for the diagnostic process, Miss Cavendish's replies from henceforward are so punctuated with incomprehensible little squeaks and gasps and moans and expressions of, as Dr Nostrum understands it, involuntary pre-coital pleasure, that when at last he feels it is only part of his Hippocratic duty to bring the experiment to its inevitable climax, and introduce his *membrum virile* into the diagnosis, and asks for the young lady's permission so to do, her replies are quite beyond comprehension, so that he is obliged to proceed without any certainty that she has given her express consent. But upon doing so, it appears much to Miss Cavendish's pleasure. And afterwards, reviewing the experiment as a whole, he cannot help but feel that Miss Cavendish has been a very naughty young lady and deceived him shockingly as to the nature of her affliction, which, far from being a lack of erotogenitive feeling, is rather an excess of it, to the point of a positively disordered nymphomania. So that he feels it a further part of his duty to administer to her squirming buttocks a sound chastisement. At this Miss Cavendish objects, saying that surely such a function should be fulfilled by her own father, as indeed, she confesses, with an expression of wide-eyed and innocent perplexity, it very often is, with herself stripped shamefully almost naked and, not infrequently, before the gaze of a number of her father's drinking and gambling companions. But no, Dr Nostrum is very strict on this point, and commences to administer the extensive chastisement himself. After all, he tells her between slaps, I am a doctor.

THOUGHT WAVES

'Olympia'

*L*ate on a hot night. So late that even in June the velvet of dark is caught between the large white houses by the canal. A smell of jasmine, of privet, the roar of cars on their distant arc around the city.

On the top floor, two men sit in a large room: coffered ceilings, maps, books, eighteenth-century porcelain, a Bechstein and a minstrel's gallery. Schubert *Lieder* balanced on the night, glasses – several glasses – of brandy, the sash windows hauled open and the one low light behind a chair casting their features in relief.

'Do you ever see that dark girl? Zena? Was that it? Do you still . . . see her?' The older man smiles as he raises his eyebrows to his friend.

'Zinnia. It was Zinnia,' the figure in the deep chair replies. 'Still is Zinnia, actually.'

'So Jane doesn't mind . . . I mean, she knows, I assume?'

'Yes and no. You know. But would you like to see her – Zinnia, I mean?' The younger man, not young, but younger, asks. 'Look, I have her photograph.'

He pulls out a book – one of his more successful novels – from the tall cases; the picture is hidden within its pages.

The grey-haired man looks down, tips the picture towards the light, is surprised. The woman is naked, reclining like Maya, on large pillows, one knee up, one arm behind her head, her eyes looking directly at the photographer, between her legs dusk, her dark nipples disproportionately large for her small breasts.

'Lucky man.'

He gazes, embarrassment and arousal struggling within him. He drinks deeply from his glass.

'Do you see her often? I mean, it must be difficult.'

'It is difficult,' the writer smiles ruefully. 'She loves me, passionately. I desire her. And she lives in France much of the time. And there's Jane. But there are ways. And she is very compliant. That's love, you see. She'll do anything for me; it's terrifying in some ways. Should I set her free? I often mean to but I never quite do.'

His friend looks puzzled. The writer fills his glass.

'Would you like me to show you? Not photographs, I mean, but how it works?'

At a nod, he picks up a telephone and touches keys in the semi-darkness. The older man can just hear it ringing. It rings and rings. Finally an answer.

'It's me.' The writer smiles, whether for his friend or his lover or himself, who can tell?

'Yes. I am. Of course. And you?'

'Where are you? In bed. Yes, it's late. I know.'

'So, what are you wearing?'

'Of course. It's hot. No, I knew. Do you miss me?'

Is he acting? The one-sided conversation seems unreal.

'Zinnia . . . I want you to do something for me. I'm here thinking of you. Missing you. You know what would make me happy.'

'Close your eyes. Now touch your breast. Yes. For me. For me, darling girl.'

It is silent in the darkness. Is he being teased? The older man is appalled and captivated.

'Put your finger in your mouth, sweetheart, now wet your nipple for me . . . Stroke it, stroke it for me. Is it hard? Tell me, darling? How does it feel?'

'Now, take your nipple between your thumb and forefinger . . . Squeeze it.'

'Now, the other one. Hurt it a little. Oh, I like that.' He exhales.

'Now, you know what I want you to do, don't you, sweetheart? Tell me, are you ready for me? Are you wet? Open your legs, darling. Open them wide for me. As if I were there. Touch yourself. Gently. Gently. Stroke yourself for me.'

He cradles the telephone to his neck like a lover. He looks up at his friend and a smile, sensuous but perhaps mocking, hovers and is gone.

'How does it feel, Zinnia? Tell me. Is it opening for me? Is your clitoris hard? Run your finger over it; is it slippery? Yes, darling, go on.'

He reaches forward and presses the handset, and suddenly, shocking yet wonderful, the woman's voice is broadcast to the room. Her breath uneven, vibrating very slightly.

'Oh.' A ragged sigh. 'Oh, I love you.' Her words drawn out, soft in the near darkness. 'And it feels so good.'

The older man cannot look at the younger. He shifts in his chair but he listens on.

'Zinnia . . . now I want you to open yourself and slip your finger in. Are you really wet, darling? Tell me . . . are your lips swollen for me?'

'Oh yes.' The woman's voice sounds eager. 'Yes, yes, I'm doing that now, as you tell me, now, now and . . . Oh, I want you . . . My fingers, no, my whole palm is wet.'

The loudspeaker throws her sighs around the shadows.

'Darling, put your finger in your mouth. Suck. Does it taste good, darling? Let me hear you do it.'

Unmistakably in the darkness, faint but magical, there are the sounds of wetness; the woman sucks and she gives a soft groan.

'Now two – no –' the writer looks up at his friend '– three fingers.'

'You can, of course you can. I've given you more than that. Much more.' His voice is persuasive.

The woman murmurs assent.

'Push, darling, push them all in for me. Now out, now in again. Is that lovely, sweetheart? How does it make you feel?'

'Uh. Oh, it's wonderful. Oh, I love you so much. Always. Please . . .' Her voice sounds young.

They are all three in the night with the woman's breathing, deep and hoarse, and the grey-haired man is afraid that his own must be audible. He tries not to breathe with her. The writer seems not aroused but something else, something darker, less tangible. He smiles on.

'Zinnia, darling. Stroke yourself, long strokes, are you ready for me? Would you take me inside you?'

'Yes.' The clarity of sound is so good and the room high above the city so silent that they hear her swallow, a tiny grunt . . . she moves in the bed . . . she is in bed, the older man feels sure . . . the rustle of covers. There is another long, long sigh.

'Darling –' The writer has lowered his own voice now and leans forward, curling the phone in his hand. 'You know what I want, don't you?'

'Yes,' she whispers. 'Just like usual.' He looks up, challenges his friend with a stare. He cups the receiver with his hand. 'Shall we go on?' he asks him. 'Finish it . . . or . . . ?'

The older man finds himself blushing and yet wanting her to be encouraged, not deterred. He stays silent. Does his head nod imperceptibly? He fears that it betrays him.

The writer turns his mouth to the phone. 'I want you to find something, darling, something . . . anything . . . whatever you like.'

They hear the woman move. For a few seconds her breathing dies down as she moves away. Then, although she says nothing, she is close again. Breathing. Aroused. Unknown, yet utterly exposed. The older man has never known such intimacy. There is heat and night and her.

'Have you found something, darling?' The writer's voice is low, but level. 'Lie back, bring your knees up the way I like it. Now push it into you. Go on . . . all the way . . . up to the hilt.'

For a moment, nothing but the lurching power of imagination. Then she catches her breath and it seems to last for ever.

'Yes. Oh yes.'

'Is it inside you? Is it filling you?' the younger man asks his lover. 'Now move it in and out slowly. Let me hear you, let me hear it.'

The woman calls out endearments; her moans are regular and faster.

The two men listen. She needs no instructions now, although from time to time she mutters something almost incomprehensible, then darling then please, then oh Jesus Jesus.

'Go on, go on,' the writer urges. 'Hard, do it hard. For me, sweetheart, I'm with you, it's just us, so show me, do it for me.'

The woman makes little noises in the back of her throat. The older man's erection aches and somewhere in his heart there is pain. For the obedience? For the deceit? He does not know. The photograph lies on the table beside him, just within the pool of light. There she lies naked, exposed, vulnerable.

'Oh God, I'm . . . It's so lovely, uh uh uh . . . I'm going to come, oh, I'm coming, I'm coming.' Her words tumble, echo, caught up in her falling breath.

'Darling, darling.' She cries out so loud that the great room is full of her, and then she seems to be weeping.

'Oh, I love you, I love you so much.' And her breath, her voice, her climax subside. The writer waits.

'You're so good, Zinnia, so good. My darling girl. My only love. Sleep now.'

'I love you.' The faintest fading whisper a long, long way away in the darkness.

The writer puts down the phone. He looks, almost challengingly, at his older friend.

'Did you enjoy that? She loves doing it . . . loves me . . . She was made for pleasure, so why shouldn't it be shared? No one else need know.'

The grey-haired man, his arousal still unassuaged, meets the eyes of his friend, now a stranger, and knows he sees his need.

In a small flat some miles away, the curtains billow. Zinnia, damp with sweat, bends back, sleepily, greedily. The man underneath her, spent but still slightly erect, looks up at her face.

'That,' he says, 'that was, well, extraordinary. How the hell I kept quiet when you came, when I came, doing it, knowing he was listening, and getting off on it, having to be so quiet. But God, how erotic. And you like an eel all over the place.' He laughs, lifts her off him.

'Find something . . . anything you like, eh? And you did. And you did. But did you ever feel anything for him? Did you really do it for real for him?'

Zinnia smiles her slippery mermaid smile, her skin shines in the lamplight. For once she is completely satisfied.

UNDERGROUND

Stephanie Merritt

I have made a discovery. I have realised why my sex life has been suffering from inertia. If the *Erotic Review* is to be believed, the volume of fleeting sexual encounters occurring on the London Underground is staggering. Yet I am shut out of this erotic Eden, this sensual realm of threadbare seats and carriages that smell of vinegar, barred from the chance of pressing against a beautiful stranger in the rush hour, gyrating slowly against his gently swelling erection in the hot, breathless air as the Northern Line crunches slowly to a standstill outside Kennington.

It's the claustrophobia, you see. I can't get on the tube without breaking out in palpitations and hot flushes, but for all the wrong reasons.

I can't even fantasise about sex on the tube without a mortal terror cruelly disturbing my incipient moistness. And cycling, my preferred mode of transport, affords far fewer opportunities for hot encounters. Although, if you're feeling particularly lonely, the cobbled towpath by Camden Lock can offer a pleasurable afternoon's ride.

'I need you to cure me of my claustrophobia,' I announced to my shrink, Dr Maurice Frawde, 'so that I can travel on the tube again like normal folk.'

'Have sex on the tube? Hmm.'

'I said "travel" on the tube.'

'No you didn't.'

'Didn't I?'

'No.'

He walked slowly across to the couch and stretched himself out next to me.

'Are you suffering from a lack of sex?'

Normally I would choose not to answer such a question. The great thing about shrinks, however, is that you pay them a lot of money to embarrass you.

'No. Just a lack of sex on the tube. Everyone else is doing it.'

'I believe it was Jung, or perhaps Lacan, who suggested role play and visualisation as the only way to conquer phobias,' he mused, studying his long, elegant fingers. His eyes were very blue and wide, partly hidden by his dark, glossy fringe.

'Imagine you're in a tunnel. Close your eyes.' His hand slid along the back of the couch to my shoulder, and he twisted a strand of my hair between two fingers.

'I can't.'

'OK. Imagine you're on the District Line at Wimbledon, say, on one of the outside bits. Not underground. And imagine someone you've always admired from afar – a great writer, say, or a film star – sits down next to you. There's no one else in the carriage.'

'Is the fire alarm system in full working order?' I asked nervously.

'Please,' Dr Maurice slipped a finger inside the top two buttons of my shirt. 'Try to concentrate. This man is next to you. How do you feel? Hot? Wet? Swollen?'

'I feel . . .' My eyes were closed. 'I feel concerned about the state of the brakes. It's no good.'

'You're not trying, are you?' His mouth was hot on my neck, those slim fingers skirting softly over one hungry nipple. Desire singed a trail between my legs, and for a second I was oblivious of the putative signalling problems that might possibly be encountered by this hypothetical train as it neared Fulham Broadway.

It seemed to be working. By the time I had visualised my way to Edgware Road, I was writhing naked on his zebra-skin rug, panting and bucking and on the verge of climactically overcoming my phobia once and for all, when...

Dr Maurice raised his head from where it was buried, mouth glistening, and glanced at his watch.

'I'm afraid we'll have to stop there,' he said. He was still wearing his suit. 'That'll be £50, please.'

'Dr Maurice,' I said, shrugging on my jacket. 'This theory that patients always fantasise about their psychotherapists. Any truth in it?'

'None whatsoever,' he said, lighting a cigarette.

I decided to take the Northern Line home, just in case.

LIPSTICK LOVER

Rachel King

*O*nly bitches paint their mouths, he said, on our first meeting, and he took a lipstick from his jacket pocket. It was Bourjois, I remember: the black case, the deep red angled tip that spiralled up, penis-like, crying out for the mouth. It was warm and smelt of him. You are a bitch, he said, so you must wear lipstick, nice and thick, just for me.

He had a thing about lipstick. A woman was undressed without it. It was an advertisement for other lips – lips always plump and ready to trap, squeeze and suck. He liked scarlet, scarlet topped with gloss, a bubble of it in the middle of the upper lip, and a smear about an inch long along the bottom one. It reminded him, he said, of a welcoming cunt. Sometimes he said the gloss looked like spunk I had neglected to wipe off. What would people think I had been up to?

He liked to see me put it on. He bought me a gold retractable lip-brush, watched me draw a line on the very edge of my lips. Mustn't go over now, mustn't let it feather, that's too horsy. You want bourgeois lips – a bit of brown liner and a scarlet centre – like a strawberry chocolate or a bruised, used cunt.

The line had to be perfect. To get it that way I used to prime the lips beforehand with white moisturiser (that reminds me, he said) then colour would flow on easily from the brush. The result – an unbroken line. Then, the business of filling in. All that mouth-music, those seductive movements made possible by lots of tiny muscles. Some women can almost paint them individually. That's making love with the mouth, it really is, a mouth mouthing the world, exploring all that comes its way. Babies do it on the breast. Among certain women those subtle conscious invitations are the very apotheosis of lipdom. He liked the tiny movements of the muscles as I filled in the colour. It reminded him, he said, of the tenuous grip of other muscles.

The downward strokes, starting in the cusp, working towards the edge.

Going so far, and no further, towards the dark almond of a slightly open mouth. Receptive, he said – that's how it spoke to him. Most definitely. And I'd better be.

He had video clips of fifties icons, naturally. Marilyn and her mouth, and the making-up of her mouth. The woman was a lip art-form. She had lips like satin pillows, innocent and bedroom come-hither all at once. She treated her lips as if they were continually kissing her. They were lips to get a woman into trouble; in bed, if not before. I watched and learnt.

My lips are not like hers. They are not après-lips, bed-lips. Mine are small and bowed, the top lip thinner than the bottom. But they aren't mean. They are mobile, and you can't get more generous and accommodating than lips that try hard to please. Naturally I used the most tenacious reds to catch attention. And I became a lip-watcher. I studied them. Lips are the first contact, not the eyes. Lips mimic the journey into the core of a person; from lips to lips, if you like. Size seemed not to count: he found even thin, rubber-band lips sexy if they were delineated in red. Then, he said, they look like a slit – reminds me of something else.

Put red lipstick on an innocent and everyone tut-tuts. My mother hated my early scarlet phase. It makes you look tarty, she said, stick to grape, it's much more natural. He hated grape. Hated natural. Who wants to make natural look even more natural? Let's you and I go for a walk with my lipstick.

Let's be healthy. Lip-stains? Nouvelle cuisine for the mouth, for the young and sporty, not on solid food yet. And pink? He curled his lips at that. Pink lipstick: it's token, a compromise, a cur, he said. It lacks courage. It says fluffy pink boudoirs with flounces and floppy fur dogs, but no-sex-please-I'm-too-delicate. And plum and fuchsia? They are poodle haircuts, vicar's teas.

Go and paint your mouth, he'd say, and I'll get my camera. He'd stand behind the dressing-table mirror in the bedroom, the lens an over-the-shoulder voyeur, the bathroom a whore's private chapel, seldom seen – me the ghost-whore in the half-light of the Glasgow flat, painting.

Let me kill a myth. Women rarely yank lipstick back and forth across their lips as they do in the movies. You might catch a woman doing it in public, but it'll be a performance, specially tailored for the audience: men. In the powder room women dab, honey, they dab. And this is merely maintenance, the gloss on the gloss, so to speak. The routine goes thus: prime, outline, kiss the mirror, peer closer, worm fine sable religiously around the top of the wax, assume a look of surprise, frown, hold your breath – begin. Then breathe out. Sit back, lean forward, get tissue, carefully kiss it.

Admire lip-shape. Begin again at step four. And so it goes on until the lips are positively armoured with colour. Then top with gloss. Done thus, there isn't a man living who won't feel stirrings in his loins. If he's lucky enough to see it.

But then we come to kissing. Ay, there's the rub. Kissing's out, unless you want to look like a clown afterwards. (Unless it's the one part which looks nice with lipstick rings round it, he said.) So why bother with lipstick if it gets in the way? What's it all for? Red lips are, of course, like all advertisements – an invitation for future purchases. They belong to flirtdom, to delicious anticipation: look what you could have later on. They speak of a woman who is conscious of her femininity, her sexuality. Naked lips betray a lack of consciousness, a lack of awareness of these things.

But plenty of women are token lipstick wearers. They'd be horrified if they knew the messages painted lips give out. So how does a man know who's inviting and who's not?

He doesn't.

Unless he's lucky enough to meet a girl who paints both lips. And if you're asking?

Well, he does have a thing about lips . . .

And, yes, the answer is . . .

I do...

MISDIRECTED MALE

R. H.

*D*ear Sir, I happened to be passing your ailing mother's house last week and thought I would call in to pay my respects. I was delighted to be greeted at the door by your youngest daughter, who was visiting on her way home from school. We had a long and interesting conversation about the blitz, throughout which your daughter flirted incorrigibly. She really has grown up.

Anyway, I was about to leave, having already refused a cup of tea, but hastily reconsidered on seeing your daughter bending over, with some provocation, in search of the sugar. Your mother had all but nodded off, so I raised myself from the pretty floral armchair and went to lend a hand in the scullery. I don't believe any meaningful words were spoken at all, although I was so immersed in the sight of her nipples peeking through her grey sweater I could be mistaken. To exonerate your daughter, I think that I myself may be most responsible for the outcome of our meeting. She had turned her back to switch off the kettle and was, no doubt, a little nervous to feel me gingerly lifting her pleated skirt. Having said that, she made no objection that I can recall. Her white knickers were conspicuous beneath the woollen tights and I took the liberty of pulling both garments down far enough to allow her to part her feet a little. She lay her torso flat on the workbench and, as I separated her pale buttocks, she was fully exposed. I think I must have hesitated a moment in consideration of the choices before me. Although sorely tempted by her tuft, I simply could not resist what I can best describe as the Dark Star. Not wanting to cause any discomfort to the girl, your girl, I reached for a bottle of sunflower oil and deliberately applied a generous handful. Once inside, I am convinced neither of us made a sound, which is quite an achievement considering the verve with which I went about my duties. I remember feeling somewhat clumsy with my circling fingers, but your daughter soon relieved me of that responsibility.

What happened next is apparently open to some debate. My version is as follows. At the point at which your daughter shuddered, tightening her considerable grip on me, I thought I heard your mother ask if everything was all right. I remember responding in an unexpectedly high pitch and, in a spasm or two, had evidently overfilled your daughter who soon proceeded to pull herself together in haste. On returning to the lounge we were horrified, naturally, to find your mother lying on the carpet, evidently without life. However, I am happy to report that by calculating her movements before death, from the position of her prostrate body, I have concluded that it is highly unlikely she saw us making tea in the scullery. I must say, however, that I can only feel pity for your daughter, who had absolutely no opportunity to change her underwear before answering the barrage of questions from all those police officers.

Anyway, my thoughts are with you in this time of grief.

Yours faithfully

R.H.

Dear Sir,

I am writing to you in order to explain your wife's behaviour at dinner on Saturday night. As you know, I had misread your invitation and arrived at your home somewhat early. On finding you immersed in a telephone conversation, I was asked to wait in the lounge. After ten minutes or so, I decided to take a good look at your collection of watercolours. I suppose I must have wandered a little too far because I was soon at the top of the staircase, scrutinising a rather lifeless still life, when I caught a glimpse of your wife through the open bathroom door. I imagine she thought she was alone. She was wearing only that silk shirt and her exposed bottom was absolutely bare and a little pink from the hot water. My immediate reaction was to retreat back down the stairs, but she had already spotted me after only a handful of backward steps and, although somewhat startled, I must say she made no discernible effort to hide herself. On the contrary, I found myself eye to eye with her lustrous black mound.

Like a car crash perhaps, I cannot remember exactly what happened next, but I am aware of the facts. I scurried into the bathroom and made sure to lock the door behind me. Your wife sat on the edge of the draining bath and opened her thighs quite casually. I descended to my hands and knees, struggled below her six-month belly and began to lick, probably a little too enthusiastically in retrospect. I assume she was heavily swollen although I have had no occasion to see your wife in such detail before, and certainly not unaroused. The bathwater was making an extraordinary noise as the final drops disappeared down the plughole when, to my shock, I heard someone approach as the sucking began to subside. I leapt to my feet, wiped my chin with the sleeve of my jacket and strode out to join you downstairs. I can only imagine how frustrated your charming wife must have felt. She would have had absolutely no time to finish herself off, and I expect that must be the reason for some of her rather terse remarks at dinner. Anyway, it was a delightful evening and I look forward to repaying the compliment soon.

Yours faithfully
R.H.

Dear Sir,

I was being ridden by your wife this morning when a most extraordinary thing happened. She had opened the window so that she could enjoy the breeze on her buttocks as she rose and fell on me in that selfish way of hers. I must have been on my back like this for only a minute or two when in flew a beautifully speckled thrush. I was quite enthralled by this little creature as it sat intently on the sill, barely moving, occasionally bobbing its head. A wonderfully poetic vision in your rather clichéd country cottage. I must say your wife seemed significantly less interested than me, and she even let out a vexed humph, perhaps due to my slight loss of firmness. You see, the cheeky thrush was putting me off as it stared unflinchingly at the slippery darkness of our 'meeting place'. Even your wife's bobbing, childlike breasts could not avert my eyes from the bird, as it perched inquisitively in the sunlight. As you can imagine, she became rather irate at my lack of attention, so she swivelled her torso in order to get a clearer view of the distraction, twisting my flagging member in the process. She attempted to shoo the thrush away but it simply would not budge, and as a result of this uncomfortable confrontation, my faculties diminished yet further. Clearly fed up with the state of affairs, I was quite taken aback to witness your spouse defiantly raise a middle figure to the stubborn bird, pull her buttocks apart with the other hand and drive the finger directly into her rectum with tremendous vigour and relish.

Well, I can tell you, that soon resolved the stand-off. The bird immediately took flight, I sprang into usefulness and your wife took no time at all to achieve her goal. We rarely talk afterwards and thus, unfortunately, I was unable to regale her with my keen observation that the most American of repellent gesticulations – the 'one-finger salute' I think they call it – always did seem ironically inviting.

Yours faithfully

R.H.

PART 4

Home Comforts

VENUS AVERSA

Stephen Bayley

*M*arriage generates an easy familiarity which can degenerate into a brutish sottishness. A friend of mine, who has acquired great riches and many golf clubs from a career in advertising, tells me that his idea of absolute transcendent bliss is to watch the rugby on the telly, while enjoying his wife a posteriori and eating egg and chips off her back.

This may tell you a great deal about prevalent ethics and aesthetics in the demi-monde of advertising, but you'll agree it also offers a memorable image. Whether it is a fantasy or a reality I cannot say, although with a vision of my friend's handsome and refined wife in mind, I rather hope it's the latter. I'd rather go for a little char-grilled quail breast and celeriac remoulade, myself.

Why do we find the quadruped coupling position so appealing? Sometimes it is inelegantly known as the doggy position, but when the woman brings her elbows and knees closer together, it is known, at least in Italy, in a further extension of zoological imagery, as 'the clam'. (For obvious reasons, if you inspect the desired ground zero when sex is offered in this position.) Some connoisseurs of penetration – inhabitants of what Henry Miller so charmlessly called The Land of Fuck – also believe that the clam offers a superior vaginal grip for penises experiencing what the motor trade calls 'piston slap'.

Mechanics aside, the feral metaphors may reveal an element of the attraction of this position. Its animal flavour may excite the beast in us, but there's a social aspect to it too. While I personally have no great interest in conversation with missionaries, the mating position to which this most dismal profession gave its name has perhaps the one advantage of allowing face-to-face contact so that you can discuss predestination as you pump and puff towards the moment critique. Sex *a posteriori*, on the other hand, offers only limited scope for conversation. In my experience, spoken exchanges tend to be restricted to very simple commands or appeals concerning rate, force and timing.

Those who advocate the missionary position as the more sophisticated option, argue that it dignifies the woman since she is looking her partner in the eye and implicitly condoning the act, as opposed to the much more primitive implications of the quadruped position, which has something of the hunter seizing his prey brutishly from the rear about it. Of course, even to those of us in Paul Smith suits, this offer of ready access to a more primitive and less inhibited state is powerfully attractive.

For similar reasons, Arab and Christian theologians argued against any coupling where the woman was on top because it implied moral subjection of the male. A woman bent over and offering herself in this fashion evokes those highly gender-specific pleasures of conquest and submission. Added to which is the extra benefit that you can get your dick in further too, although this can sometimes cause the egg and chips to shake.

The doggy position was known to Latin thinkers as *venus aversa* and highly recommended by Lucretius and Ovid when they weren't writing poetry. However, some medieval clerics suggested that three years' penance was required if it was practised regularly, although I cannot comment on Egbert & Co.'s concepts of frequency. The fact that evolution has seen more changes in the female function of sex than in the male's again emphasises the significance of the position in mankind's long, slow journey from the primeval goo. Without prejudice to the thrillingly primitive and potent character of entrance from the rear, there is an aspect which acknowledges woman's progress in this area: there's a good deal of scientific (and, speaking personally, some very patchy intuitive) evidence that *a posteriori* offers as good a deal for the woman's clitoris as it does for her partner's prick.

The conversational restrictions of the quadruped position enhance its erotic significance among hard-pressed married couples who, having first spoken in the day during a fight over Fruitibix and maths homework in the kitchen, have not much taste for muttering sweet nothings when they are on the job. Equally, the impossibility of kissing (at least within the normal range of human flexibility) enforces a concentration on the organs of penetration and acceptance. Those of us whose fantasy women howl foul-mouthed imprecations ['**** me hard in my hot, wet ****' is the sort of thing I tend to have in mind in moments of reflection on these matters] do so, at least in my own mind's eye, when they are vulnerably bent over, rather than when they are comfortably supine.

The thing about marriage is that while its compensations are obvious and sanctified by a well-established tradition, you do inevitably tend to lose those elements of mystery and danger that are important components of the erotic. Granted, in terms of physical and spiritual pleasure, what you lose is more than amply compensated for by crazy little things like love, respect, familiarity, which, of course, have enormous erotic force all of their own, but the fact remains: mystery and danger you lose.

I can't claim that rugby on the telly with egg and chips have mysterious and dangerous elements, but perhaps the *a posteriori* position has some non-threatening aspects of them. The same taste for mystery and danger may also account for the persistent fantasy of voyeurism. Here I find most men maintain a rigidly contradictory theoretical position. I certainly do. Yes, it would be absolutely fascinating and a capillary-busting turn-on to watch one's wife heaving and groaning with pleasure (and, if at all possible, howling atrocious foul-mouthed obscenities the while). No, you cannot even begin to think about it being with a real man.

Although there is a subversive school of thought that says a woman is never so enjoyable to have as she is immediately after another party has vacated the premises, the focused thought of another person, a disgusting specific hairy male, going flat out through the most intimate procedures, actually enjoying your wife, is murderously repellent. The fantasy man has to be a cipher: no other personality should be involved. The erotic basis of this fantasy resides simply in the pleasure to be had from witnessing uninhibited carnality in the one you love. This you don't get at breakfast.

But these are imaginative games, not real life. Real life tends to brutish sottishness. The way to avoid this condition is to stop listening to pop music and to refine the subtle minutiae that are the authentic scriptural source of the erotic. *Venus aversa* is all very well. *Venus aversa* is absolutely splendid. But I can tell you one little detail that sticks in my mind as more powerfully erotic than a whole zoo of quadruped couplings. Sitting one evening in a quiet and rather bad Mexican restaurant in Camberwell, talking about nothing in particular, I realised that peeking out of the half-undone buttons of a Jil Sander jacket was that very familiar, but very beautiful, left breast. She had an odd and maddeningly seductive smile, so much more arousing in fact than the 'asterisks me hard in the hot, wet asterisks'. I couldn't even play with my nachos. I think it's so often all about context.

MUMMY'S BIRTHDAY TREAT

Simon Raven

What an attractive woman,' said my old Cambridge friend K, who had popped in to sponge my Calvados and was now prying through one of my scrapbooks.

'Which woman?'

'The one with very short shorts, sitting on the steps of a beach hut, drying a small boy. She's just beginning to get his bum-bags down.'

'That was me and my mother,' I said, 'in 1938.'

'What a pity we can't quite see your dear little doodah. I bet you were as stiff as anything, being mussed about between a pair of thighs like those.'

'I was only ten.'

'Byron got hard-ons at the age of nine,' said K. 'He says the nursery maid saw to that.'

'As it happens,' I said boastfully, 'I got a hard-on at the age of eight. But with chums at prepper, not with my mama.'

'Didn't you fancy your mama – as young and pretty as that?'

'It is not permitted,' I said priggishly, 'to fancy one's mama.'

'You'd be surprised how many boys do. Remember that French film some years back – *Le Souffle au Coeur* it was called – all about a very pretty little *garçon* who was in short, white socks when the film began, but was just getting pubescent. He couldn't find anyone to do it with because he was so delicate that his *maman* wouldn't let him play with the other boys and girls; so he began to nag at her to have it off with him, and eventually she was part bored and part flattered into the thing. They both enjoyed themselves like all get out; they got a lot of amusing ideas for the future, and the boy's health improved *instanter*. One of the critics said that any proper boy would fancy his mother if she was as sexy as that boy's was.'

'That was only a film, and a French film at that. I never,' I said resolutely, 'fancied my mama.' Time for getting a bit of my own back, I thought. 'Did you?' I asked.

'No,' said K. 'She fancied me.'

'What an unchivalrous thing to say. Were you upset . . . disgusted . . . frightened?'

'Frightened of my own mother? No. I was interested.'

'But you said you didn't fancy her.'

'Once things were getting started,' said K, 'it would have been ungrateful and ill-mannered not to join in.'

'But your mother,' I said, 'wasn't a bit sexy, not at all like that lady in the film.'

'This was all a goodish time ago. My mother was handsome then. Well made. Lots of wholesome flesh to – let's say – handle. When I think of her now I think of that poem of Browning's, the one where the dying bishop promises his sons that if they build him a splendiferous tomb, he'll pray to the Virgin Mary to send them mistresses "with great, smooth, marbly limbs". That was what my mother had,' said K, with relish: 'great, smooth, marbly limbs. Very appetising.'

'I never looked at your mother's limbs. I didn't think they were relevant.'

'Neither did I,' said K, 'until the night before my fourteenth birthday. I'd been taken to the cinema (Michael Redgrave and John Mills in *The Way to the Stars*) and I was in my room, having a glass of milk and putting on my pyjamas. I'd just put on my pyjama jacket and taken off my underpants, when midnight struck and there was my mother, stark naked, posing in my bedroom doorway like the *Venus de Milo*. "Happy birthday, darling", she said. Then she beckoned and vanished. By this time I was thoroughly alerted. So I set off down the corridor in my pyjama top – I'd grown a lot lately and it only came down to my navel. Suitable kit for what seemed to be in train, I thought.

'The bathroom door was open and the light was on. "In here, darling", said my mother's voice, and there she was, sitting on the loo with her legs splayed, pissing like a carthorse.'

'How very off-putting,' I said.

'Nonsense. There is nothing more exciting,' said K, helping himself to a quintuple Calvados, 'than a woman with her legs splayed, pissing. Rowlandson has a special picture about it, called *The Family Outing*. The mother is peeing from the "at ease" position, holding up her skirts so as not to wet them. The two daughters (seventeen and twelve, by the look of it) are squatting. The family dog is careering round with a dotty look on its face; and the son of the family is standing on the box of their barouche, clutching a colossal erection in one hand and his driving whip with the other.'

'The trouble with Rowlandson,' I said, 'is that he can't do penises properly. They all look like pencils with angry red ends.'

'Still, he got the micturating women right. In my mother's case there was a bonus. She had a very prominent, Brigade-scarlet, semi-erect clitoris.

"Hullo, darling," she said: "if you want to go pee-pee, there's just room through here." And she pointed to a triangle made by her two thighs (which she now splayed a little further) and the front of the seat. She took my cock and depressed it to aim through the gap. "Thank you, Mummy," I said, "but I don't actually want to pee." "How silly of me," she said, "of course you don't, with a boner like that." She let it return to its former angle and fondled it very lightly with both her capable hands.'

'Boner?' I inquired.

'American for erection. My mother,' said K, 'was American.'

'Perhaps that explains it all.'

'She was also Jewish; but she didn't take that very seriously,' said K, 'she never had me circumcised. So now she was able to slide my foreskin backwards and forwards . . . "My little boy," she intoned, "with his pretty prick standing up stiff for his mummy." Then she suspended her operations on my foreskin. "You mustn't worry about a thing," she said. "I'm not worrying. Darling Mummy, just go on . . . doing what you were doing." "I promise I shan't keep pestering you," she said, in a bright chatty voice. "I'm only doing it this once, in honour of your birthday and because you're growing up and I think I ought to show you things. But I find I'm enjoying it much more than I ought to be, considering that it's all supposed to be educational. I've never been so wet between my legs in my whole life. Perhaps I really ought not to carry . . ." "Never mind all that," I almost shouted, "please, Mummy, don't stop." "Well, all right," she said, "so long as we're both quite clear that it's just for your instruction."

'Then she stood up,' K continued, 'and slipped her left knee between my legs. She cupped my bottom with her left hand and arranged me in such a way that when she put gentle pressure on my bum, my willy skidded up and down the inside of her thigh. "I'm still not sure it's quite right," she muttered, "so much pleasure in teaching." "And in learning," I said.

'"I wonder . . ." she began again, and stopped her rhythmic propulsion of my bottie. But by then I was fully able to keep going on my own. "Too late now, Mummy," I said, "much too late . . . CHRIST, MUMMY, CHRIST, MUMMY, JESUS, JESUS." Four fierce squirts and a long, juddery dribble. When I started, my mother got some of my stuff on the fingers of her free hand. She applied it liberally to her clitoris and then guided my hand down to massage it under her direction. By the time I'd almost finished coming but not quite . . ."

'While the long, juddery dribble was going on?' I suggested pruriently.

'I felt Mummy's thigh start to quiver and the muscles just under her bush jerk like a jack-in-the-box. Then she started to laugh, not a normal laugh, but a high, thin, tweeting giggle . . . followed by a kind of sepulchral moan, while the whole of her stomach seemed to heave.

'She sat down again on the loo so suddenly that I found myself riding cock-horse on her thigh. "My little boy has made his mummy come," she sort of crooned: "what a dear, good little boy." "My lovely mummy has made me come," I babbled: "lots and lots and lots, what a dear, kind, beautiful Mummy." Then, visibly trying to take control of herself, my mother said, "His mother always knows a boy best; she should always be the one to show him. Now back to beddy-byes." She prised my buttocks off her thigh with a kind of squelching noise, turned me round, patted my head, and, "Off you go, darling," she breathed. "Happy Birthday".

K helped himself to more, much more, Calvados.

'And was that the end of it all?' I said, sadly.

'Not quite. A few days later I went to her and whispered in her ear that I hoped another round of "educational activities" would be in order as I'd missed some of the finer points the first time. She put her fingers on her lips and shook her head, not guiltily or crossly, but very firmly. So I rather lost

heart. After all, she had stipulated "just this once". However, when my fifteenth birthday came, and my sixteenth and my seventeenth, there she was naked at my door at midnight, and off we went to the bathroom, to do what we had both been longing for the whole year. Every time there were a few appropriate variations in the dialogue . . . "my big rorty boy" when I got to be sixteen, "Mummy's brave soldier laddie" when I'd started my National Service. And there was always something new on the agenda, in the cause of education, of course. The year I was commissioned into the Dragoons ("Mummy's knight with his long curving sabre") she went down on all fours above me and rubbed me off between her dangling breasts. And on my first birthday after I was demobbed, she tickled my fesses and my balls and my peego with a peacock's feather and a power puff, till I ejaculated so violently I almost fainted. "Very instructive, that," she said: "it'll teach you not to overdo it." And so on, till the end.'

'When was that?'

'Not long after I first went up to the old college. We'd been celebrating my twenty-first by *soixante-neuf* in the bath. Wonderful. Being in a hot bath solves all the hygienic problems. Anyway, I was just leaving in my short pyjama top – I kept that going as a tradition – when my mother called out, "*Helas, cheri, ils sont fini, tes amours avec maman.*" She'd been teaching me the French words, you see, for everything like pubic hair and masturbate and spermatozoon, so she found it easier to carry on now it was time for the bad news. "Why?" I called back. "I was hoping to fuck you next year, Mummy."

"That's just the trouble. I knew you'd want to fuck me, sooner or later, and if you really wanted to I shouldn't be able to resist. So I shall make a point of being as far away as possible on your next birthday. However educational it might prove, fucking would really be going too far." "Why, Mummy?" I whined at her. "It's really desperately simple, darling," my mother said. "One must not commit incest."'

THE SWIMMING POOL

Justine Dubois

W here will we go?' The girl's voice is plaintive, like someone whose fate depends on his reply. 'To Italy maybe, Rome or Venice?'

'I should much prefer France.'

They sit on a low stone wall by a swimming pool. Music filters through the stillness around them, emanating from the kitchens of the big house. Their hostess approaches, crossing the lawn, her body at a slight tilt as she weaves her way amongst the miniature army of sun loungers. Did she imagine it? Were they about to make love? She had once made love to him herself, many years ago when her husband was away. But the girl, once loved, has become a stranger, difficult to decipher and no longer especially liked. She is also very beautiful.

'How are you?' The man takes her wrist. She shivers slightly at the empty casualness of his touch. He seems to sense her dismay.

'Come and join us.' She takes off her dress, a simple construction, much like an old-fashioned pinafore, made more elegant by the delicate printed silk of its gauze-like texture. Beneath it she wears a black swimsuit, cut high at the legs. She is tall and slim of build, with high rounded breasts, her legs long. Her figure is that rarity, it looks better undressed than dressed. Had her face not worn such a look of anxiety she, too, would be beautiful. She puts on her dark glasses and stretches out on the sun lounger nearest to them. The music continues to play.

The man stands up. His erection is clearly visible beneath the film of his swimming trunks. The girl watches him. He approaches their hostess, leans over her briefly and, with a deft movement of his fingers, lifts the tight elastic at her pudenda, revealing the flattened tangle of her pubic hair, slips his finger caressingly towards her clitoris, and then withdraws. It might almost not have happened. Their hostess struggles to sit up, lifting herself on to the flying buttresses of her arms, searching his face for answers, her legs slightly splayed. The man says nothing but, seeing his hostess now further exposed, kneels on the foam covering of the bed, placing one knee between her legs. She can feel the tickling warmth of the hairs on his leg.

He again lifts the black elastic to one side to reveal the pink honey moisture glistening between her flurry of pubic hair. As he does so, he also lifts the long loose leg of his swimming trunks and, taking his erection firmly in hand, strokes it up and down the length of her groin, up and down, a melting lubrication between them. But he does not enter. Her clitoris is engorged. He understands. He touches her briefly with his hand. She can feel her energies mounting towards delight. From behind the veil of her dark glasses she sees his penis, heavily veined and columnar, and as angry and alert as a whip. Desire settles on her like a dream. Her hand reaches to caress him. But no, it is not what he desires.

Instead, he bids her remain lying, receptive but uncommunicative. He wants to do it all. He places his hand under her waist to reach beneath the small of her back, raising her pelvis up to him. Briefly, he examines her, preparing her, stroking the glistening hairs outwards, so as not to impede his entry, allowing his finger to delve between the corrugated folds of her flesh. She spills warmth and moisture. Again he teases the tip of his penis against her, before entering her unhesitantly, following through in one swift movement to the core of her. Her body clasps him and he can feel the drag of her grip on his flesh. The fingers of his hand beneath her pelvis stretch out towards the sweet softness of her vagina. They caress her. She is ready to reach orgasm. He stretches his free hand towards her breasts and teases the nipples erect. He senses her mounting excitement. But, not yet.

Still within her, he raises her on to his now-kneeling lap, wrapping her legs around his waist like a scarf. He places his arms around her slender waist and kisses her breasts, all the time moving heavily within her. The moisture between them now is such that her clinging to him is less exact. He takes off her glasses, exposing her pale blue eyes, and almost without preamble places his tongue in her mouth. She welcomes it, lacing her tongue with his, and he reclines her on to the cushions of the sun bed. The black elastic falls back, leaving her partly exposed. He gets up, his erection still high. She watches him.

He turns from her, stripping off his trunks, handsome, yet curiously brutalised. He dives into the swimming pool, deserting her. She sits up to watch him. He calls to the other girl, who has sat still and carefully observant throughout their coupling. She joins him in the pool, stepping lightly down the tessellated blue-green steps to greet him. But, on the final step, he stops her and stands before her in water at waist height. Her body is tanned. She has fine, delicate features, with a mystery of a smile always implicit in their manoeuvres. He detains her entry into the pool until he has slipped the straps from her pale golden swimsuit, revealing the gentleness of first one breast and then the other. He kisses her gently and lovingly, hugging her to him. He peels off the last skin of her swimsuit and arches her backwards to place kisses between her legs, both he and the blue water lapping at her blonde exposure.

Their hostess witnesses the tenderness and trust between them, jealously sensing a difference of approach. He lifts the girl on to the side of the pool, and, remaining in the water, he widens and caresses between her legs. He picks up a stray leaf and tickles her secret flesh with it. He massages her thighs, the soles of her feet and spreads her out, encouraging her abandonment. She feels toasted and warm from the sun. And then he tugs her forward and, as she falls into the water and into his arms, slips her directly on to his erection and holds her to him.

She too is full of excitement now. Her body quivers at the completeness of his touch. He seeks out her mouth and together they dissolve in the sweetness of mutual kisses. She reaches climax almost immediately. He holds her pinned to the side of the pool as she falters in his arms. Her orgasm racks on and on, beginning again just as it stops. He feels the empowering gratitude of her response to him. As her body subsides and relaxes, he re-manoeuvres her to the topmost step of the pool and kneels before her. He enters her again and then retreats briefly whilst he turns her round on to all fours to ride her. They are now both facing the wide-awake face of their hostess. Briefly their eyes engage with hers, and then the girl, bent beneath the power of his body, subsides to the floor, the better to receive his fierce energies.

He beckons the second woman closer. Hesitantly, she eases herself forward to the very edge of her bed. His energies invade and beat at the young girl, seeking fulfilment, whilst at the same time, his free hand strays to caress the woman. Again he deftly lifts the elastic at her groin. Again, his fingers tickle her moist flesh and, as he judders in orgasm, so does she, their mutual calls startling the birds and defying the music.

The girl raises her slender neck, a look of concern on her fine features. 'Are you happy, Mummy?'

PART 5

Dirty Work

A LENDER, NOT A BORROWER, BE

Henry Hitchings

Stags. To you they are – what? Male deer? Men who venture out to social gatherings without female company? Priapic archetypes of masculinity? Your reaction is the reaction of any normal person. But to me, a stag is an investor who seeks to profit from an issue of new equity.

Nine years of investment banking have done deliciously inflationary things to my bank balance and my ego, but they have, I confess, defiled my vocabulary. If you attempt to regale me with details of recent white nights, I shall probably think you are talking about 'white knights' – which is to say, companies who impede hostile takeover bids by outbidding predators. I talk of 'due diligence' and 'adding value', of 'playing hardball' and 'no-brainers'; and my thoughts, both at work and at rest, are tainted with knowledge of zero-coupon bonds, Egyptian ratchets and Gross Yield to Redemption.

I know all about the anaphrodisiac properties of language. Bad language drives out good, and my office life is a lexical wreck. But power and money remain exciting, and in my line of work I tend to come into contact with the sort of people for whom this excitement is most intense.

Last week it was Frankfurt. I picked up a Slovenian junkie in the *Hauptbahnhof* and bought her starved little body with pizza and Coke. Two weeks before, I had been in Bologna. Did you know that in Bologna there is a Via Fregatette, which means 'Tit-wank Street'? Neither did I up till then, but I found a tart who looked like she'd walked straight off the set of an Antonioni film, and she showed me what a narrow, suffocating place Via Fregatette can be.

I enjoy being able to buy people; I enjoy being able to pry them out of their shells. But it's better when there's no actual transaction; when it's the stink of riches, not the riches themselves, that opens up for me some hitherto unseen inlet.

It's happened, of course, but only once has it been magical. That was in Budapest, when I was just an apprentice, a raw little analyst, eight years ago. I was staying in Buda, in a sleepy suburban *panzió*. It wasn't a business trip; I'd just fancied going somewhere I knew none of my colleagues would bother to go. I had decided to pay a visit to the Széchenyi Baths. I'd surmised that they'd afford a good opportunity to meet the locals and see them at play.

In my baggy, olive-green trunks I looked out of place among the blondes in skin-tight swimsuits and the cocksure men in thongs. I wallowed in the warmest of the indoor pools, watching the sexual tension evolve. The guys hunted in packs, and for their benefit the women preened themselves.

I watched a girl in a bathing cap who was parading her pertness with a quietly casual air that only served to draw attention to the nipples speared through the creamy film of her bikini, and to a bronzed face lit by dazzling eyes and a half-smile that looked like it had been carved out of a swatch of walnut velvet. She vanished, and I was disappointed. I flicked away the embers of my interest, and then a moment later she was at my side, treading water, smirking at me from beneath those viridescent eyes, and I knew instinctively that she had picked me out as the one man there who was, shall we say, a serious player.

I spoke no Hungarian. My only phrase was 'Reménytelen', meaning 'It's hopeless.' And she spoke next to no English. We managed to converse in a nursery hybrid of sign language and German.

I told her about my job. Told her I was sizing up some new venture capital opportunities (although, of course, I wasn't). She didn't seem too interested. Maybe I'd mis-remembered the German for 'emerging markets'. Maybe she was fantasising about a dinner of deep-fried catfish. Without thinking, I kissed her. She had a mouth that tasted of condensed milk, and when my tongue snagged on her teeth I was overwhelmed with a sun-soaked aroma – pulp and blousy fruits and gritty slivers of coconut.

She pushed me away. People might see us. They might object. Nothing was said, but I could feel that her reflex was one of fear, not refusal. I spread myself a smile for her, and she returned it nervously, and the afternoon contracted into a single bloodshot moment. My hand swam between her legs. Bracing myself against the side of the pool for balance, I teased her bikini bottoms down, and with an exploratory finger undid the leaves of her. She made no sound, but I could read a spider of a smile in the knot of her lips. My one tentative finger became two, and she enfolded my touch. I felt the trefoil beginnings of her, the nubbly ridges of her petioles, and then the mangrove warmth within, the furled convulsions as my hand opened her like a ploughshare.

I wanted to hoist her up on to the side of the pool, but my eyes were fixed on hers, and even though she had stifled her emotion, I could feel my way beneath the lie of her expression to the truth that she was imploring me, begging and begging me, not to expose her. Yes, of course it felt good, but she was fit to blush to her very root.

'I could stay here for ever,' I thought. I didn't want to see another copy of the *Wall Street Journal* ever again as long as I lived. Instead, my mind conjured with workaday words that were resonant, specially resonant, at that moment: capped floaters, and opening a trade, and apportionment, and interchange, and leverage, and inflation. Higgling. Haggling. For an instant I was . . . well, I was long; and then the whole fiduciary currency of my performance spent itself in a single, unwilled gout – my golden hello turning so soon to a leaden handshake of goodbye and good riddance.

My semen poached in the water. My Magyar girl paddled away and swam to the steps at the far end of the pool without a backward look. I shrivelled, nursing my incompetence.

I said it was 'magical', and now you are wondering how I could mean that. Well, it's like this: for a moment I was gloved with all the spore-and-stamen pleasure of a sprig becoming a spinney, but then it was gone, and then I had to recompose myself – and I found that I could. I found I had the knack of not caring. And then, as I lay back once more on the stone mantle of the pool and allowed a jet of water to massage the insides of my thighs, I had a yet more life-affirming thought: after that little disaster, it was fair to say that interest rates could only be set to rise, and my yield curve would soon once more be upward-sloping.

AT THE SIGN OF THE PHOENIX

Michael Bywater

When I am feeling low and out of sorts, I tell myself that one day I shall wake to find myself owner of the finest brothel in the world, which makes me feel better.

I know where it will be: in an old stone house dating back to the early baroque period, in Tiefer Not Allee, which forms the darkest corner of the great cathedral close at Freiburg, for seven centuries the brothel quarter of the most luxuriously licentious city in the history of the world. There are other towns called Freiburg, it is true; but they are mostly dreary, rain-haunted, middle-of-the-litter places of licit and infrequent copulation; quite the opposite of my Freiburg, where inchoate lust is a source of wonder and the occasion for a party.

Hier alles macht mit alles; a perpetual Saturnalia, where the laws do not run. Whatever your dreams, you may indulge them; whatever your darkest desires, here at the Sign of the Phoenix they will be cause not for contempt or disgrace, but for delight. If you have lived your life holding your most profound erotic yearnings in check – playing your fantasies close to your chest for fear of (if a man) a woman's anger or (if a woman) a man's disgust, the Phoenix will seem a paradise and the garden of earthly delights, drenched in voluptuous flesh, dripping with civet and attar of ross, the air close with gentle heat and soft (or fierce) cries. See what is here, behind the doors, which, if not locked, may be considered open in invitation. Here, in Wahnfried, a gentleman is dining; his dining-chair is of my own design; one after another, the waitresses enter, carrying silver chafing-dishes, which they place at his feet, lifting the lid to reveal a pastille, a distillate, the absolute or *concrète* of their own bodily perfume, which suffuses the air.

And the food?

They are the food. He devours them one by one, after their separate kinds. First is a gentle blonde, vanilla and myrrh, prepared in the kitchen by four labouring and muscular Ethiopians, who mould and fondle her to such a pitch of deliquescence that as she stands above him and smears and strokes her body over his face and lips and tongue – her oiled breasts, the axillary sudor, drenched pudenda, slick limbs – she seems pure unguent. (Did I mention that he cannot move his hands, restrained as they are on the arms of the chair? They are, and he can't.)

Next, a brunette, dark, musk, oakmoss and Jasmine de Grasse: the richer odours of a richer flesh, prepared not with the demulcent caresses of the *ouverture* but under a compulsion fierce as the fire which roasts or the red-hot pan which seals the juices in the emollient flesh to flood the mouth at the first, sharp slash of knife or teeth. This woman has been brought to sacrifice by her lover, who, even now, is waiting for her in the room called Überhäuf, reclining easily in his chair – another of my own designs – sipping a glass of Trockenbeerenauslese with a drop of bitter Underberg in its soft and icy heart. Soon his woman will be brought here, stripped, and laid outstretched, her head cradled in his arms, and then the others will enter: five men, liminal creatures picked at random, who will take his woman again and again before, spent and saturated, she is repossessed by her lover. She knows that if she is not ardent and liquefied before she goes to him and to the liminal men, she will be handled harshly, seized and spread-eagled and almost certainly flogged, and here in Wahnfried it is hard to say who is devouring whom as she writhes and squirms, clutching first at herself and then at the seated gentleman, pulling his head on to her, smearing his face with her musk, plunging her fingers into herself and then into his mouth, drawing herself repeatedly to the edge of a smoky, autumnal fruition then back again, until, alight with an ardour so deep she can barely stand, she leaves him and moves on hands and knees through the connecting door that leads from Wahnfried to Überhäuf, where she will be consumed and reclaimed.

Finally, dessert, the *Nachtisch*: a Titian voluptuary, a phoenithrix, tumbling flame above milky skin, a milky odour in her silver dish, styrax, tonquin, ylang-ylang and the tiniest note of butyric, buttery corruption. A cardinal flash at the oxters, a flare of red gold below the belly, moving before him, dancing like Salome and now the *chef de cuisine* enters – see him? This man can take a human being and turn her into a banquet like no other – with two assistants who seize her from behind and bend her over the man so that he drowns in her hair, heavy with sandalwood, the hair which is then seized and held taut and sheared away with one stroke of the knife; and now she is bent back again, her arms outstretched, and the room is filled with lavender and tuberose as kitchen-bearers appear with brushes and blades, with golden soap-dishes and pitchers of scented water, and she is shaven to sweet perfection and held up for his delight. And beneath the glory, behold: more glory. Now they retire, the *chef de cuisine* last, who, with a courteous bow, releases the gentleman's hands to fall upon his denuded, silken *Nachtisch* to part and penetrate, to stroke, scratch and tear.

The door now locks with a soft click. I know my customers: where they draw the line (because there is a line, though drawn far further out than you could ever have hoped) and now it is time for a little chat, a glass of wine while I explain to you what is required of you before you may be accepted as a client of the Phoenix. My room is comfortable; bookish, almost. You'll be surprised. Enjoy it, observe its details, try to work out what it says about me. You'll not succeed, but do your best, because you won't be seeing it again unless I have to ask you to leave, not to come back. Nobody comes back. There are no second chances, and you might ask yourself what you could do that could shock a brothel-keeper. Because there are things that shock us, you know. Not what you might think. You might be embarrassed about patronising my little establishment; you might think that I am looking at you, thinking, 'Poor fellow, can't get a woman to enter into fathomless sensual complicity with him; has to pay for it' or 'Poor woman, lover no longer finds her arousing so she has to come and play the *Hobbyhüre* here.'

Not at all. Paying for it? I have nothing against paying for it, and not just because I am grown improbably rich on your money. No; you'd pay for a meal in a restaurant, you'd pay for fine perfumes or beautiful clothes, you'd pay to travel to an unseasonable sun or to be ravished by Bruckner. How much more warrantable an expense, then, to pay for the gratification of your most fundamental appetites and desires? 'But Don Giovanni never paid for it,' you'll say to me – they all do, when we have our little chat – and you're very probably right. I don't suppose Don Giovanni ever would have paid for it. Well, I don't pay for it, either. Not any more. Not now I am a brothel-keeper. Brothel-keepers don't pay for it. To be frank (since we're confidential, here in my private room), brothel-keepers don't do it. Brothel-keepers listen to Bach and drink too much. *Le patron mange ici?* Bollocks; *le patron ne mange plus.*

You're probably not surprised about that. Or about the drinking. Probably surprised about the Bach, though; but if you can't see the connection between high baroque counterpoint and the *Ultima Thule* of sensual self-indulgence, then you're a fucking pervert and I don't want you in my whorehouse.

Understood? Good. Now we can begin.

THE MISTRESS

Lizzie Speller

'I shall not say why and how I became, at the age of fifteen, the mistress of the Earl of Craven.' Harriette Wilson, Memoirs

Whereas once, only the sound of pencils being sharpened accompanied the diligent critic at work, the heavy-breathing reviewers of Victoria Griffin's book *The Mistress* write against a background metallic buzz of knives being honed and axes being ground.

From Margaret Cook onwards, the reviewers have been a partisan crowd. Indeed, in this case, a female partisan crowd. I would like to have seen what Alan Clark, or Steven Norris, or the Duke of Devonshire made of *The Mistress*. Complete bewilderment probably; you keep a woman because she's pretty and you like fucking her and you'd rather do it out of the rain.

But I think it is important to state from the outset that I am as biased as my sisters. I am, or was, a mistress; a proper Mistress with a capital M, not the office slapper in an ill-judged Bacardi-coda embrace with her boss, or a generous housewife providing blow-jobs in the overflow car park of Birmingham Airport to a stressed middle manager in a company Mondeo.

Because, so often these days, a Mistress is, lamentably in my opinion, synonymous with any woman having any affair with a married man. As with everything else, the tabloids are to blame.

For the more discerning semanticist, the word 'Mistress' has the allure of the expensively illicit, of glamour with slightly foreign overtones, and resonances from the better-dressed eras of history. The perfect Mistress is desired for her occult sexual promise. She offers not just a body but wit and a good brain, the better, it is believed, to develop recondite sexual practices, which might become onerous, even injurious to health, if explored on a more than part-time basis.

Hours of oral sex on her knees? She is adept and malleable. Anal sex? She turns, all compliance. A whip to her back or in her hand? She will. She will. Or, at least, she might; it is what Mistresses might do that excites. There are, after all, only so many ways to skin a . . . cat. It is a matter of attitude; with a Mistress, all is potential. That is what a man invests in.

Most dictionary definitions of 'Mistress' emphasise her power, not her social powerlessness. Mistresses have influenced political decisions, brought down governments, holy men, bankers. They are usually establishment undoers; amongst the literati irregular liaisons are too mundane to thrill, and no self-respecting Mistress wants to pick up the tab after a long evening at the Chelsea Arts Club.

My own definition would be a woman in a relationship with a married man who is supporting her in a parallel *ménage* to the one in which he maintains his wife and children. The financial aspect is crucial; a Mistress is the possession of a wealthy man; she is an extra, and the gifts he gives her must be, like her, entirely beautiful, costly and unnecessary. Fifty grams of Sevruga, lilies smelling of the sweetest corruption, lunch in Nice, a Bichon Frise. What she cannot expect is a Black and Decker, new jeans, an iMac or five days on an outward-bound course; nor could she be offered Anne Summers red nylon panties; the lover, too, has to have a certain innate expertise.

I was in many ways a stereotype. My lover, twenty years my senior, was a charming, accomplished, charismatic man. Above all, he was a rich and powerful man. We met at a small party; the next morning he called at my house and for over a year afterwards sent cuttings, brief letters, the occasional book. He played his harpsichord on to my answering machine, sent anonymous roses.

I was driven nearly insane; that he was interested was certain, that he felt a sense of urgency was not. In the best tradition, when he moved it was sudden and unexpected, and afterwards he took me to a table booked in one of London's best, but most discreet restaurants – a table booked in anticipation of success. Our relationship was to flourish for over a decade.

But being a Mistress is not an anarchic sexual *divertissement* outside the conventions of marriage. On the contrary, its rules are as rigid as any other establishment institution run by men. Over that first dinner my lover made the explicit suggestion, somewhere between the scallops and the guinea fowl, that we should come to an 'arrangement' and even now the erotic charge of the word is potent. But looking back, I can see that the material advantages of my relationship have increased incrementally; a trajectory any career woman might hope to emulate.

I started part-time, as it were, with the free use of a studio in a notorious – as I discovered later – block in Chelsea and, three or four moves later, have a charming small house by the Thames in my own name. In the early days it was Giorgio Armani suits and wine deliveries. Later, it became rare editions, a piano, first-class travel abroad and a new car. My domestic bills are paid, I have his credit card. No underwear, no jewellery. My mother would have approved; it was one of her strictest rules.

What she would not have approved of – or even understood – is the £200 cash each time we meet. It is the cash, I have to say, that gives me a buzz and perhaps that's the key. To be a Mistress, or to keep one, you have to be turned on by power, by control, the apparently anti-romantic notion of exchanging sexual favours, time and focus for material advantage.

But what is interesting about the dynamics is that it is very hard to perceive from the outside where the power lies. With the man who gets to have two *ménages*? Two bedmates? The woman for whose occasional company and sexual favour he will risk social and professional disaster and expend sometimes staggeringly large amounts of money? Or the wife, whose daily companionship and security he will not, even in a time when divorce is relatively easy and accepted, compromise? It is the elusive, even perverse, manifestations of power which give this particular alliance its charge.

Griffin is right in claiming that serial relationships of this type can be no coincidence. The high-intensity emotion, the laser focus they engender, can be addictive and the gentle glow of more mundane, domestic intimacy is quite extinguished in the phosphorous flare of adultery.

Sex remains exciting, particularly in the head, for far longer than in more equal partnerships in my experience. The old joke about oral sex and Chinese food never rang more true than for the Mistress. Her sexual repertoire is a series of virtuoso performances; her entire libido focused on the night or hours a week her lover spends in her bed.

She is, briefly, a sexual Scheherazade. The other nights she may recover slathered in Annick Goutal body lotion, cashmere bed socks and *The Story of O*. She may, equally, be in jeans and a baggy jumper eating *Star Wars* cornflakes and working on the footnotes of her doctoral dissertation. A Mistress can endlessly reinvent herself; can turn her little fantasies into cash in her spare time. She is no victim, she is not even, as Griffin seems to suggest herself to be, shying away from intimacy; she knows her worth and is complicit in the contract. One day she may become a wife – but not of any man who also keeps a Mistress.

But as the law trundles on its way to reflect the increasing variety of irregular liaisons, the exotic allure of the Mistress may disappear completely. A court recently awarded a call-girl a share in the flat her foreign lover had bought for their rendezvous. It is not, I think, that men will object to the risk of having to maintain an ex-lover, but that the relationship will become ordinary. Once the Mistress has legal and financial rights, the electricity that zaps in the gap between her and the Other Woman fizzles away. The sexual thrill in the illicit, in having time and money at one's disposal, to be sufficiently self-directing and powerful to buy and keep a human being for pleasure, or *to be that garden of forbidden delight*, with no future assurances, may be quashed by being perceived as an entirely reasonable arrangement by the man or woman on the Clapham omnibus and recognised as such on the statute books.

Victoria Griffin's *The Mistress* is really two books in one. A brief survey of Mistresses in history, and a personal and psychoanalytical view of the contemporary Mistress. But, although this makes for an interesting, if sturdy, read, the two hardly exist in the same sphere of reference. Historically, women had restricted social and sexual choices. More rigid class barriers and the impossibility of divorce institutionalised the kept woman. Crude contraception made pregnancy an inevitable concomitant of sex, and such children, except where the father was of royal blood, were stigmatised.

Choice is what makes the modern Mistress sexy; but where once Mistresses scandalised society on the grounds of their sexual impropriety, now they are more likely to offend the shibboleths of feminism.

And, in the end, Chinese food is fattening, only satisfies the appetite ephemerally, and can bring you out in a nasty rash.

> 'A mistress should be like a little country retreat near the town,
> not to dwell in constantly, but only for a night and away.'
> William Wycherley, *The Country Wife*

A LIBRARIAN'S WEEK
(THE LOST DIARIES OF PHILIP LARKIN)

Gary Dexter

June 4th, 1958 – God, I'm ugly. Who'd fancy me? Bald. Three chins. One dead eye behind thick specs. A suggestion of madness in the other. A nose like a reject on a sculptor's floor, well trodden in. Thin lips that long to kiss.

10 July 1958 – At the library, Sarah bent down to sign a receipt, lengthening a fat cleavage. Buttering the phone handset with an opened cheese sandwich, I tit-fucked her where she stood, forcing my cock into her mouth and then fucking, fucking, my own throat swelling and despair filling my spine and brain like hot cream . . . I put a cross against her in the wank-book.

30 August 1958 – Letter from Reggie; disappointing read. I expect people like him to at least raise a laugh. He's going downhill fast.

1 July 1959 – I do admire the Monarchy. Saw Prince Philip on television, looking amazingly shiny and awkward. Went into the stacks and had a wank, God knows what I glued up this time. Then thought, fuck it, I'll have another, and stayed in the bogs for two hours beating it to a pulp, but to no avail.

2 November 1960 – Oh bum bum bum and more bum, I've got a bloody speech to make to the student body on Wednesday – well, tomorrow. What

on earth do they want from me? I'd like to see the whole filthy lefty boiling strung up by the balls, ditto the women over twenty-six, the remainder receiving a sustained assault from elephant dildoes RIGHT UP THE ARSE except my little bunny rabbit.

9 January 1963 – Sexual intercourse began. Rather late for me as it happened. The first signs became apparent about eleven o'clock, just as Brenda brought the coffee in. She seemed at first unremarkable, loaf-haired as normal, everything was in place, but then I looked outside – the lawn in front of the library had been shaved and oiled. I won't say what the air smelled like, but up till then it had been my favourite smell in the world. A crow flew past, and said 'Cunt'. I wonder if it meant me.

22 November 1963 – Heard about Kennedy, but couldn't remember where I was. Ha! Ha!

25 January 1965 – So Churchill's gone. Silly sod wanted us to fight the Russkies in 1945, not that it would have made any difference to me. Too short-sighted for history. My X-ray glasses arrived from Juggs International, and with Brenda's help I taped them on to the end of my binoculars. I then taped the entire assembly to a music-stand, enabling me to look out on to the concourse at the students and still have one hand free. This must be paradise.

11 June 1966 – Looking at the wank-book on Monday, I see it's nearly full. A hat-trick of tits, arse and cunt for every female member of staff since 1952. Opened a new bottle of Gordon's to celebrate, and watched *Zorro*.

I've lately noticed a curious sensation in my balls just as I'm about to come. As one reaches the point of no return, it's as if time lengthens and an aged little man, sitting in a chair in one's scrotum, sighs, stretches and takes out a rusty key; he unlocks a large, nail-studded door which creaks back, then hobbles away, climbing with some difficulty and much complaining a little ladder into a tiny alcove near the ceiling, reaching safety just as a furious torrent of spunk howls and rages into the room, battering and destroying all his furniture.

12 September 1966 – Right little, tight little Hull. Everyone thinks it stinks of fish, but it doesn't – it stinks of industrial effluent, particularly I'm told from the paint factory. The people of Hull seem shorter than anywhere else except Wales, the elderly more corrugated, the weather filthier, the curry-houses more numerous. Here, cancers come earlier; here, suits are cheaper; here, the traffic is half-hearted. I like it. To Hull, Hell and Halifax, the Good Lord deliver me.

3 January 1969 – Found an old photo of Penny yesterday, just the head and shoulders, caught with her head inclined, looking down at something in the garden, her blouse half unbuttoned. Summer . . . I was wonder-struck by her beauty, smooth and plump and young, young, young, so incredibly young; that perfect kissable neck, those lovely tits – not that you can see them in the photo – I don't have a photograph of her naked and I can't decide whether I'd want one – if I'd had one, I'd have inundated it in a Niagara of semen so prodigious that its wash could have lit a continent . . .

2 May 1974 – Bought three French loaves of all things today, the rest of the bread at Chester's looked so bloody stale. The girl wrapped them and said simply, '69'. Not '69 pence', but '69'. The look in her eyes, puzzling at first, seemed to say, 'You can either suck me right here in the shop, or walk out never to return, both alternatives mean EXACTLY the same.' I'd reached home before I'd worked this out, however.

7 April 1981 – Jonathan R. visited and we went for a curry in Albany St. In the bestial, flock-wallpapered peace of the restaurant a girl, naked, hooded, was brought to the table along with the polished dishes, warming racks, etc. and a very large serving dish was placed in front of us. The girl got on to the table and reclined in the serving dish with one leg outstretched and the other bent with the knee up and her heel resting by her buttock. A waiter quickly approached with a small tureen and ladle. He filled the ladle with a thick creamy sauce and served it expertly over her cunt, smiled and withdrew. Silence. After a moment's hesitation, Jonathan picked up a miniature gherkin from a bowl on the table and bit into it. There was an audible crunch.

Actually, he bored the arse off me and made me visit the be-buggered little yacht he's sailing around Britain in. He then left me with the promise of Paul Theroux coming round the other way.

12 July 1984 – Fucking titting bollocks! The arrogant bum-fuckery of it! The shitting, titting, clit-frotting, turd-biting, mum-licking, dad-sticking, piss-guzzling, arrant cuntery of it! How dare they ask me to be Poet Laureate! Here's a poem for them!

Suck fuck prick lick arse tit bum,
Twat crap scrote toss balls cock come,
Muck-hole fuck-hole cunt frig clit,
What-a-shower-of-fuck-ing-shit.
Poet Laureate for a day! CUNTS!!

13 July 1984 – Mind you, I'd have been offended if they hadn't asked me.
7 March 1985 – Look in the mirror, Larkin. Faint heart ne'er fucked the
pig. And so the pig remains unfucked, unfucked . . .

AFTER HOURS

Daren King

*P*icture the scene. Moonlit starry night. Office party on the back of a
boat, cruising the wrong way up the River Thames. Overstuffed
sandwiches and one too many glasses of sparkling wine. Conversation
revolves around the ins and outs of Accounts Payable. Smart chaps crack
crap jokes while junior staff members listen and learn, and bearded bosses
shake their bearded heads.

Among them is a man who hasn't had it for a bit, and a woman whose
next period is due. She once photocopied herself at a Christmas do, the A4
sheet finding its way into the man's in-tray. He remembers taking it home and
wanking over it, then using it to clean up the mess, smearing toner over his
tool. She made him promise to show it to nobody, and he assured her (saving
her the details) that he had destroyed it the moment he had got it home.

But tonight the air is full of romance and grit, and such memories fall away.

As their four eyes meet across the streamer-festooned deck, the two
individuals come together, stepping over sausage rolls and weaving between
cavorting colleagues, joining hands in the passage that leads to the ladies'
loo. The man compliments the woman on her make-up, and she confesses she
wore it because she felt ugly. He recalls a joke he once heard about women
wearing perfume because they smell, but keeps it to himself, instead
commenting on the woman's outfit. This makes her feel special, and gives
him a chance to feel her tits and arse.

Lights are blurring now, as alcohol works its magic and tiredness
intensifies its effect. To him, her skin takes on the pallor of a princess, the
cones of her Wonderbra forming turrets in the fairytale landscape of
her dress. To her, his stubble suggests untamed machismo, and she wonders
if it is true what she has heard about men with big feet.

As the boat comes in to dock and the revellers say their farewells, the
man and the woman link arms and step on to dry land, setting off in the

direction of the nearest taxi rank. On the cab's back seat, in the heady haze of cigarettes and disinfectant, the woman snuggles into the man's sweat-stained armpit, dropping her hand on to the Alton Towers of his lap. He mutters something about not being able to wait, and she hopes he is referring to eagerness rather than premature ejaculation.

Back at his place, he sneaks off to tidy his socks while she makes coffee in the kitchen; coffee that will not get drunk. Then, in the bathroom, she pees whilst picking her teeth with her hairpin, thinking only of her period, wondering if he is squeamish, praying it won't come on.

The man, meanwhile, has stripped down to his underwear. He sits on the side of the bed wishing he looked like David Hasselhoff, wishing he had bought boxer shorts instead of pants, wondering where he put the condoms, wondering if he should put one on.

She masks her finger-buffet breath with toothpaste and enters the bedroom.

He watches the way she moves, the way her dress moves, the way her body moves within it, wishing her tits would move, cursing the inventor of the bra. She writhes like an enchanted snake, copying something she saw in a television advert. He stands and holds her, kissing one of her corners, unhooking the strap of her bra, lowing her knickers, pausing while she steps out.

On the bed, she crouches, arse in air and leaves the hard work to him.

And so begins a fortnight of blissful soreness, of genitals like jellied eels and unforeseen days off work. A fortnight of scattered Polaroids and a bedroom that changes shape, stretching down the stairs to the lounge.

PART 6

Transports of Delight

ANOTHER COUNTRY

Richard Smithson

*A*s the century ends, perhaps we will stop taking the piss out of the Victorians, and admit that either (a) there is not much point in complaining that our great-grandparents did not behave as we do, or (b) that we are much more like them than we think. After all, if, as is commonly believed, the sex lives of the Victorians were limited to brothels and pornography, it is unlikely that there would have been any Edwardians, Georgians or New Elizabethans.

In the 1920s and 1930s, our grandparents were content simply to behave differently. By the 1960s, it was necessary not only to shag on our ancestors' graves, but also to berate them for not applauding. Nowadays we seem to be heading straight back to where we were in 1900. Consider the case of R. v. *Baker*:

1876. Poor Miss Dickinson, wicked Colonel Baker.

In June 1876, Miss Dickinson (aged twenty-two) was on a train from Hampshire to Waterloo, and was chatted up by Colonel Valentine Baker (aged fifty), a distinguished soldier and the author of an improving book on Russia. He eventually got a bit frisky. When he put his arm around her waist and tried to kiss her, she screamed and tried to get away from him, eventually opening the door and standing on the running-board outside (like Indiana Jones) as the train thundered along, with the Colonel holding on to her to prevent her from falling. Eventually the train stopped, she complained, and the Colonel was prosecuted for indecent assault.

The judge told the jury, 'If a man kisses a woman against her will and with criminal passion or intent, such an act is an indecent assault.' Which sounds quite reasonable. The jury convicted him, he was sentenced to a year's imprisonment and the judge concluded with the following rebuke: 'Prisoner at the bar, when this appalling story was first published, a thrill of horror ran through the country at learning that a young and innocent girl, travelling by a public conveyance, had been compelled to risk her life in order to protect herself from gross outrage.' Eventually he was rehabilitated, rejoined his regiment and ended his days as the Chief Inspector of the Egyptian Police.

1969: poor Colonel Baker, wicked Miss Dickinson.

This tale was retold by Ronald Pearsall in 1969 in his book *The Worm in the Bud: The World of Victorian Sexuality*. He had no doubt about the identities of the good guys and the bad guys: 'It never seems to have occurred to [the judge] that here was a case that was farcical in the extreme . . . The Baker case was a triumph of a rather smug, period damsel against a distinguished fifty-year-old man . . . He should have travelled third class, where the women were not so fussy about a bit of slap and tickle.'

1999: poor Miss Dickinson, wicked Colonel Baker, wicked Ronald Pearsall.

Ms Dickinson is travelling by train to, let us say, a lecture on Gender Studies at Essex University. Colonel Baker, the great-great-grandson of the original Colonel Baker, makes a pass at her. She takes fright, tries to climb out of the window of the train and narrowly avoids being killed. Colonel Baker is charged with indecent assault, and elects to stand trial at the Crown Court. He read *The Worm in the Bud* when it first came out. He was twenty-three years old at the time and it made a great impression on him. He decides to defend himself.

He is surprised to see, when he turns up at court, that it is surrounded by GROLIES (*Guardian* Readers of Limited Intelligence in Ethnic Skirts), waving placards calling for his castration and chanting, 'What do we want? Women on top! When do we want it? Now!' The Colonel has prepared a speech in which he reminds the jury that we have come a long way since 1876 – but unfortunately, though this is true, we have not only come a long way but we have also started on the journey back.

The peroration of the Colonel's speech, which is reported in every newspaper and flashed worldwide on the Internet, is as follows: 'It never seems to have occurred to you all that this case is farcical in the extreme. Here we have the cumbrous machinery of the law directed on behalf of a rather smug young lady against a distinguished fifty-year-old man. I should have travelled second class, where the women are not so fussy about a bit of slap and tickle.'

The jury takes fifteen minutes to find him guilty. The judge sentences him to twelve months' immediate custody – which would nowadays be a lenient sentence for a sexual assault that a woman risks her life to escape. The judge concludes by saying: 'Innocent young girls are entitled to travel on public transport without being the subject of sexual assaults and having to risk their lives in order to protect themselves.'

As he sits in the prison library the next day, a warder dumps a thick packet of letters on the table. The first is from the Ministry of Defence, relieving him of his commission. The second is from his club, saying that the committee much regrets, etc., etc. The third contains a divorce petition. The fourth to the hundredth are hate mail in surprisingly similar terms from a number of independently minded members of the public. Many are written on lined paper in green biro, with much underlining and go a long way to disabusing the Colonel of the idea that he should have travelled second class.

Meanwhile, Ronald Pearsall, now a distinguished elderly academic enjoying a trip to the University of Berkeley to conduct a seminar on nineteenth-century pornography, is surprised to see, when he turns up at the Andrea Dworkin Lecture Hall, that it is surrounded by DILLIGAFs (Do I Look Like I Give a Fuck?), waving placards calling for his castration and chanting, 'Ronnie, Ronnie, Ronnie! Out. Out. Out!' He is stripped of his professorship, his publishers cancel the contract for his next book (*Victor, Victoria: Transvestism at Balmoral*) and he is forced to flee the campus with a bag over his head.

There is an alternative modern scenario, however:

1999: ironic Ms Dickinson, laddish Colonel Baker, postmodern Ron Pearsall.

Trish Dickinson, a former aerobics instructor, presents *Gazonka!*, a children's TV quiz show. Colonel Baker is a crinkly-eyed soldier with a chiselled grin and a grizzled cheek. They appear together on a pro-celebrity edition of *Gladiators* in aid of Save the Children. On the way back to London by train after the show, Trish pulls up her T-shirt and says, 'What are you going to do about it?' The Colonel drops his trousers and starts to fuck her. They are interrupted by the Transport Police, who prosecute them under a bye-law which prohibits sexual intercourse between holders of Awayday tickets. They are fined £250 each.

Trish is fired by the BBC, the executives of which immediately rehire her to present an ironic late-night celebrity chat show in which the guests are interviewed naked in a gigantic lavatory bowl. The Army holds an inquiry into the Colonel's conduct, which concludes that though the incident was regrettable, it was a private matter with which the Forces cannot concern themselves.

The Colonel becomes a regular columnist for *Loaded*, and leaves his wife for a twenty-two-year-old researcher whom he meets at a PR party to launch a new brand of curry-flavoured lager.

Ron Pearsall, the BBC's media commentator, writes an amusing article about the whole affair for the *Spectator*, comparing Trish Dickinson to the Mona Lisa and the Colonel to Flashman, and including the passage:

'It never seems to have occurred to anyone that here was a case that was farcical in the extreme. The Baker case was a triumph of late twentieth-century triviality, the cumbrous machinery of law directed at a rather smug damsel and a distinguished fifty-year-old man. They should have travelled second class, where the Transport Police are not so fussy about a bit of slap and tickle.'

THE DISCREET CHARM OF THE MEXICAN MUSTACHIO

Lucy Moore

Ah, the lure of foreign parts. Nothing is as rich in erotic possibility as a journey. There is the getting there, of course. I am partial to trains, but I know others who prefer aeroplanes. And then, once there, the gradual shedding of inhibitions. There are as many variations on this theme as there are people who love to travel. First, there's nothing like sampling the local delicacies. I am writing this in Mexico, where, for the first time in my life, I am finding curling, waxed mustachios strangely alluring. Just across the border, the south-west of the United States begets in one the overwhelming urge to lasso a cowboy, boot-legs, shy grin and all. The Greek Islands also have a well-known effect on middle-aged women; we have only to remember Shirley Valentine, the Patron Saint of Waiters in Tavernas.

I have a friend who spent a year in Italy, ostensibly to learn the language. She never got any further than a huskily whispered, '*Non capisco, sono Inglese*,' which drew black-eyed Lotharios to her like bees to honey. She would lie back ecstatically and let their words of passion, none of which she understood or ever hoped to understand, wash over her. Who needs the past imperfect when you can communicate in the universal language?

As a child, I was taught that to travel hopefully is better than to arrive. What could compete with the pleasure of a holiday driving through France, where every day is both voyage and vacation? To wake in the morning in a provincial hotel, coitus interrupted by a frothy-aproned *jeune fille* with sulky dark eyes, bearing a tray of coffee and croissants (if only she'd stay). To drive through small towns, perhaps stopping by the roadside to skinny-dip in a mossy stream. After dinner, the local *boite de nuit*, that summer's pop song blaring over and over again, as hormones and tequila surge through your blood in a way they haven't done since you were seventeen, on your first skiing holiday without your parents.

And when you go home, you can leave it all behind you. Any indiscretions (that rapacious little Asian girl with a suitcase full of dildoes, that night with your wife's best friend, whom you encountered in a shabby hotel lobby in Lima) will be forgotten. Nothing, save the happy memories, will remain as part of your daily life. Perhaps that's the best part of all.

WANKERS

Rupert Wates

I was having this conversation with my friend Roy. Roy's a writer. You wouldn't have heard of him until a few months ago, when he started writing stories for this new magazine, which is a big noise at the moment. To be published in it, your stories have to be poised, elegant, intelligent and, above all, about fucking. And since Roy's stories started being about those things, he's won himself a record readership. You might well have come across his stuff yourself. It's nothing to be ashamed of. The editor of this magazine is a pretty dynamic lady, a crusader, and not shy of publicity. You've probably heard her on the radio or seen her on TV. And the whole thrust of her argument is that stories about fucking can do more (or less, depending on your point of view) than give you a hard-on or make you a bit wet at the top of the legs. They can also be things of beauty and a joy for ever. There's something in them for everyone, in fact, and to prove her point, everyone's buying her magazine.

Of course, most of the people who read it are probably wankers. I said so to Roy, and he agreed, but he said the biggest wankers were the writers, including of course, himself. And not only were the writers who wrote for the magazine wankers, but so were all writers. He wasn't being bitter or defensive or chastising himself for his own sudden success. Nor was the conversation the kind in which words like 'wanker' crop up indiscriminately. Roy was making a serious observation. All writers are wankers, he said, no matter what they write about, because whatever it is they're writing about, they get more of a kick from writing about it than someone else gets from actually doing it. As a wanker gets his kick from reading stories about fucking, or from looking at pictures, mental or real ones, of people fucking instead of fucking. And whereas wankers tend to read their stories, or look at their pictures only some of the time, writers look at pictures all of the time, in order to tell their stories.

No matter what they're doing, even if they are just sitting in a pub having a conversation, they can never let go, they can never just let it happen, but in some part of their brain they're watching themselves doing it. They'll be making a note of what it looks like and feels like, and smells like and tastes like, so they can write about it, and make it as real for you as it was for them. Except it was never real, it was already a picture. You end up looking at a picture of a picture. Writers are wankers by vocation, creating a co-fraternity of wankers who spend their whole lives on their knees, peeking through keyholes at themselves and other people. And the greater the writer, according to Roy, the bigger the wanker.

I was glad in a way to hear it, because between you and me I've always been a bit of a wanker, sometimes two or three times daily in the summer when the girls are out, and now I could take comfort from being in such exalted company. And I was reminded of a little story, of something that happened to me and my girlfriend Kate.

It was near the start of me and her, when we were still new and always wanting each other. Even better, we were in Paris, which as everyone knows is the sexiest city there is. It breathes sex and it's as natural as a glass of wine in the afternoon. Of course, like most cities these days, they're cleaning up the red-light parts. If you go to Pigalle, and stroll along the gently sloping Boulevard de Clichy, as I used to do when I was alone, to see the dull red replica of the old Moulin Rouge, or browse in the shops that sell videos and magazines of the kind you can't buy in London without a fine at least, or watch the whores in the hip-length wigs sitting on the café terraces, while the touts tout on the rain-wet pavements in front of the strip-clubs and fleapit cinemas showing hardcore porn flicks round the clock in half-hourly rotation while you'd get a hand-job from the man in the next seat, you'll find that some of those people and places have gone. And where they used to be, there's now something called the Museum of Erotic Art, which is causing a new generation of punters to get off the *metro* at Blanche; people who have less need for, or interest in, the other things that area used to be famous for; normal healthy adults in stable, loving relationships, who appreciate beauty and have enough curiosity to pay the museum at least one visit, two of whom this January afternoon were Kate and me.

It had suddenly begun to rain and it was splashing down on to the pavements when we came out of the *metro* doors and climbed the steps to the street. We put our heads down and ran through it. Soon it was streaming from our cuffs and had turned our hair to seaweed and there were big drops on Kate's eyelashes, and we were gasping and feeling as happy as children. Kate had always loved the rain, the smell and feel of rain, just as she loved the smell of flowers and to have incense burning while we were making love; and I liked the rain for the way it made her face shine and her sweater cling more tightly to her. But it must have kept the other people indoors, and then Paris itself was out of season, and it was already late by the time we found the museum with the huge Man Ray naked woman's back several storeys high over the door, and there weren't many people besides us shaking the rain from their collars and stamping it from their shoes in the little entrance hall.

All round the walls there were glass cases full of things. There were totem-like figures from Africa and Asia, carvings with pricks big enough to worship or ride on. There were little laughing Buddhas mounted on glass, innocent enough until you looked in the glass and saw that under their robes at the touch of a little lever they masturbated and ejaculated. There were Japanese prints of wide-hipped women, their faces like masks and each one with a kimono drawn up to show her vivid, swollen sex about to receive a purple-headed, veined and craning cock.

It was all grotesque, but it piqued your curiosity while you were paying for your ticket. The main feature of the month was an exhibition of paintings in the gallery upstairs, stuff that hardly anyone had seen because the artist had always forbidden them to be shown until after he was dead. He was still alive, actually, so he must have become too broke or changed his mind, or maybe he'd always intended to change it. It did the trick, anyway, because you wondered what the paintings could possibly be like. We bought our tickets from the girl behind the counter, fed them into the machine by the turnstile, pushed through it and then went up.

The paintings were in several rooms. And at first I thought I was in for a disappointment. They were just big splashes of paint. I remembered now that he was that kind of artist. It turned out they made a series that told a story; and the story, in crude terms, was the story of a fuck, which the artist had had with his lover, from the first subtle inkling that a fuck was in the air, through to the first kiss, the first touch, all the many positions and variations, right through to the orgasm. You could tell that much from the titles. You certainly couldn't tell it from the pictures.

I'd look at them and see if I could get the shapes to make up a form that had something to do with what the painting was supposed to be. But it was no good. All I could see was mess. It looked like he'd taken a running jump, brush in hand, and just let the paint explode on to the canvas. Still, I could hardly ask for my money back. There were a few other couples ahead of us, moving slowly from room to room, and it was a turn-on, in a way, to watch them looking so seriously at all the paintings and secretly imagine their sex lives. And after a while I started noticing the colours in a new way.

They made an impact all of their own if you let them. They'd take over until the whole room became that colour and you felt like you were walking in it and breathing it like a diver walking on the sea floor. The paint was all knobbly and blotchy, and some of it was shiny, as if it was still wet and you'd be able to smell it. You wanted to run your hand along the strange lunar surfaces it made. But of course, you couldn't touch it. It was all under glass.

Anyway, it had an amazing effect on Kate. She kept coming up to me and standing very close, pushing her breasts against me and whispering in my ear, like you do in galleries, even though there was no need to whisper as by now the other couples had gone and there was no one in any of the rooms except in the first one was the attendant, who might have been asleep. And Kate wasn't saying anything that needed to be whispered, but her wet hair on my neck and her breath on my ear sent shivers down my spine, as they always did, and I got hard at once, which I always do whenever I get the signal from any woman. I knew she was exciting me.

And standing there, with her head on my shoulder, she moved my hand to the top of her jeans and started discreetly rubbing it up and down, slowly at first and then faster. I whispered, for fuck's sake, can't it wait until we get back? and, still whispering, she said it couldn't. She'd never seen anything as beautiful as those paintings; they were alive and coming right off the wall at her, and while it was there, all that beauty, it was our last chance to be surrounded by it. We just had to do, it surrounded by all those beautiful things.

I thought we'd be all right if we were quick. I took her into the next room, the smallest room, where the last painting was. I had time to notice that it was nothing, there was nothing there at all, just an empty canvas under the glass. But Kate must have liked its white purity because she got down on her knees in front of me and I knew what she wanted. We were both laughing like kids and our hands were trembling with excitement and the fear that someone would come in or the bell would go and they'd close up and we'd be locked in for the night, and that made Kate move all the more fast and hard.

But it wasn't Paris, or Pigalle, or the rain, or the things in the cases downstairs, or the names of the pictures, or the pictures themselves, or the fact that we were supposed to be just looking at them and anything else would be all the naughtier for not being done in the hotel bedroom, where no one else would be about to walk in. It wasn't even the pressure of Kate's lips that was the final trigger for me.

None of those things was as exciting as it was to look over her head and see us both, her and me, in the reflection behind her on the glass, to see the frame round the canvas of the painting called 'Orgasm', that was the only one still empty of splashes of paint, and see us making a picture there, where there used to be nothing.

That was the story. I told it to Roy, and he said I ought to write it down and send it to the magazine. The readers would appreciate it, and what was more, I was obviously a born writer.

UNDERGROUND

Nicholas Royle

*T*he most flattering light in the world is not to be found under the Mediterranean sun, at Cap d'Antibes or the southern tip of the Algarve, but on the London Underground. The eyes and skin of a woman do not look at their dreamiest, most fuckable best as she lowers the front of her swimsuit in the frothing surf of Western Australia or floats naked in the turquoise shallows of the Indian Ocean off Zanzibar, but as she travels west along the Central line scanning the route map above your head for her destination.

Whatever it is – the limpid lighting in the creaky trains or her awareness of being confined underground, the film-star lighting on the modern trains or your awareness of her being confined – women are more alluring on the tube than anywhere in the world.

Ten years ago I saw a woman I will never forget. She was on the Northern line, and she was sitting opposite me, wearing a shift dress. And nothing else. Apart from the rats.

Three rats, two brown and one white, ran over her body, in and out of her dress, where it hung loosely under the arms. One would pop out from between her breasts, which were neither supported nor in need of it, while another wriggled across her tummy, burrowing under the thin material. She spoke to them in a low murmur and I admired her composure, her lack of self-consciousness, qualities that added to her immense sexual appeal.

Her auburn hair was straight, falling to her shoulders, clean but not fussed over. The dress was thrown on. She knew that men would be looking at her breasts as they walked alongside her and two steps behind. She knew also that when she bent forward to get out of her seat on the tube, my gaze would be drawn to the front of the dress, where the generous cut would reveal everything that I had ever wanted to see. She didn't care. It wasn't important. Possibly, just possibly, it was a game.

She wasn't expecting me to follow her off the train at Tufnell Park, one stop before my own, and talk to her on the platform. I wrote down my number and gave it to her, but, of course, she had nowhere to put it.

She never called, but when I see her, these days on the Central line, she hasn't aged and she still has the rats. They still tickle her skin as they roam over her body. Their claws still catch her nipples and their soft pink noses still moisten her thighs as they crawl between her legs. I stand, even if there's a seat available, so that I can see down the top of her dress, the same dress. Her skin has a permanent, year-round glow.

We get off at White City and walk to Ariel Way. As we cross the road, we feel the trains rumbling beneath our feet – hers are bare. We shin the wall and drop into the overgrown ruins of Wood Lane station, disused since 1947. I don't touch her until we take the branch line leading to the White City depot and even then I wait until we've walked fifty yards down the tunnel along the old westbound platform.

As she raises her arms above her head and I peel off the dress, the rats scatter to join their brothers and sisters in the shadows. There's enough light to see the tiny hairs that stand up on her skin as I run my hands over her body, my palms brushing her nipples, which become hard. She moves her legs apart and I kneel in order to press my face into her warm thicket of pubic hair, my tongue tasting salt, touching something softer than velvet. Her hands enclose my skull, pushing me in closer, grinding my mouth against her. When I feel the sweat begin to run into the cleft between her buttocks, she arches her spine and vocalises a tiny, high-pitched keening, as if calling to the rats. I pull away and, by the light of an incoming train, read the forties sign on the wall: 'Wood Lane. Alight here for Exhibition.'

MAJORCAN DREAMS

Henry Sutton

*H*i! Can everybody hear me at the back? No? Yes? Okey-dokey. My name's Zara and I'll be looking after you while you're on the island. So I hope you're not going to be too naughty.'

I always say this and the punters always laugh and, yes, invariably they are incredibly naughty. They get smashed and start fighting. They shag their best mates' girlfriends. Some of them get to shag me behind their girlfriends' backs, behind Pedro's back.

Pedro's my current fella. He runs the Autos Serra car-hire franchise in Alcúdia. And he has a thick Spanish cock. It's not the longest cock I've ever encountered but it's certainly the thickest, which is sort of odd because Pedro is tall and skinny (for a Spaniard).

I can't believe I'm thinking about Pedro's cock while I'm sitting here at the front of the coach with sixty-eight punters in the back, as the coach pulls out of Palma Airport en route for the Hotel Gran Sol, Las Gaviotas, Alcúdia, which is in the north-east of the island, some 50 minutes away. Plus it's only 6.45 a.m. It's not fully light. Judging by the smell of alcohol on their breath, their bloodshot eyes and the way they struggled aboard the coach, most of my punters are still pissed from last night. They were delayed at Manchester for three hours and had to wait another hour and a half at the airport in Majorca because their luggage was sent to the wrong carousel, in the wrong terminal building. It happens every time.

The bigger tour operators like JMC and Thomson never seem to suffer such problems. But the company I work for doesn't have much clout with the baggage handlers. In fact, we're like the lowest of the low on the island, except in one department. We have the best-looking reps. We're all dead fucking gorgeous, especially me. I'm five-three, have a thirty-eight-inch bust, blue eyes and a yard of bottle-blonde hair, which drives Spanish men nuts, without fail. Take Miguel, the coach driver today, he can't keep his eyes off me. I would tell him to keep his eyes on the road but I don't want to reprimand him in front of the punters. Besides, I like to be noticed, whatever the time of day. He's also making me feel rather hot and tingly (and wet). Or perhaps that's just because I can't stop thinking about Pedro's stubby cock – rolling back his foreskin and sucking the bulbous end into my mouth, so it's like I'm chewing a squash ball. A squash ball with a split in it.

Looking over my shoulder, I notice there's this complete hunk sitting just behind Miguel – brown eyes, black hair and deep tan already. How come I missed him earlier? And the fact that he appears to be on his own? The way I'm feeling right now I wouldn't be surprised if I found myself burying my head in his lap before we hit Inca (which is about half-way to Alcúdia, bang in the middle of the island). I'm pretty experienced at giving guys blow-jobs on buses. I used to do it on the way to school. I turn back to face the road, through the giant windscreen, wondering what it is with me and this job, and sex. Kim has this idea it's to do with the sun and being reps, like we're in charge, we're in power – and, wow, do the punters look up to us. It might be a cliché, but it's true.

Kim's my best friend out here – she works in the Hotel Regina, also in Las Gaviotas – and so far she's shagged two more men than me since the season started. I'm determined to even things up by the end of August, despite wanting to hang on to Pedro – you might have some idea why by now. And guess what? I already know who's going to be the next lucky fella.

'Before you lot nod off,' I say, having picked up the dicky mic (they're always dicky), 'I'd just like to tell you a little bit about how we organise things at Majorcan Dreams, what to expect at the resort, and how – are you all listening at the back? – we guarantee that you have the holiday of a lifetime.'

I can recite this spiel without even thinking about it, on automatic. The thing about being a rep, as Kim keeps pointing out, is the repetition. Kim's on her third season. I was a virgin when I came out in April. Well, not a virgin virgin of course, but a virgin to this business. Which is perhaps why, it suddenly occurs to me, Kim's two up. She knows the ins and outs better than anyone, those tucked-away places in Las Gaviotas which are perfect for a quickie. Still, I haven't done too badly – I'm not going to reveal my total so far, I'm far too modest, but I will tell you about the first punter I shagged. I'm particularly proud of that one.

He was called Warren and Warren was here with his girlfriend and another couple. They were all from Stockport or somewhere. The moment I spotted him boarding the coach I knew I had to have him. The feeling went straight to my crotch. He was dead gorgeous – muscly (I usually go for men with a bit of meat on them – Pedro's an exception, of course, though I suppose he has it where it counts, at least in one direction), swarthy (I hate guys with pale complexions) and with this wicked-looking grin permanently on his face (and they absolutely have to have a sense of humour).

For the first couple of days we were like giving each other the eye – passing in the Sol's lobby, by the pool, at the bar, when I was 'doing my rounds' (as we reps call it). I could tell he was coming on to me. Then one afternoon (we do get some time off in this job, about three-quarters of an hour a week), I managed to squeeze into a spot on the beach just in front of him and his gang – the others didn't notice me at first, but he did, straight away. It was as if he'd been looking out for me. I pretended I hadn't noticed him as I unrolled my towel, making sure my bum was pointing right at him as I bent over. I used to think my bum was rather low-slung, but I have this great bikini at the moment which seems to disguise that. Don't ask me how, because there's so little of it.

I settled on my tummy, undid my top and let the boiling, and I mean boiling, sun go to work. However, I soon found that I was gently playing with myself, having slipped my right hand under my tummy and into my bikini bottoms. I think it helps being neatly shorn, particularly in the heat – I hate it when your fingers get tangled in your pubes. I'm not sure what exactly Warren could see, but the next thing I know he's kicked a slab of sand on to my arse and he's weaving through the crowd heading for the water. I didn't even think before I was up after him. But there were so many people playing by the water's edge I lost him.

Desperately needing to cool off, I waded in anyway. I normally stick to the pool because I like to be able to see the bottom, but I didn't mind the murkiness then. Whoever said the Med was crystal clear? I was sort of half floating, letting my boobs support me, when Warren suddenly surfaced about six inches away, that stupid grin all over his face. I immediately reached for his shoulders and hooked my legs around his waist. The first thing I felt was his erection, pushing against the waistband of his trunks.

Somehow, with me still clinging on to him like that, he managed to free his cock, push aside my bikini bottoms and enter me. There were some lads on an inflatable banana nearby and a para-sailer floating just above us, but we didn't care about them. You see, I'd never done it in the sea before – I didn't even know it was possible. It's the weirdest sensation. It's sort of wet and dry at the same time – all slippery then abrasive. I'm not sure I'd recommend it, but I have one up on Kim here. She hasn't done it in the Med, yet.

I replace the mic in its slot by my seat, knowing I've gone on for too long, again. The thing about 'giving the spiel' (as we reps call it) is that part of my mind always switches off and thinks about other things, like Pedro's cock or doing it in the Med. Plus I'm one of those people who once they get going are impossible to shut up. I reach for my bag and my sunglasses because I'm now flooded with sunlight. Miguel has already put on his shades but I still don't know how he can see where he's going. I look over my shoulder, checking on the hunk. He's now sprawled across the two seats, his head resting on a scrunched-up jacket. He's fast asleep – I sent him to sleep. Never mind, I've got a whole week to work on this one. And then there'll be another coachload of potential shags. And then another and another. Bliss.

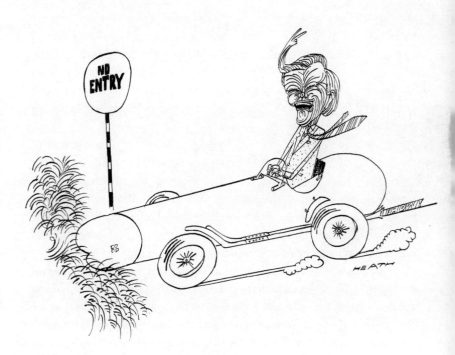

PART 7

The Island of Seduction

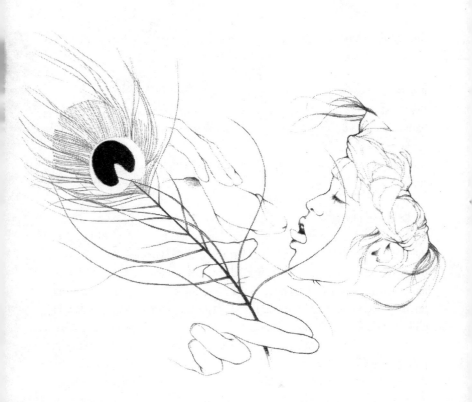

DESERT ISLAND FRISKS 1

David Aaronovitch,
journalist and broadcaster

Where is your island?

Oh, you know. Turn left at the North Star and keep right on until Thursday – something like that. To be honest, now I'm here it doesn't seem to matter where the island is in relation to this great continent or that craggy land-mass.

How did you get there?

One wet day before Christmas I took a packed tube train into central London to do some emergency Christmas shopping. As I stood there suffocating between warm, smelly bodies, my eyes met those of a beautiful androgyne, peering out from beneath the armpit of a man in a shell-suit. Exactly how she (or he?) teased a slim, brown, teenage body out of my thickening forty-plus frame, and sent it through the stratosphere to Neverland, I neither know nor wish to know.

What season and what year?

Every season and any year are available in Neverland. If you want snow badly enough, you usually only have to wait a day or so before the first flakes settle on the slopes. But usually it seems to be late Mediterranean spring: you can hang-glide naked from the Shining Cliff without fear of frost bite or sunburn.

Are the natives friendly?

Better, the natives are exciting. Take the Lost Boys. It wasn't until I first saw them down at Great Waterfall that I realised their wonderful secret. As the patched trousers and dirty shirts were thrown off on to the rocks, their short-haired owners revealed themselves to be gamine with an 'e'. Their long, boyish limbs are set off by small, firm breasts and unmarred by the dangling giblets of adolescent males. I suppose the French accents should have alerted me to the truth much earlier. When, beside the limpid pool, they discovered that I was different to them, their desire to explore every aspect of that difference at every available opportunity was both exhausting and satisfying.

What about the pirates?

Lesbians, of course. Very, very beautiful and butch lesbians. Hook herself is both dangerous and magnificent, her silver arm glinting in the sun, her eye scanning the horizon for signs of the crocodile. And always looking for a fight! What the pirates do to us when they (as they sometimes do) catch us and tie us up is too wonderful to relate. You may be reading this in the tube yourself, and be unable to cope.

And the mermaids?

Nice, but a bit dim. What can you say about girls who spend all day reclining on smooth rocks, combing the seaweed out of their hair? Also, the fish element makes conventional sex impossible. I mean, where is the G-spot on a haddock? But they're a caring bunch, and they like being read to.

Who is your Girl Friday?

Wendy. Do you remember the young Lauren Bacall in *To Have and Have Not*? Those sloe eyes, that cocked eyebrow, the lips, that husky voice? That's Wendy. Sassy, intelligent, strong, fearless and the sexiest thing on two legs.

What is she wearing?

Right now? If I use my telescope I can just see her telling the Indians rude jokes down in the village. Yes, a pair of tan chinos, a man's white shirt, and I think she's carrying her Indiana Jones whip.

What are you wearing?

Green tights, of course. They show off my legs to advantage and make even a modest package look good – I have to say I'm not exactly small, but since I'm the only person with a dick for a thousand miles, I don't really need to boast.

What is your shelter? Palm-tree or palace?

Shelter? An odd concept. If you mean where do I sleep, the answer is, wherever the last adventure ended. In Wendy's house, with the Lost Boys under the tree, next to Tiger Lily in her wigwam or Hook's stateroom on the *Jolly Roger*.

What are your provisions?

Bacon sandwiches, when I can get them. Berries, otherwise. Hook has a good chef who can be persuaded to cook the odd steak if we've captured the ship that evening. The mermaids are not worth dining with unless you have a Japanese-type yearning for algae.

What record is playing?

For some reason, all the Lost Boys will ever play on their battered old gramophone is *The Best Seventies Album Ever*. I think it's because they enjoy my Rod Stewart and David Bowie impressions. Wendy likes Hot Chocolate's 'You Sexy Thing', and can usually be persuaded to remove her chinos in time to the music.

What book is lying casually to hand?

The Count of Monte Cristo. Great adventure, terrific revenge. Everyone on the island loves it, even the mermaids (they particularly go for the bits with fishermen).

What movie is showing at the island drive-in?

Just about anything with Errol Flynn in it. Robin Hood always goes down well, and gives us ideas for the next day's adventures. And Flynn really knew, if ever a man did, how to wear green tights.

You are allowed one prop. What is it?

My twelve-inch dagger, of course. Useful for cutting fruit, bonds and whittling obscene figurines from driftwood.

What is the scene as the sun sets?

Nine times out of ten I find myself being explored and caressed by a gamine Lost Boy, an Indian, a lesbian pirate, Wendy or (on a bad night) a mermaid as the sea laps the sand and the *Jolly Roger* creaks at its anchor. It's tiring work, but on this island I'm the only man available to do it. What a shame I cannot give you directions on how to get here.

DESERT ISLAND FRISKS 2

Adam Buxton of C4's Adam and Joe Show

Where is your island?

My island is far away to the south just across from an old tavern frequented by sailors and pirates. There is a lot of traffic around the island. In a way, you could call it a traffic island. In fact you could call it the traffic island across from the Vauxhall Tavern in south London.

How did you get there?

I cycled, as I'm on my way home from visiting my ma & pa in Clapham. Half way there, I decided I'd make a stop at the traffic island on account of my boxer shorts getting rucked up and all, and I thought I'd have a nice fag break.

What season and what year?

It is autumn, nearly winter now, of 1999. Can't you tell by all the leaves and the coldness? Maybe you never go out, but still you can check the weather on TV and stuff. Come on, there's no excuse for not knowing what season or what year it is, unless you've been time-travelling, or on the booze for five days solid.

Who is your Man/Girl Friday?

People are coming out of the Vauxhall Tavern. They having been watching a drag act. After a while, a man crosses the road and walks towards me. It looks like David Bowie. It is David Bowie! He's had a barny with Iman and he's left on his own. He wants to hail a cab.

What is she/he wearing?

He is wearing a brown duffel coat and his hair is orange, but long and floppy as it is on the cover of his album, *Low*. He looks hot for a man of fifty-odd.

What are you wearing?

I'm wearing jeans that are too tight. The tightness caused the rucking of my boxers. I just don't think I can get away with cycling shorts is the thing.

What is your shelter?

There's no shelter, and I wish there was, because there is a light drizzle. I hate this country sometimes.

Describe the soft furnishings.

The saddle on my bike is new. I bought it at Halfords yesterday because for the fifth time in as many months some little shite stole the old one from outside my flat. There are no cabs around and I think David is wishing he could cycle off on my bike. Suddenly he asks me if I have a cigarette. As coolly as possible I reply that I do and begin to search through my ridiculously large backpack for one, frantically thinking whether or not I should acknowledge his top pop status.

What are your provisions?

I've got everything in my backpack. My laptop, a few DVDs I just borrowed off Joe, a couple of beers I nicked out of my parents' fridge and a whole bunch of tapes for my Walkman, plus a spare set of batteries. I always used to think, if I ever did get stranded on a desert island, as long as I had enough tapes and batteries for my Walkman, I'd be happy. A lot of them are Bowie tapes. Not too many new ones though, which is a shame because then I could have enthused to David about how he's still on top of his game, in a lame bid to endear myself to him.

And what is in your hip flask?

There is no hip flask, what do you think I am, a raving ponce? In fact I am a raving ponce, but I do not have a hip flask.

What record is playing?

'Be My Wife' from Bowie's album *Low* is leaking out of my headphones. 'Please be mine, share my life, stay with me, be my wife,' sings David. I used to imagine he was singing it to me. I so badly wanted him to share my life, but I had to be content to share his. I wasn't fussed about actually being his wife, I think we'd both find that a little revolting.

What book is lying casually to hand?

I borrowed an audio book of *The Moonstone* by Wilkie Collins from my sister. It's opium! He's on opium! In the future there will only be audio books. I always thought David would be great doing an audio book. I bought the *Peter and the Wolf* album he did, but his narration is too brief and that frigging music keeps interrupting. A good book for Bowie to narrate would be *Bridget Jones's Diary* as he was christened David Jones and it would be poignant.

What movie is showing at the island drive-in?

There is no drive-in here. The nearest multiplex is probably in Fulham. Call the Odeon Cineline for programme times and credit-card bookings. It'll take about forty minutes to navigate the never-ending key-pressing options only to be told they've sold out. DVD, that's the future of cinema! Ask David.

You are allowed one prop. What is it?

Goldie, Tricky or Trent Reznor, basically any vaguely modern duffer that David thinks is cutting edge. If I had one of those guys to hand, I would be so in there with David. He loves the cutting edge. I wish I was cutting edge. Think of all the chatting we'd do about, you know, the edge and the cutting. Oh balls, he's spotted a cab with its light on and we still haven't bonded.

What is the scene as the sun sets?

Actually the sun is beginning to rise now, and David is pulling away in his cab. All I said to him was 'Here you go,' as I handed him a ciggie. I admire the packet of Marlboro Lights he touched. Perhaps I will keep them, unsmoked forever. They seem almost iridescent in the morning light. It's ciggie stardust.

DESERT ISLAND FRISKS 3

Anne Billson, novelist and film critic of the
Sunday Telegraph

Where is your island?
It is rumoured to exist between Orkney and Shetland, a dark silhouette
glimpsed only by female ferry passengers who wake after midnight, their
loins stimulated by the deep throbbing of the engines, and peer through a
predesignated porthole on the vessel's starboard side.

How did you get there?
As I strolled along Birdcage Walk one morning, I was kidnapped by the string
section of an evil orchestra. I was drugged, gagged, blindfolded, stripped and
taken on a long, arduous journey by train and boat, throughout which the
first violinist never stopped fiddling with my erogenous zones.

What season and what year?
This was the height of a summer so dripping with humidity that I was soon
awash with salty perspiration, which, of course, was soon licked from my
trembling breasts and thighs by a brace of double bassists.

Who was your Man Friday?
The cellists were about to have their way when there was a sudden duel to
the death and I was rescued! Or was I? The top secret agent whipped off his
hawk-mask to reveal himself as none other than . . . Maximilien Robespierre,
idealist and doomed revolutionary. He'd arrived with orders to decapitate
me, but decided first to have some fun. Barely able to contain his amusement,
he now informed me that the instant I achieved orgasm, he would be forced
to cut off my head. Then he started to fondle me, mercilessly.

What was he wearing?
Robespierre was wearing his customary green-striped nankeen coat, blue-
striped waistcoat and cravat of red and white stripes. I soon became aware,
however, that beneath the pristine and virtuous exterior lay a simmering
hotbed of seething lust.

What were you wearing?

I was wearing nothing but crimson lipstick, head-to-toe clingfilm, and a pair of stilettos so vertiginous that the only way I could walk in them was with the help of a zimmer frame.

What was your shelter?

A ruined hotel, fronted by crumbling ivy like a mausoleum. In the basement we found a fully equipped medieval torture chamber, a fully stocked mini-bar, and a hot-and-cold-running bathroom complete with little bottles of shampoo, shower gel and mouthwash. Sheer heaven!

Describe the soft furnishings

The soft furnishings were made up from a squirming, wriggling ocean of velvety Labrador pups and tabby and white pussycats which whiffled and purred, occasionally rolling over with their paws in the air to have their tummies tickled.

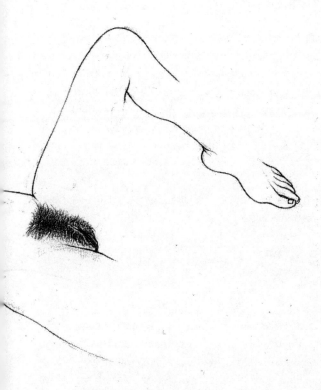

What were your provisions?
Our hamper brimmed with herring roes, Reece's peanut-butter cups, individual fruit pies with apricot or fruits-of-the-forest (but not apple) fillings, cheese 'n' onion crisps, raspberry bear-claws, rabbit-flavoured Whiskas, a French dictionary and fur-lined nipple clamps.

And what was in your hip flask?
Absinthe.

What record was playing?
Scriabin's late piano sonatas, but not a recording – Robespierre, an accomplished pianist, pounded out the music himself after strapping me, face down, to the top of his grand piano. The vibrations, needless to say, drove me all the way up the escarpment of desire (a well-mapped feature of the island), and it was only with a supreme effort of will that I was able to stop myself tumbling over the edge.

What book was lying casually to hand?

Smitten by the erotic possibilities of Euroculture, Robespierre next chained me to a handy tombstone and forced me to listen to selections from André Breton's *Nadja*. He was particularly fond of the line, '*La beauté sera CONVULSIVE ou ne sera pas*,' chanting it repeatedly to himself while passing a low-voltage current through my nipples. He was having so much fun that he decided not to decapitate me after all.

What movie was showing?

The movie, naturally, turned out to be *Daughters of Darkness* – the best Belgian lesbian vampire movie ever.

You were allowed one prop. What was it?

The *Daily Telegraph* cryptic crossword.

What was the scene as the sun set?

As the shadows lengthened, the vampires emerged from their resting places. Pale of face and sharp of fang, they pinned us down and drained our blood before setting us back on the road to civilisation, where even now we mingle with mortals who go about their business unaware of the dark secrets we share. We pass for normal, but I have only to catch my lover's eye as we pass each other on the street to become aroused to the point of dementia.

PART 8

True Confessions

I AM

Sharon Black

I walk like the Devil in these shoes, with an evil, scarlet bounce. They have a deep, hand-stitched cleft that runs between my first and second toes. Black leather as soft as if it had been chewed by a tribe of toothless squaws. They are built so high at the back, it feels like my ankles would snap if it weren't for the lacing. From the side, I must look kind of equine: thoroughbred fetlock, ergot and pastern terminating in a well-turned hoof. But stand before me and look down: pure goat. I like to think of myself as strong as a horse. See the hard, flat planes of my muscle, my long limbs and giant stride. I am abnormally tall for my age. However, I do not eat like a horse.

They would like to run their feeble hands along my bones to measure me, I know. They can't. I will not allow it. Their eyes on me are all I need. It is as if there is bombproof glass between us, and I can do anything I want, commit the most outrageous acts in complete security. I could say, Come on, fuck me, and watch them rip themselves to shreds in the attempt. But where's the fun in that?

I am trying to think and someone is pulling the hair from my head, twisting and pinning, twisting and pinning so tight it feels like my brain is being exposed. She is creating two great gold-braided ram's horns. Her hands are bleeding from the wire she had to coil around my hair. The same copper colour as coins at the bottom of a well. It almost drowns me in the bath. I can knot it into a bun at the nape of my neck and be almost invisible apart from when the sun sparks.

Past lovers often tried to wrap themselves in my hair – fingers, feet, prick. On occasions I have caught a total stranger caressing the dead ends of me. Once, on a plane, an old man teased a tendril from between our seats. He had too much skin for his hands and I shot him such a look his eyes watered for the rest of the journey.

People like that make me sick. Furtive, tiny gestures when they could be ripping out my heart. Now they are painting my face, fixing the pale base with duck-egg blue powder which smells of violets. Reminds me of the Devon violet sweets my grandmother used to keep in a china dish on top of her TV. I keep my eyes downcast, pretending to myself that I am a demure girl. I even manage to blush. But I am naked apart from the boots and cool as marble. I once read somewhere that, 'The greatest strength is to commit a crime in the certainty of denying it to everyone.' I am that brazen. I practise. It does not come naturally.

Now he is inking around my eyes. I could roll my eyeballs back into my head and present the whites for him to modify but, in truth, I like my eyes. Green with gold splinters, black pupils rectangular as an open door. When I blink, my lashes click. My lips are sticky. This stain is made to look and taste like blackberries. I have to fight my tongue. I can smell sweet fruit and flowers, and I want to cram my mouth with them – taste taste taste – but instead, the mask hardens. Only my mind is mobile, ranging, voracious . . .

Two people dress me, uniformly thin and clad in grey. They grab my wrists with their bony fingers, push, bend, bruise me. The garment shines like steel but moves like water, encasing me from nipple to thigh. One makes adjustments at the front, exposing most of my breasts. The other is stitching me in at the back, muttering as he tugs the fabric so close around my thighs it will be difficult to walk. I imagine cantering down the catwalk, this silly dress lifting and flashing my cunt at the punters. They would probably topple off their tiny gilt chairs, squeaking in distress. They think we are smooth down there. Dresser Number One grabs a make-up brush and resheens my shoulders, tits and arms with professional disdain. Dresser Number Two bends close to bite off the thread, straightens up and slaps me on the buttocks. I am not playing. I wheel round, pivoting on my bespoke heel, and slap him hard. My palm, his cheek, flush to match. He looks surprised but happy. I want to do it again but there is no time.

I hold my head up, balancing the great weight of my horns. Someone pulls gloves over my fingers, made of stretchy metal thread. I practise swinging my arms. I gauge my optimum stride, calves quivering on my new hoofs. I am the tallest person in the room and I like it. They all bow down to me. Oh yes, and I am wet and naked underneath this thin disguise. Can they see? Not that it matters, because I am behind glass. I touch myself for reassurance, slip an abrasive finger into the groove, then between the lips . . .

My time has almost come. It seems like I am peering over the edge of a mountain. I feel dizzy and sick, and about to scream with excitement. Obscenities spring to my painted lips. Here in the wings I have to bite them back but out there, in the music and the packed auditorium, I can curse at full voice, rain contempt on their heads like blood-specked sputum. Which they will lap up. Such a perverse relationship!

I have the runway to myself. I am bathed in lilac light and the heat of all eyes is upon me. There is such an ache now between my legs. My head is

floating. I am breathing fast and shallow. Applause. Palms pinking. The memory of the sharp slap is still warm on me. The gloves scratch my thighs. I reach the limit of my trajectory and pause, fists on skinny hips. One nipple fully exposed glitters, hard. I swing my head, tilt my horns, steam escapes from my nostrils.

There is the detonation. . .on my side of the glass all is blood and heartbeat and ecstatic relief. I bite my lip, savour the sweet fruit of myself. They look pinched, cold, maybe even a little dreary. As I turn to leave, my knees are trembling like a dazzled foal, but I soon recover. I only have to look at my feet to be reminded of my strength.

I don't walk like the Devil in these shoes: I AM.

CONFESSIONS OF AN AMATEUR: EROTIC DIPLOMACY

Sir Leslie Colin Patterson

(Exclusive extracts from The Extended Tool, *forthcoming sequel to Dr Patterson's famous manual of 1985,* The Traveller's Tool*)*

I'm a diplomat, an Australian diplomat, to boot, and I have been in some pretty sticky situations over the years. Like most readers of this horny little publication (sent to you under plain wrappers and printed so it can easily slip inside the innocent covers of *The Economist*, *The Lady's Home Journal* or the Gideon Bible) I am a married man. Furthermore, I love my wife, even though she is nearly at least 13,000 miles away from the motel suites and commodious back seats of limos in which I might be currently slipping a Girl Friday or a research assistant the irresistible eight inches. I think I can hear a few puritanical readers making disgusted noises at this fearless admission. I can hear them saying, 'We subscribe to this publication because we believe eroticism is a viable art-form which can be appreciated in the same way as a lovely hand-done painting or a show by Shakespeare. Why does this Australian diplomat have to drag our elevated concepts through the shit?'

Let me explain. I wear a lot of hats. I'm not just a politician but I am also a world authority on cheese – in case you didn't know it, I put Tasmanian Camembert on the map. Not to mention Gulla-Gulla Gorgonzola, a delightful spread cultivated by our own Aborigines in the privacy of their preferred accommodation. As a matter of fact, whenever I'm having my photograph taken, I never forget to say 'Cheese' because there is always a bit of it under my fingernails to remind me of home.

It will not surprise the reader who has followed me thus far to learn that I am also a world authority on aphrodisiacs, which is where my qualifications and the preoccupations of this little mag cross over, in a raunchy kind of way. Remember, aphrodisiacs are not just potions. I've pumped enough pulverised rhino horn, ginseng and Spanish fly into attractive young church-going lasses of my acquaintance to keep the old purple-headed warrior in business until the millennium.

But I have found that the success rate of these products is practically nil compared with the infallible power of the aforementioned eight inches. It isn't always eight inches. It could be a bit shorter or a bit longer too, no worries. I well remember a trainee secretary I had called Wendy. She was a delightful young woman from a good home and she always wore a tasteful little cross around her neck. She must have had a few of them because she would swap it for the larger article if there was a love bite to cover up, bless her. I have to say, little Wendy and me really hit it off, particularly if I had a few letters to answer late at night. 'There's no doubt about you, Les,' she'd say, 'you're the bloke who put the dick back into dictation.'

I must have had Wendy on my mind that night last year when I popped into the Adonis fitness club. This is a bona fide establishment – it's certainly no rub and tug shop – and I usually do a few minutes on the exercise bike, which they reckon limbers up the old prostrate. It was in the sauna that I got the fright of my life. Right next to me sat a great big West Indian bloke, completely starkers. He was a bit of an O.J. lookalike, funnily enough, with the same innocent expression on his face. Not that I was looking at his face, at least. My eye did move involuntarily to the area where his towel ought to have been.

I hasten to say that I always drape a towel over the wife's best friend when I'm in a sauna situation. Why give a perfectly nice bunch of blokes an inferiority complex? is my motto. However, he could have knocked me over with a feather when I glanced down at this ethnic minority's old fella and saw the name Wendy tattooed down the side of it. I'm a pretty sensitive organism

– actually, I'm a sensitive organism with a sensitive organism – but it really hurt me to think that little Wendy might have been doing the dirty deed with the six-foot stallion sweating like buggery on my right.

Now, starting up a conversation about intimate appendages with another bloke in a health club could brand you as a bit of a poofter. Not to put too fine a point on it, you could convey the impression of being a card-carrying mattress muncher or even a turd burglar or Vegemite driller. Fortunately, there are still a few blokes around who are sufficiently politically incorrect to take exception to pillow biters coming on strong in the steam room, heaven be praised. Still, I was sufficiently jealous to take a big risk. 'Excuse me, mate,' I said to the black bloke, 'I notice you've got a tattoo on the old blue-veined junket pump.' He gave me a funny look – but don't they all?

'Yes, man, I have,' was all he said, the dirty bastard.

'Well,' I persevered, 'I just can't help observing that it's the name of a sheila – Wendy.'

'Is that so?' my dusky perspiring neighbour replied, looking down at the tattooed member.

'I just wondered,' I said diplomatically, 'if, er, your Wendy might happen to be the same tart as my Wendy.' He had another look at it and after a long pause, when I thought he might be on the verge of giving me a knuckle sandwich, he said with a lovely smile, 'It doesn't say, "Wendy", man, it says "Welcome to Jamaica, Have a Nice Day"!'

But I'm getting off the track, and scholars and connoisseurs reading this, please forgive me. The eight-inch aphrodisiac I was referring to in a previous paragraph is a British Airways Business Class International ticket, and BELIEVE YOU ME, slip one of those into a sheila's clammy hand and she'll be on her back, inspecting the ceiling of a foreign hotel and screaming for more.

I've never known the eight inches to fail. Sometimes it's not a bad idea to say you're on a business trip to New York or Paris and your secretary's copped a dose of salmonella or rabies, or something, and there's a vacant seat going begging. That lets a nice girl off the hook and she can PRETEND she's just going for the ride. But every woman knows that there's small print – invisible to the naked eye – on every airline ticket, which entitles the donor of the ticket to sexual liberties, lawful and unlawful, at journey's end.

I began by saying that I love my wife, and I do. Her name is Gwen, and she is an amazing woman. Most people are amazed when they first set eyes on her, but after a few drinks they generally adjust to her appearance. You see, readers, Lady Patterson is not a conventional beauty, which is why I have never taken her to a convention. Furthermore, she spends most of her life in an old dressing-gown, the Lord be good to her.

She has become a little bit of a substance abuser recently, but the family doctor has put her on a vigorous regime of Prozac and Valium, and told her to drink plenty of liquids. I have to say I was a bit worried about her recently when I found her watching the same video (*The Return to the Valley of the Dolls*) sitting in the same chair as she'd been sitting in seven months before, when I took off on a business trip. But Gwen did ask for help. As a matter of fact, she asked me for help. You see, there was a bottle of Smirnoff out of reach on the top of the wardrobe and she asked me to get help to get it down and put it on her bedside table.

I've got a picture of Gwen that I always carry around with me. It was taken a long time ago, before she started shaving, and it's a beauty. Whenever I'm doing some young lady a favour, I always whip it out of my pocket surreptitiously and Blu-tack it to the wall above the hornbag's head. Let me assure scholars and connoisseurs who have read thus far that there is no more steadying or prolonging influence than the face of a beloved spouse staring at you between the ankles of a compliant research assistant.

I think of Gwen very often, readers, but I think of her the most whenever I'm driving the old pigskin bus into Tuna-town.

FAMILY

Sebastian Horsley

When I was young I thought the recipe for happiness was devastating good looks, a blazing talent and a colossal income. I was right. As for love? The rich think that the most important thing in life is love. The poor know it is money. It's the only thing poor people do know. Given that money is the root of all evil, they should be very virtuous. But they're not. No, they just moan, groan and drone, looking for a loan. Why don't they just get rid of such luxuries as food, clothing and shelter, and give us all some peace? Give me the luxuries of life and I will dispense with the necessities. I learnt this very young. It was the only thing I did learn.

You see, I didn't have a childhood. I had an apprenticeship in human depravity. My mother and father only slept together once. Money changed hands – probably a dime. When my mother found out she was pregnant with me, she took an overdose. (As mothers do.) There's nothing like being made to feel welcome. Unfortunately, the overdose didn't work. Had it, I would have been a very happy man – there is nothing worse than being born. And had mother known I would turn out like this, she would have taken cyanide.

And so, very reluctantly, I was born. My mother took one look at me and succumbed to severe post-natal depression. Thirty-five years later and she's still got it. She still talks about committing suicide (actions speak louder than words, Mother). She assumes it is normal to spend an hour each day contemplating the advantages of carbon-monoxide poisoning over a leap off a high building. After four unsuccessful attempts, I can proudly proclaim that Mother is a failed suicide. On the evolutionary scale you can't get much lower than this. Beneath her, there is only primeval slime. I know it is wrong to throw stones at your own mother; as a rule, I prefer bricks.

The only great thing my father did was produce me. As far as I know, that is. I also have a brother and a sister. (I wasn't consulted in the womb; had I been, I would have been an only child and an orphan to boot.) They claim to be related to me. I shall demand a DNA test. How could one as glorious as me possibly have come from such a middleweight, middlebrow, middle-income, middle-class, middle-of-the-road, middle-England, middling gene pool? I ask you.

My father is a drunk and a cripple. In fact, the one thing I am really grateful to him for is that he has broadened my emotional range as a result. I never thought it was possible to want to murder a drunk cripple. There is nothing else to be grateful for. I often think of taking a bag, filling it with sperm and sending it to him. It is the only thing I owe him.

I grew up in an orgy of drink. Every night our house was hit by a tidal wave of alcohol. The consequences were devastating. Father, because he was a drunk and a cripple, was always falling over. Mother, because she was a drunk, a manic depressive, and lazy, never got out of bed, and my stepfather, who was a drunk and had a faulty pacemaker which kept conking out, spent his life holding on to the floor. Indeed everyone in my life who should have been vertical was horizontal.

There is a photo I have of them taken around this time. Mother is on the floor, face down in what appears to be a pool of her own vomit. On the sofa sits my grandmother, her wig lopsided and her lipstick smeared across her face. Next to her sits father, a drink in one hand and his cock in the other. 'Home Sweet Home' was obviously written by a bachelor. You can see why I have the odd problem now and again. Occasionally, one member of the family would try and rein one of the others in. Mother's behaviour was always the most admirable. She would lock my sister in a room all day; she would set the house on fire; she burnt all my father's possessions skipping round the bonfire like a wild banshee; she was arrested for shoplifting from my father's own shops; she once ran over a crocodile of nuns; and she wrote off three of father's Jaguars by driving drunk to the off-licence. Finally, in exasperation, he confiscated the car keys, hoping to kill two birds with one stone, only to find her driving to the liquor store on a motorised lawnmower.

Certainly the wind of the wing of madness has passed over my family. My grandmother was clinically insane. Mother was in and out of the nuthouse. She would oscillate wildly depending on the treatment she was receiving. After electric-shock treatment she would feel 'rather sparky, actually' and have a zing to her step; after Mandrax she would be depressed and wander around the house like a tortoise on a lettuce hunt. I often wonder how it is that I, who have always had the mind and the nerves and the history, everything necessary, really, to go mad, have never actually done so. Instead, I spend my life poised between Savile Row and Death Row, trying to find a balance between vanity and insanity, wandering aimlessly like the dispossessed king that I am.

My parents didn't operate an open-house policy. It was more open bed.

Lovers cascaded from the sky like confetti. Sex sat enthroned; her drawbridge pulled up to keep intellect at bay.

They were more interested in penetrating orifices than penetrating insights. Father tried to be faithful – to his mistress. He had three wives – of his own. It was not unusual to come home and find him in bed with various people, none of whom bore any resemblance to mother. Stepfather tried to screw sister. Father screwed stepfather's wife. Brother (me) tried to seduce stepsister. Father tried to screw son's girlfriend. Mother tried to seduce son's best friend. Father did seduce mother's best friend. You get the general idea.

There were compensations: money, chiefly, and lots of it. Some people talk of morality and some of religion, but quite frankly I'll have the cash if you don't mind. In fact my main problem in life is that I was born with a silver spoon in my mouth. It should have been platinum encrusted with diamonds. Unfortunately, we were flash, brash, trash. To my horror I am a parvenu. (How could you have misread those signs?) Father would come off the phone, mother would put her perfume and outfit on in front of the mirror, go to the toilet, and then they would have a meal, wiping their mouths with serviettes, before retiring to the front room to sit on the couch. Pardon?

Not that I am too worried about all this, you understand. After all, *nouveau riche* is better than no *riche*. Years later, mother came to visit me in a drugs clinic. I was lying in bed, withdrawing savagely from crack and heroin. I was looking and feeling fit only for the undertaker. Out of the corner of my eye I saw a blazing Technicolor explosion which I took to be a fruit cart. It was mother. She waltzed in, clad toe to crown in velvet and silk and perched on the end of the bed.

'Have I failed you as a mother, Sylvester?'

'It's Sebastian, mother.'

They say that you choose your own parents. If this is true then I seem to have made a terrible mistake. When I was born I took one look around and said, 'This will not do.' I invented myself. I am a self-made man in love with my creator. I have sacrificed myself on the altar of artifice. I am a shell of velvet enclosing an abyss. What on earth does 'good' or 'bad' parenting have to do with this?

Yes, it is true, my mother and father were uninterested, unloving and unconscious. But did this make me unlucky? I think not. It is frightfully common to be loved by one's parents.

CONFESSION

John Gibb

*F*ather Anthony rises from his stall in the choir, eases his collar and genuflects stiffly towards the high altar. Morning Mass is over and the monks have gone about their business, but the airy vaults of the Abbey Church are still fluttering with echoes of Gregorian chant. The priest glances at the sunlight loitering in the misty archways and sniffs the incense in the dusty air. Comforting sensations; familiar and reassuring; what he is used to.

On Friday mornings, Father Anthony processes the sins of the community in the confessional beside the Chapel of St Agnes. He walks across to the south aisle and, with familiarity born from a lifetime of ceremony, kisses the chasuble, slips it around his neck, settles down on the hard wooden seat and shuts the door. This is the best time of the week; a time to be alone with one's thoughts; anonymous, secure and vulnerable only to muted admissions of human failure. Most of his penitents are regulars, rural Mass-goers who have to scratch around for something worthwhile to get off their chests. Half a dozen Hail Marys for penance and see you again next week. Nothing too challenging.

He sighs and raises a buttock to emit a discreet, low-velocity fart before opening his breviary and turning to St Peter's Epistle to the Apostles. A silence, broken occasionally by the faint chime of a clock somewhere in the distant sacristy falls upon the old building. Father Anthony dozes.

After a while, the door of the Abbey Church swings open and lets in a flood of sunlight. A girl in a flower-patterned dress stands on the threshold. She is black, perhaps of mixed race, and tall; shiny hair swept back from her face and tied in a ponytail. She wears trainers and carries a small leather bag on her back. Her eyes are prominent and limpid, framed beneath a pair of gently slanting eyebrows. Her mouth is generous and her lips are deep. She walks across the nave and into the south aisle. A card slotted into a brass frame on the door announces that Father Anthony will hear confessions between 11.30 a.m. and 1 p.m. She notes the socks and sandals beneath the door, kneels by the grille and says, 'Bless me, Father, for I have been a very bad girl.'

Father Anthony, who has slipped into a sensuous dream of roast pork, potatoes and crackling, drops his breviary, sits up sharply, crosses himself and mutters, 'God bless you, child. How long is it since your last confession?'

Deborah, for that is her name, sits back on her heels and says, 'Look, this could take some time, I'm going to get a chair.' As she walks towards the nave, Father Anthony, squinting through the grille, sees her body in a halo of sunshine outlined through the filmy fabric of her skirt.

Settling down, legs crossed, some moments later, Deborah says, 'Look, Anthony, I have no idea how long it is since that catechism shit. I was at school, you know? I need to tell you some of the tricks I been up to lately and get them off my mind, OK?'

The priest, now wide awake, says, 'You must confess your sins, my child, but you must realise that I am no more than a vessel; you are speaking though me to Our Lord Jesus Christ and you must truly want to repent. Remember that he laid down his life for our sins.'

'OK,' says Deborah. 'What can I say? I live in Crouch End with Gig, my boyfriend, and we work in the clubs but not together. He's a barman and he took me in when I arrived here from Los Angeles four years ago. I am still with him. He's cool and he lets me get on with my life, you know? We may go our separate ways, but we have our own friends and we have things in common. I mean, for instance, we do a lot of drugs.' Deborah takes a tissue from her knapsack and wipes her nose. The priest can think of nothing to say.

'Anyway,' she continues, 'during the summer I meet this man. He is a writer and he comes to the club while he is researching his book. Sometimes he sits in the corner and scribbles on his own, as if he is in another world. This turns me on; I never mix with the customers but writers have a powerful effect upon me so I talk to him a little and we get along. After a couple of weeks, he asks me to have lunch and I say sure, why not? I have never been unfaithful to Gig, but after a while I realise I am starting to like this guy. His name is Hubert and sometimes he writes stories in the papers and I like his style. He makes me laugh.

'It happens like this. There is a Thai girl working in the club and she is getting married to one of the waiters, so we all give her a big lunch at Quadroon's Bar and Grill in Ladbroke Grove. I am there with Gig but I notice that my beautiful Hubert is also there, standing at the bar, drinking with his photographer friend, Dennis. I catch his eye.

'Well...' Deborah pauses, opens her bag and takes out a small pot of cream with which she anoints her lips. 'To cut a long story short, we nip into the cloakroom to do a line and, oh boy, that's when it happens.' The priest, now very wide awake turns towards the grille and asks, 'What happens?'

'Well,' replies Deborah, 'we are in "the disabled" and I turn towards him and kiss him with some vigour. In fact, I smother him with my mouth. I am very oral.' She smiles self-consciously. 'This is a big event for my writer. He stands with his back to the wall and it occurs to me that I have lost control of myself and I have no means of stopping and so I kneel on the floor and I take him in my mouth and I blow him.'

'Blow him?' says Father Anthony.

'Yeah, look, I take his beautiful cock out of his pants and I suck it and play with it on my tongue until he comes in my mouth.'

The priest, in what he hopes is a world-weary but reasonable tone, says: 'There is no need to be explicit, my child. You have confessed to taking drugs and committing a sin of physical impurity and that is all I need to know.'

Deborah uncrosses her legs and leans forward towards the priest's disembodied voice. 'Look, baby, I am not confessing the blow-job,' she says. 'It's not on offer. I have a serious sin here and I need to give it to you.' Father Anthony sits back and reaches once more for his crucifix.

'So, after the event in the toilet, Hubert and I are a fixture,' she continues. 'I call him every day and I see him whenever I can. Sometimes we take a bottle of wine to Airlie Gardens and drink it beneath a chestnut tree and I will sit on his lap, and we do it, slowly and gently, until I am weak-kneed and slippery. We go to friends' houses on wet afternoons and fuck each other until we are raw. I love his body and every time I see him or talk to him on the telephone, my pussy gets wet. I cannot get enough of him. One afternoon we go to the Halcyon Hotel and we slide under the bed. There is only eighteen inches between the base of the bed and floor, and I lie on top of him in the space. We can hardly breathe because of the pressure and we are covered with sweat and his cock is as hard as an iron bar and hot as a poker, and my knees are on either side of his thighs and somehow he slips inside me and I come with a bang; it's so strong because I cannot move my legs or my body.'

The priest, now starting to experience a sensation of claustrophobic unease, says, 'You are telling me a story; there is no need to describe your actions in such detail. It is sufficient simply to say that you have committed an unnatural act.'

But Deborah has stood up from her chair and is walking slowly round the aisle of the church. After a few moments, she returns and says, 'I'm talking about love here, baby, this is not unnatural, this is no sin. I am coming to that. Keep your habit on, OK?'

'Well, this goes on throughout the summer and I begin to see that Hubert is becoming more than a little fervent in his regard for me. He gives me flowers and calls me when I am at home with Gig. He drinks more than he used to and he comes to see me late at night when I am counting out the takings at the club. He is interfering with my domestic arrangements. We still fool around from time to time because I find his body so fine, but he is beginning to make me feel nervous. I think he understands this. Things have changed.

'Then one night, about a month ago, I get a call from his friend, Dennis. He says, 'Have you seen Hubert?' And it appears that my writer has disappeared, vanished. None of his friends know where he is and his publishers are looking for him. It is as if he has evaporated. So I talk to a detective I know in the Vice Unit at Charing Cross because I am worried.'

It occurs to Father Anthony that, were he a newspaper man, what he was about to hear would probably make the front page. 'What are you trying to tell me, child?' he says. 'Remember that Our Lord has infinite powers of forgiveness.'

Deborah leans forward until the vapour from her mouth condenses upon the metal grille. 'I have found him, Anthony,' she says softly. 'Just now. He's here, in the monastery. I saw him in the garden sitting beneath an apple tree in the orchard. He has a rosary in his hand and is shaved to his skull. He is in the novitiate. My friend the policeman says he has taken the name Paulinus. I thought you should know. He has come here because of me.'

Deborah rises from her chair, pulls her skirt tight about her hips and walks down the aisle and out of the church. After a moment, the priest closes his breviary and stands up. There are no more penitents; the morning sun has vanished behind the clouds and the church suddenly has a sombre feel to it. He raises the chasuble to his lips, folds it carefully on the wooden bench and wanders slowly from the confessional, through the porch and into the garden.

PART 9

Play Time

TALLY HO!

Tom Holland

*C*rops, leather harnesses, riding one's mount? The vocabulary of equestrianism is an eroticist's dream. The horse, noblest and most beautiful of the beasts tamed by man, seems always to have been identified with specifically sexual qualities: vigour, passion, to say nothing of enormous genitals. And the mastery of such an animal still conveys a special aura of power. Perhaps it is not surprising that on the outer fringes of erotica, where fabulous creatures may often be found, one of the most fabulous of all is a human-pony hybrid, a man or woman literally treated as a horse. Like the centaurs supposed to haunt the wilds of ancient Greece, such a figure might seem almost too fantastical to be true, and yet the pony-slave, although elusive, is not as rare as the casual student of erotica might think.

Ironically, the earliest-known person to be associated with such a form of bondage, the philosopher Aristotle, was also the first zoologist to argue that different species could never mix. A celebrated Renaissance woodcut shows the Stagyrite bitted and bridled, with his mistress, Phyllis, in the saddle on his back. In a foreshadowing of almost every such subsequent illustration of the theme, the rider lashes the rump of her human steed with a whip.

The inspiration for this portrait, however, was not classical but drawn from a medieval poem, in which '*Aristote chevauché*' was offered as a warning against the capacity of lust to overwhelm reason. But as is so often the way with such fables, the lesson titillates more than it instructs. The very extent of the philosopher's fall, his debasement from the heights of logic to a bestial status lower than a slave, becomes, to those predisposed to see it so, delicious in itself.

When Christopher Marlowe, a man whose sadism was evident in almost everything he wrote, came to pen that other Renaissance masterpiece of pony play, *Tamburlaine the Great*, the thrill of humiliation was openly acknowledged: 'Holla, ye pampered Jades of Asia.' With this celebrated – and much parodied – line, Tamburlaine lashes the backs of two kings he has defeated in battle and harnessed to his chariot. Other kings follow, tethered behind him, and Tamburlaine loses no opportunity to revel in their transformation. They will sleep in stables; they will drink from pails; they will 'die like beasts'.

What gives added piquancy to this role reversal is that Tamburlaine had originally been a shepherd, very much lower class, and a foreigner to boot. The vertiginous drop which separates human and beast is widened yet further by class, for it is a curious feature that in almost all the classics of pony-slave erotica the victims are exquisitely well bred.

In Anne Rice's *Beauty* trilogy, for instance, the princes and princesses who are sent to the village suffer a humiliatingly utilitarian slavery, in which their iron-shod boots and horse-tailed dildoes, their harnesses and bits, have no function save to make their wearers more efficient as workhorses. And all this is taught them by rude-handed grooms, strutting around the stables, 'scrubbing down their charges or rubbing them with oil, their attitude one of casualness and busyness'.

This could only seem utilitarian in a fairy-tale setting, of course.

Even scenarios in ostensibly contemporary settings are invariably located in remote fantasy fiefdoms, whether in the deserts of Arabia or amidst the jungles of South America. Yet while this hardly serves to make them any the more realistic, it does enable one further tooth to be added to the ratchet of equine humiliation. For the victims of your typical pony-girl-rearing sheik, or hacienda-owner are pointedly not only aristocratic; they are also very white or, to be specific, Anglo-Saxon. This perhaps comes as no surprise when one realises that the earliest and most influential examples of pony-girl literature – and the emphasis is very much on pony-girl – were French. In a succession of anonymous novels published on the theme in Paris during the 1920s and 1930s, diabolical humiliations were practised by assorted subject peoples upon the Miladies of the British Empire. *In the Rajah's Stable*, reads one typical chapter heading; *Race Day at the Wadi*, another.

One sequence of illustrations in particular does more to highlight French attitudes towards their imperial rivals than a whole series of historical tracts. In the first illustration, a duchess poses snootily at a viceregal *soirée*; in the second she cowers in a stable before the pawings of two Sikhs; while in the third she has recaptured the *hauteur* which she wore in the first.

But gone are her gown and glittering tiara, and in their place are all the appurtenances of the fetishist's art: harness, bit and bridle, blinkers and nodding feathers, rings through the nipples with tinkling bells. A rajah looks on at her proudly, a curling whip in his hand, and it is evident that he is preparing to take his new pony for a ride, for haughty though the duchess may appear, yet she is fastened by elegant chains to the shafts of a cart.

The implausibility inherent in this image (that if you wanted to go for a spin, the last type of pony you'd trust to last the course would be a delicate former duchess) is so obvious that it scarcely seems to need pointing out. But it is also the case that human ponies are not confined to novels and fantastical illustrations; as with every erotic fantasy, there are those who seek to make it true. Dildoes with horsetails can certainly be found; so too boots in the form of hooves; so too farms with stables fitted for humans. Yet if anything illustrates the power of the erotic as opposed to the pornographic, it is to compare a photograph of a human pony, however handsome and muscular, however beautiful and slim, with a line illustration of a similar sight, or a paragraph describing such a scene.

The appeal of 'equus eroticus' exists not despite but because of its being a contradiction in terms. Sometimes the erotic becomes more powerful for being an exploration not of the possible but of what can never be.

X-LARGING IT

Nicholas Blincoe

I was fifteen, Charlotte was thirty-eight, so what happened between us was inevitable. It was the summer of '96 and I'd been skating the paved undercroft on London's South Bank. Walking back across the river, I held the skateboard loose in my hand, the deck towards my thigh. The grip tape made a sawing sound against my jeans, sanding away at the double seams around the pockets. The jeans weren't that old, but they were pretty ripped up.

The week before, I'd popped an olly, almost pulling off a frontside bluntslide down the school steps, but I bailed. I ended up skidding across the playground, ripping my jeans. They were X-Large, which was the brand name but also the size. They were way too big for me. As I slid on my backside, they pulled down to my knees. I was lying in the schoolyard, face to the tarmac, bum to the air. Charlotte stood there, grinning, as she stared at my hole. I asked her if she had seen enough. That's how we set up a date.

She was lying on the grass in St James's Park. I dropped my skate next to her; she looked up. I couldn't see her eyes because she was wearing shades. I was staring down the front of her shirt, anyway. What she was wearing was like a bikini top rather than a bra, made of a dark, shiny material. The design was the type that worked to separate her breasts. I imagined, if I could skate her, I'd want to pull a straightleg channel launch across her cleavage. I had my fingerboard in the pocket of my X-Larges, so I pulled it out. I stood there, flicking it between my finger and thumb, and looking down at her boobs. Charlotte asked me, wasn't I going to sit down?

She stripped down to her bikini top and jeans. The jeans were low-slung, as low-slung as mine. The way they hung on her hips, I was guessing they were only like an inch above her pubes. She lay back on the grass, using my skate as a headrest. I lay on my side, resting on my elbow. I used my free hand to show her my moves. I came from way up on her right shoulder, tall nosegrind along the bone of her clavicle. I took it slow and smooth to the highest point of her left breast, where the skin met the seam of her bikini. Then it was an f/s 5-0 along the bikini line and back down to airwalk the gap and a nice wide carve across her right breast.

She was walking her fingers along my thigh, right where the grip tape on my deck had worn the seams to threads. A long fingernail found skin, sending prickles to my spine. I had to work to concentrate, this time pulling a switch heelflip across the boob gap and coming back up the right breast to grab air. It was a huge revert, taking off from the mound that her hard nipple made in the cotton-lycra of her bikini. I landed it and then took the drop on to her stomach. The sun had warmed her skin, warm and granular as a paving slab at the height of summer, pale brown as plywood. She said, What now?

I said, I go freestyle.

I pulled an olly to skip across her navel. Then a boneless 180 to turn as I skated south. I rolled slowly towards the flies of her jeans, letting the fingerboard spin on its wheels. I imagined how I would go into a handplant, if I was using a hand and not my fingers. But my fingers weren't even touching the board at this point. They had slipped beneath the waistband of her jeans, quickening as they met a film of oil. Charlotte said, We need an indoor arena. She called ahead, booking a room at a hotel on Piccadilly. I had a fingerboard; she had a credit card.

THE GIRL CAN'T HELP IT

Gavanndra Hodge

I had my first encounter with that sticky sensation of erotic arousal when I was twelve. At home, my father's vintage copies of *Playboy* and *Men Only* were proudly stacked in the same way as *House and Garden* or *Country Living* were in other houses. As a girl, I would browse through their pages with a mild curiosity. But the award for activating my nascent sexuality belongs to the books I discovered in my father's variegated panoply of porn. The thin tomes stashed under my parents' bed were filthy literature that eschewed plot and characterisation for page after page of sexual *tableaux vivants*.

Alone in the house, I would seek these books out, choose one and hurry back to my bedroom with my prize. Once securely ensconced, I would read greedily for hours until the book was finished. I was helplessly captivated by the stories of girls like Layla: the prostitute/wife who lived on a yacht, who had a red bikini that could barely stretch over her pert nipples and who delighted in being taken simultaneously by her husband and her bodyguard. It was a newly discovered world, where all the men had cocks and were invariably called Rock or Giorgio. And it was while reading these boudoir books that my hand was first compelled to feel its way downward, tracing the dip of my ribcage and eventually finding the barricade of my knickers. Holding the book open with my left hand, still reading, I would allow my other hand – now strangely foreign – to tug my knickers to one side and explore the novel territory within. It was a revelation.

After this, I became more and more voracious in my quest for pornographic reading material. There were only about half a dozen of these books at home and soon I had read and re-read all of them to the point of over-familiarity. But they had taught me how to give myself an orgasm and established in my mind an unquestionable relationship between reading and masturbation. I am not alone. There are legions of women for whom a book, an imagination and a clitoris constitute the most fun they can have on their own. And it does seem a peculiarly female pastime. It is a common theory that women are aroused by words whereas men respond sexually to images, and this hypothesis can be backed up by statistics – women buy 80 per cent of erotic fiction. Perhaps this is because reading and masturbating are the two most enjoyable self-serving activities women can do when they are completely alone. But part of the pleasure is the subconscious acknowledgement that indulging in these two practices is somehow inherently wayward for a girl; society takes a dim view of those who pursue their pleasure in solitude – particularly ladies.

Most cultures seem able to normalise male masturbation. Graeco-Roman culture considered it a positive hobby, an act of natural elimination for men. The god Hermes had imparted the art of pleasing oneself to the love-struck Pan, who coveted the inaccessible nymph Echo; and Pan, in turn, taught the libidinous shepherds. In Greek literature the very imagery of masturbation was male and martial; *cheiromachein*, the word that was used, literally means to fight by hand.

But the wanking woman has forever been considered an affront. She rarely figures in Greek or Roman literature. The only time I have ever encountered her is in the bawdy context of Aristophanes' *Lysistrata*. The heroine laments the scarcity of dildoes from Miletus in war-stricken Athens: 'We can't even buy a decent twelve-inch dildo. It is not the real thing, but at least it is something.' But here Lysistrata is bemoaning the lack of a dick, not celebrating the delightful treats at her fingertips.

A woman alone with words is also objectionable. Words seduce and delight; they penetrate the mind and can debauch it with improper thoughts and desires. Billets-doux and sonnets are the weapons of the adulterer, capturing women's minds and ensuring their bodies will follow. The writer is always a seducer, and I have been smitten by words innumerable times. I remember travelling on the Number 31 bus from Camden to High Street Kensington. It is a long journey so I bought myself a wicked little gift: *L'Histoire d'O* by Pauline Réage. (For me, the procurement of erotic literature is like buying Chanel nail varnish or Guylian chocolates – a purely self-indulgent delight.) It was a sultry July morning; I wasn't wearing any tights. I lodged myself in a seat, which seemed moulded to fit my body, and opened the book. Within moments I was riveted, my breathing became fast and audible, and my face flushed. The bus was fairly empty, so, as it bounced over the speed humps, I allowed myself to succumb to the tremor of sexual agitation that was creeping over my entire body. I rubbed my thighs together, dewy with sweat; and let my arm brush my nipple more than once. But as the bus neared Kilburn it began to fill, and soon I had a rather dubious-looking man sitting next to me, so close our elbows banged whenever the bus jerked. I was aware of my heightened state of arousal, and embarrassed lest my neighbour catch sight of the page I was on, replete as it was with treacherous words. But I was so intoxicated I was incapable of taking my eyes from the page; I was wetter than I had been for months.

The journey was over maddeningly soon. Dejected, I put the book in my bag and went to work. All day I was agitated and irascible, the book kept peeking at me seductively from my bag, and my only thought was of the thrill awaiting me at home in bed with my fabulous new paramour. Finally, it was six; I was too impatient to take the bus, so got a cab. Once home, I raced up the stairs, shedding clothing and got into bed. I clasped the book with one hand and let my eyes drink in the lusty language. Obediently, my other hand performed the duty it had been aching to do all day. In no time at all, I was sated, content in the knowledge that in a few hours time we could do it all over again.

THE SECRET HISTORY OF THE SEX WITCHES

(PART SEVEN: UNDINE UNBOUND)

'Musidora'

*U*ndine tingled with excitement as she planned the evening's entertainment. As you may already know, it was the Sex Witch's lot to exist in a state of constant sexual arousal, a frustrating situation so long as she was an ephemeral creature composed of nothing but ether, without a body to occupy. But lend her a living vehicle of flesh and blood, with a complete set of organs (Sex Witches can avail themselves of corpses too, of course, but that is another story), and nothing can stand in the way of her sensual gratification.

After a close and exceedingly pleasurable encounter with the chinchilla-covered couch, she rose refreshed and sauntered naked into Adèle's well-stocked kitchen, where she kicked off her schedule in traditional Sex Witch style with a series of frenzied sexual attacks on the kitchen gadgetry. The blender, the electric kettle, the various baffling components of the Parmesan cheese grater, even the dark and deadly waste disposal unit offered temptations that proved well nigh irresistible, though in order to avoid serious physical mutilation she was forced to employ a fair amount of caution and not a little skill in order to wind-surf the waters of the Bay of Euphoria. But such risks only added to the fun, especially with the concomitant joys of fresh mango pulp, squashed banana and a few judicious spurts of maple syrup smeared all over her breasts and bottom. A Sex Witch is supple as an early-spring satsuma, and she can lick herself clean, like a cat. Undine was thus able to obtain both erotic satisfaction and nutritious sustenance in one bountiful swoop.

Then it was time for the usual round of saucy phone-calls, made to numbers plucked at random from Adèle's leather-bound address book. Adèle's elder brother, several of her old school chums, her bank manager, dentist and cleaning-lady all found themselves on the receiving end of Undine's elegant entreaties for them to bury their heads between her thighs and nibble on her golden nugget. Even the telephone receiver was pressed into use as an extemporare dildo. Two of the recipients, it has to be said, hung up in shock and disgust, but the remainder responded with unexpected enthusiasm to the Sex Witch's uninhibited animal pantings and squeals of ecstasy, joining in the game with such gusto that she was able to count several satisfied customers at the other end of her telephone line.

For her next port of call, she'd arranged an appointment at a pornographer's studio, but half-way there she changed her mind. She simply couldn't resist popping in to see that poor sap Quentin, whom she was forced to admit she was beginning to find oddly endearing. There was something in his willingness to forgive his fiancée her every peccadillo that made Undine want to prod him further and further into the valley of naughtiness, just to see how far he would let her go.

He wasn't at home, but she tracked him down to his club in Pall Mall, pausing long enough en route to perform an act of gross indecency with a Ford Mondeo parked in St James's Square (not her first choice of marque naturally, but there was a dearth of Alfa Romeos in the vicinity). Trollope's was an *ancien régime* establishment, but a strict edict forbidding women access to the main library proved no barrier to the wily Sex Witch, who swiftly fellated the doorman, cloakroom attendant, a passing MP and a TV celebrity into submission as she wended her way through the entrance hall and up the grand staircase.

She found Quentin sunk in a shabby leather chair in front of the fire. He was in a state of evident distress, chain-smoking Bolivian cigars, his brow wreathed in a nimbostratus of consternation. 'What's the matter?' she asked, feigning an Adèle-like innocence and ignoring the loud hurrumphing from the half-dozen or so other gentlemen scattered around the room. 'That damned orchestra,' he muttered without removing the cigar from his mouth. 'Things just haven't been the same since yesterday evening.'

'Do tell,' she purred, genuinely curious to learn what had happened after she had abandoned him, drained and senseless over the tubular bells, and hastened to the Glove Club for a merry night's frolicking among the timpani. The memory sent an eddy of white-hot desire coursing through her torso.

'Take care, Adèle,' he growled. 'I'm not feeling myself today.' But Undine couldn't help herself; her pilot light had already been ignited. She tried to concentrate on the matter at hand, but the sight of that fat brown Bolivian torpedo clenched between his teeth was too much. She felt suddenly hemmed in by restrictive undergarments. She needed to be free, so, without further ado, she hitched her skirt up over her lightly stockinged legs, inserted her thumbs beneath the waistband of her white cotton panties, and, with much wiggling of her bottom to facilitate the process, began to slide them down over her hips and thighs.

It was shameless behaviour, she knew, especially in such august surroundings. Quentin couldn't believe his eyes, and neither, it seemed, could the half-dozen or so other gentlemen in the room. One or two of them rattled their *Daily Telegraph*s in indignation, another started to examine the contents of his briefcase, but the rest were unable to do anything but stare at Undine in amazement, their eyes almost popping out of their florid faces. One of the more elderly codgers began, very gently, to drool.

The sensation of their collective gaze fixed on her arse gave Undine an added thrill. 'Oh, Quenty,' she breathed, her eyes filming over with lust. 'Wha . . . what are you doing?' faltered Quentin, letting his cigar drop on to the parquet, where it busied itself in making a small but pertinent scorch mark in the wood. 'Adèle, I must insist . . . '

In reply, Undine bent over him and, with firm yet teasing fingers, unbuttoned his flies and eased his jewelled sceptre out of its restraining pouch so that its magnificent purple head thrust proudly up out of the brown corduroy nest of his groin. Then, planting her feet on either side of him, she lowered herself, inch by inch, on to his lap. When she was fully impaled, she began to rock backwards and forwards, uttering small chirrups of ecstasy like a dainty pheasant having its feathers plucked.

The book-lined walls faded into oblivion as Quentin's member was engulfed and tightly caressed in a Mexican Wave of rippling muscle. Adèle's luscious cherry-ripe lips bore down to meet his tobacco-tinged mouth, her questing tongue stopping up his protests before they could burst from his throat. Meanwhile, her hands roved eagerly over his shirt, tugging the buttons undone so her fingers could riffle in his sparse, but manly chest-hair like explorers in the African veld.

But something was not quite right. All of a sudden, she stopped foraging and drew back in puzzlement. 'For God's sake, don't stop now,' he panted, his Adam's apple palpitating madly.

'But I can feel something beneath your shirt . . . ' said Undine.

'You want to know what happened after the concert,' he groaned. 'Well, this is what happened, Adèle. The Van de Villes happened. They bundled me naked into their Mercedes and took me back to their Mayfair apartment. Dotty and Drogo tied me to a mahogany hat-stand and whipped me while the Baron watched from his wheelchair and the Contessa sat with her whippets in the adjoining room, eating custard and entertaining a succession of young men with moustaches. The twins ruthlessly probed my every orifice, and then they . . . they . . . ' He sobbed.

'Then they what . . . ?' asked Undine, leaning over him and licking her lips like a hungry velociraptor.

'Then, in full view of everyone, they did THIS. And since then I've been able to think about nothing but sex – sex with women, sex with men, sex with animals and vending machines. Sex with EVERYTHING.'

He tore his shirt wide open, baring his left breast to her astonished gaze. The nipple still looked sore. Dangling from the fine gold ring that had been passed through the areola hung a tiny pear-shaped emerald that glimmered in the firelight. 'My God, Quentin,' Undine gasped. 'You're a Sex Witch too!'

She fell on him with renewed ardour, dragging him from his armchair like a combatant unseating a mounted opponent. Whether or not it was the Sex Witch within him, he responded magnificently and presently they were rolling around on the floor, biting each other in front of the fire. Only when several of the other Trollope's members attempted to take down their own trousers and join in did Quentin come to his senses and lead her up to one of the private rooms at the top of the club. There they engaged in various ingenious forms of sexual congress – forms conceivable only to Sex Witches, alas – until the wee small hours, when one of the porters started hammering on the door and threatening to call the police. He quietened down, though, once they invited him in for a threesome and he found himself hanging upside down with his testicles wrapped in tinfoil.

But later, as Undine rode alone in the cab back to her apartment, she began to feel, if not guilty (for Sex Witches cannot feel guilt, per se), then at least a little troubled. What was she thinking of? It was Pongo whom she loved, dearest Pongo, and not this milksop Quentin, even if he was currently playing host to a Sex Witch as nutty and voracious as she herself. There were fewer than thirty-six hours to go before the love of her life was married to a thoroughly unsuitable young woman.

Undine made up her mind there and then. She leant forward and told the taxi-driver there had been a change of plan, that he was to take her directly to the station.

Her course of action had suddenly become dazzlingly clear. She would take the night train to Percy Manor and stop the wedding . . .

To be continued . . .

Musidora's identity is shrouded in mystery. She lives in an hotel, once had her portrait painted by Paul Delvaux and makes infrequent television appearances after the nine o' clock watershed. I could tell you her real name, but then she'd have to shoot you.

PART 10

Talking Dirty

SMALL TALK

Luke Jennings

*A*nother drinks party at the Sandy Hills Golf Club. The company tends to be on the conservative side at the club – almost all of the husbands commute to the City, very few of the wives work – and I had no high hopes of any great repartee. In fact, it would be fair to say that I could identify in advance every single topic of conversation that was likely to be raised.

It was, however, a lovely evening. The heat of the day had ceded to a golden stillness, and long shadows were painted on the lawn and the clubhouse veranda. And I would venture to say that we ourselves made a brave enough picture – the men distinguished in blazers and open-necked shirts, the women charming in print dresses and light woollens. I arrived just as the fray was warming up, and after arming me with a gin and tonic – longish on the gin, shortish on the tonic, as is my regrettable wont – the club secretary introduced me to a new member, Davina Harvey-Clissold.

Mrs Harvey-Clissold was an attractive woman of some thrity-five summers. She was wearing a navy-blue linen suit with a pretty sapphire brooch. Her intelligent features displayed a light honey-coloured tan – Barbados, perhaps, or Gstaad – and her smartly cut blonde hair was restrained by a black velvet band.

'So,' I said, when she had accepted a cigarette and I had lit it for her. 'Tell me something about yourself.'

She smiled politely and examined the frosted glass of her drink. 'I love to guzzle cum,' she told me. 'I love it when some big-cocked stud hoses my dirty slut's face with his creamy wad.'

'And have you and your husband moved to the area recently?' I asked her.

She coloured slightly at the intimate nature of the question. 'I love to feel a massive rock-hard prick between my juicy stiff-nippled chest-puppies,' she said, drawing absently at her cigarette. 'But how about you, Mr Corbishley? Do you like to drive your rock-hard piston into the drenched twat of a barely legal cumteen? Or do you prefer to gag on the swollen ebony shaft of a super-funky Brazilian she-male?'

Her question went unanswered, for at that moment an acquaintance of hers hove into view. They air-kissed, and Mrs Harvey-Clissold turned to me. 'Mr Corbishley, I'd like you to meet Consuela Vasconcellos. Consuela is a filthy spunk-chugging Latina slut-bitch who likes nothing better than to spread her hungry twat for the casual pleasure of strangers.'

Consuela Vasconcellos smiled, and we shook hands. Sensing a directness in her manner – and, I confess, a hint of mischief – I dared a personal question.

'How do you find Berkshire, Mrs Vasconcellos?' I asked. Her jaw dropped, and for a long moment she stared at me, appalled. Then, with every fibre of her being quivering with outrage, she turned on her heel and marched into the clubhouse.

'Well, that was hardly tactful, was it?' murmured Davina Harvey-Clissold. 'I've heard you have a reputation for plain speaking, but . . .'

'I'm sorry,' I said, 'but don't you sometimes feel you want to cut to the chase with people? To dispense with the formalities? I mean, would you really be offended if I asked you your opinion of the property market, or where you and your husband were thinking of sending your children to school?'

Hardly were the words out of my mouth than a stinging slap connected with my face. The report was like that of a gunshot, and I could feel my cheek blazing with the force of the blow. When my eyes had finally cleared, Davina Harvey-Clissold was nowhere to be seen and the club secretary had materialised at my side.

'Dickie, old boy,' he began. 'You must stop behaving like this. People are beginning to talk.'

'I'm sorry,' I said. 'I'm afraid I just don't seem to have the gift of small talk.'

George Arbuthnot looked at me kindly. 'Let's just forget about it, shall we? Why don't you help yourself to one of my panatellas and come and say hello to the Hoarwithys. Guy loves chocolate sex-play and wears a hardened rubber butt-plug and Sophie dreams of being orally and anally violated in a Transylvanian dungeon.'

The sensible chap, I have always thought, knows when it's time to throw in the towel.

'Lead on, George,' I said.

PILLOW TALK

Kate Copstick

I love words. Words are my art-form, my recreation and my weapon of choice. Words are my first line of defence and my first recourse for comfort. My favourite pornographers arouse me with words, and my favourite bawds tickle my humorous fancy verbally.

I love to talk and I love to be talked to. But not in bed. As the conduit to the parting of the Egyptian cotton, of course. As an incitement to repeat . . . Even as an apology for . . . But never during. There are many, many good uses for tongue and lips where the lilac love lance meets the bearded clam. But talking is not one of them. Once flesh has met flesh we are – to quote Oshima – In the Realm of the Senses.

Honest-to-goodness pore-opening, scalp-tingling, toe-numbing sex is beyond words. It is body-to-body, nerve ending-to-nerve ending, hormone-fuelled, mindless and thoughtless. Words reduce it.

Because words don't just describe . . . they circumscribe . . . And worse. There are various categories of copulatory conversation . . . some more pupil-constrictingly anerotic than others.

For example:

1. 'Tell me that you love me . . . '

How to kill passion in six words. Let's face it, grown-ups, this moment is not about love; this moment is about sex. You may as well be told, 'Tell me that you think I'm an innovative cook,' or 'Tell me that my last feature was coruscatingly funny and intelligent.' Nice for a person to know, but irrelevant while attempting a game of Mr Happy Hides His Helmet.

2. 'Tell me what to do . . . '

Brow-furrowingly anti-sensual. I like to assume that if someone has got themselves behind the wheel of the Lamborghini of my body, they will have more than a provisional licence. Apart from which, shouting 'left a bit, right a bit, higher, higher' turns sex into some sort of ghastly crash between a biological Brucie's *Play Your Cards Right* and a genital *Golden Shot*.

3. 'Tell me how that feels . . . '

A very dangerous can of worms to open . . . not least because it has a tendency to lead on to . . .

4. 'Tell me how good that feels . . . '

Which can only lead to embarrassment, leading to lies, leading to disappointment. There are so many more effective ways of expressing satisfaction with what he/she/they is/are doing . . . a screaming orgasm for a start. And one only has to take part in a couple of market surveys to be aware of the linguistic quagmire that is the comparative analysis of enjoyment. The logical corollary of this line of chat is one of those forms in which you are faced with a statement ('I love it when you insert your whole hand into my vagina and clench and unclench your fist in a four/four rhythm', for example) and have to opt for a rating from one to five, where one equals 'strongly disagree'.

5. 'Tell me what you're thinking . . . '

AAAAArgh! I blame feminism for this one. It came in with New Man who cries and cooks, shares and respects, practically lactates . . . and asks you what you're thinking just as, in an ideal world, your blood supply has migrated south.

Let's face it, if all is going well, you will be incapable of speech. If not, then he is not going to want to hear what you're thinking. I have encountered no one who is comfortable with this one.

6. 'Talk dirty to me . . . '

Oh, God! If I'd known I was meant to provide cabaret you should have booked me through my agent! Although, it has to be admitted, this one is popular amongst those of the species who stand to pee.

7. 'Fuck me, fuck me, fuck me . . . '

Among male friends I have canvassed, a BIG FAVOURITE. Along with its variants: fuck my ass/fuck me hard, harder, etc. Although I don't know many who need that much encouragement.

8. 'You are so beautiful . . . I love your thighs/tits/bum etc.'

Dangerous . . . as it is frequently chanted, like a litany, as a perceived duty, and can, in the mouths of the inexperienced, or worse, the honest, inadvertently lead to a ghastly mistake along the lines of 'I love the curve of your tummy . . . the way it kind of sticks out', and I quote from experience there. Worse still, when a boy feels obliged to say something complimentary and, at a loss, comes up with 'You are the . . . oldest person I have ever been to bed with.' (A painful experience involving an eighteen-year-old with the body of a Greek god and the intellect of a whelk . . . sing it with me, that's the way uh-huh, uh-huh, I like it . . .)

Now you can play games with me . . . you can be my master for the moment . . . instruct me and humiliate me, be my mistress and discipline me.

At this point words become important.

I can be your virgin or your whore, if you will be my savage or my trick, and we will use words to weave the fabric of the fiction. And words arouse. But fantasy games play with my head much more than my body.

And we must flirt . . . a game of verbal fellatio in which you and I are the cuddly toys on the conveyor belt of prizes. And I can feel my nipples erect and stiffen to the point of calcification.

But later . . . when the Sloggis slide to the stripped pine . . . and body fluids shamelessly seek each other . . . don't whisper sweet nothings.

Whisper nothing.

A man I know has a single line he uses to great effect on bringing home a take-away. 'Shut up, bitch, and open your mouth.'

And he's a psychologist.

So, follow the doctor's advice, and let actions speak louder than words.

I LOVE IT WHEN YOU TALK DIRTY

Jonathon Green

*I*n October 1973, the American comedian George Carlin recorded a twelve-minute-long monologue in front of a live audience in a California theatre. In it he talked about the words 'you couldn't say on the public airwaves, the ones you definitely wouldn't say, ever'. He then listed the words in question: fuck, shit, piss, cunt, tits, cocksucker, motherfucker, fart, turd, cock, twat and ass, then repeated them in a variety of colloquialisms.

A few days later a New York radio station broadcast the monologue. A man who had been driving with his young son complained to the Federal Communications Commission. The FCC referred to its own regulations and stated the while the monologue was not obscene, it was certainly indecent and 'patently offensive'. The list, subsequently apostrophised as 'filthy words', remains a broadcasting touchstone.

The niceties of American law, and the fears of those who nanny the US airwaves, are irrelevant here, but for the wordsmith, especially the slang collector for whom such words and their infinite synonymy are the very essence of professional life, there emerges an inevitable question. Are words, those agglomerations of neutral vowels and consonants, prisoners of human use and interpretation, 'filthy'? Is there such a thing as an innately 'dirty' word?

Let us consider the term. Dirty: 'Not nice', 'nasty', 'unwholesome', 'insalubrious', and of course 'dirty' as Roget has it. Synonyms being *risqué*, ribald, improper, indecent, indelicate, not for the squeamish; vulgar, coarse, gross; broad, free, loose; strong, racy, bawdy, Fescennine (no, I didn't know either. It's something to do with *Fescennia* in Etruria, famous for a sort of jeering dialogues in verse), Rabelaisian; uncensored, unexpurgated, unbowdlerised; suggestive, provocative, piquant, titillating, near the knuckle (what *is* this knuckle? That with which we perform the *knuckle shuffle*?), near the bone (and as for *bone* . . .); spicy, juicy, fruity; immoral, equivocal, nudge nudge, wink wink; naughty, wicked, blue, off-colour; unmentionable, unquotable, unprintable; smutty, filthy, scrofulous, scabrous, scatological, stinking, rank, offensive; indecent, obscene, lewd, salacious, lubricious;

licentious, pornographic; prurient, erotic, phallic, ithyphallic (lit. rendering one's prick 'straight'), priapic; sexual, sexy, hot.

Those words, OK? Now wash your mouth out.

The idea of dirty as morally unclean and impure, or 'smutty' as the *Oxford English Dictionary* carefully defines it, is hardly new. The idea of 'dirty speaking' can be found in 1599; Ben Jonson savages a character as 'dirty' in 1637 and Sterne has a 'dirty fellow' in *A Sentimental Journey*. (Note: *arrive at the end of the sentimental journey*, [nineteenth century slang] to have sexual intercourse.)

Rupert Brooke offers the earliest citation for *dirty stories* in 1912 and adds *dirty jokes* a year later. Maugham has *dirty postcards* in 1916, while *dirty bookshops* appear (surely only the dictionaries could be so laggard) in 1960. The *dirty weekend* is a coinage of 1969. Surprisingly, *dirt* as a noun has no place, at least on a morals rap, in the lexicon. Only *do dirt on*, with the perversely puritan D. H. Lawrence and his definition of porn as 'doing dirt on sex'. So 'dirty' is all over the shop. Never more so than in the supposed 'Confessions' of Mr Patel's top shelf, where gorgeous, pouting slappers and their lubricious exploits are routinely paraded as 'dirty'. The use, I assure you, is not pejorative.

Paradoxically, it is only in slang, where all these 'dirty' words abound, that 'dirty' is quite devoid of sexual content. Here at least the word can actually mean bad, terrible or objectionable, or, in a tradition that has continued since the sixteenth century's *rum*, 'good' to villains and 'bad' to the respectable; 'good', 'wonderful' and 'excellent'. It refers to the possession of or addiction to drugs, or the holding by criminals of incriminating evidence; it can mean rich or at least comfortable. In phrases such as *dirty great* it works to intensify; in Australia it means resentful. None of which even ponder on sex.

But then you start thinking. 'Dirty . . . words'. I mean tell me, what are we on about here? Words have no substance. No dimension, other than conceptual, no depth, no width, no dusty corners, no nooks and crannies wherein such filth may hide. So what are we talking about?

Lenny Bruce used to do a 'bit' in which, accused of telling 'dirty toilet jokes', he pondered on the literal meaning of the phrase, railing against the mute porcelain, before 'I'd thunder out of the bedroom and dash open the door and . . . "Look at you, you *dirty, dopey, Commie* toilet, you! And the tub and the hamper – you should know better." OK, it's all metaphorical, and once you do take this stuff too literally, you're hand-in-glove with the morons for whom the pursuit of 'dirt' is an apologia for their gruesome *vitae*, but words, even the most excoriated, are not of themselves dirty.

What they can be is highly apposite. Why has *fuck* lasted the course since its first sightings six centuries ago? Because it works. *Swive* didn't make it, *jape* fell away (outside the world of Jennings and Billy Bunter – and does such a usage cast new light on those dormitory romps?); *sard* has been lost for years. But *fuck* makes it. Rooted most probably in the Latin *pugnare*, to fight (thus parent to that ever-expanding list of terms that mate sex with violence), and satisfactorily echoic of the slap of copulatory flesh, it does the biz.

Is *cunt* 'dirty'? Cunt comes from *cwm*, redolent in its native Welsh of streams and valleys. I know they're probably polluted, but not morally. *Turd* means 'torn' (as in 'from the body'). OK, *shit*, which comes from the Anglo-Saxon *scite*, means 'dung' and yes, I wouldn't deny the dirt here. Physical dirt, though, not mental dirt. But *cock* relates to a cockerel, *tit* is from teat, *twat* from the dialect *twitchel*, a narrow passage, *prick* began life as a female term of endearment for the male beloved, and so on and so forth. Half the goddam stuff was standard English anyway until the missionaries of repression began weaving their sick webs over nineteenth century language.

Is sex dirty, as Woody Allen once famously asked? It depends what you mean by dirty, really. One man's spiked heel, G-string, white thigh and black stocking is another woman's . . . other woman. Far be it from me . . . But words, those I *do* know. And are words dirty? If I may choose the *mot juste*: bullshit.

GOOD SEX, BAD SEX, NOVEL SEX

THE EROTIC NOVEL

Auberon Waugh

*F*ive years ago the much-loved monthly magazine, *Literary Review*, under my editorship, launched its Bad Sex Prize. The prize itself – usually a semi-abstract statuette vaguely reminiscent of bad sex, designed or chosen by R. M. Posner – goes to whichever novelist has published the clumsiest, most embarrassing, or most otiose and redundant description of the sexual act in the year under study. There is, in fact, very little good sex in fiction nowadays. Perhaps readers do not have the patience for it. A good erotic novel is a novel of sexual tension and suspense. It must be single-minded and rather humourless, concentrating on eventual arrival at the moment of penetration. Thereafter, it tends to reduce to anatomical description. There is much to be said for leaving them at the bedroom door on the first occasion, returning to the bedroom for subsequent episodes. Erotic writing (unlike erotic illustration) is really effective only for the sexually deprived. Those who have a partner or two, or a rich and varied sex life, have little patience for reading about straightforward sex. It is a curious market. I have noticed time and again that where the intention is frankly pornographic, the age of the female partner is given as fifteen. An experienced fifteen-year old seems the ultimate fantasy, although a sixteen-year old will do at a pinch. This surprises, because the young are as rotten at sex as they are at everything else. Brooding about this, I decided to track down the first dirty book I ever discovered, which had an electrifying effect on me between the ages of fourteen and my first genuine heterosexual adventure at eighteen. This was Robert Graves's 1950 translation of *The Golden Ass* by Lucius Apuleus, which had somehow crept its way into the Classics Library of the Benedictine college in Somerset where I was a sex-starved boarder.

I found I had lost my copy, but a solicitor friend lent me his to take to a health farm, remarking that the *Satyricon* of Petronius was much – ah – racier. Here, the first love-object, a slave girl called Fotis, is obviously very young, but that would not have worried me at a time when a fifteen-year-old girl seemed frighteningly mature.

Fotis is obviously no stranger to the amatory arts. Their courtship is perfunctory. When he sees her cooking a casserole, he says, 'Dear Fotis . . . the man whom you allow to poke his little finger into your casserole is the luckiest fellow alive . . .' She replies, 'Yes, I certainly know how to tickle a man's . . . well, his palate, if you call it that.'

Within minutes, she was smothering him with kisses, saying, 'I love you – I'm utterly yours. At torch-time tonight, I'll come to your bedroom.' And so she does.

'She climbed into bed, flung one leg over me as I lay on my back and, crouching down like a wrestler, assaulted me with rapid plungings of her thighs and passionate wrigglings of her supple hips . . . at last, with overpowered senses and dripping limbs, Fotis and I fell into a simultaneous clinch, gasping out our lives.'

Which is all very well for a susceptible, inexperienced teenager, but even a sex-starved adult might be a trifle suspicious of the ease of it all. Thirty pages later, there is a variation:

Before we had quite finished discussing my plan, a sudden wave of longing swept over us both. We pulled off our clothes and rushed naked together in Bacchic fury: and when I was nearly worn out by the natural consumma-tion of my desire, she tempted me to make love to her as though she were a boy; so that, when, after long hours of wakefulness, we finally dropped off to sleep, it was broad daylight before we felt like getting up again.

The most memorable episode, however, comes towards the end, after our hero has been turned into an ass after experimenting with the phials of a sorceress. A beautiful noblewoman falls in love with him and decides to seduce him:

You must understand that she was a beautiful woman and desperately eager for my embraces. Besides, I had been continent for several months now . . . All the same, I was worried, very worried indeed, at the thought of sleeping with so lovely a woman: my great hairy legs and hard hoofs pressed against her milk-and-honey skin – her dewy red lips kissed by my huge mouth with its great ugly teeth. Worst of all, how could any woman alive, though exuding lust from her very fingernails, accept the formidable challenge of my thighs? If I proved too much for her, if I seriously injured her – think of it, a noblewoman, too . . .

But her burning eyes devoured mine, as she cooed sweetly at me between kisses and finally gasped, 'Ah, I have you safe now, my little dove, my little birdie.' Then I realised how foolish my fears had been. She pressed me closer and closer to her and met my challenge to the full. I tried to back away, but she resisted every attempt to spare her, twining her arms tight around my back, until I wondered whether, after all, I was capable of serving her as she wished . . .

Perhaps not many people, in their lonely moments, fantasise about being turned into an ass and seduced, in that guise, by a beautiful noblewoman. But it is the novelist's job to lead his reader down unfamiliar pathways. Subsequent writers may find it galling to discover that the perfect erotic novel was written eighteen centuries ago and has never, really, been improved upon. But it would be nice to see some new prints of this famous scene between the ass and the noblewoman.

PART 11

Carnal Appetites

CHOCOLAT AND MONSIEUR

Clare Naylor

*T*he girls had been in the hot south for a week though they hadn't ventured outside the walls of the garden. They had mostly sat about the swimming pool like Gauguin's Tahitian maidens – naked save for the odd flower tucked behind an ear or a new coat of pink applied to toenails. As a consequence, they had acquired a way of walking around that would have suggested nakedness even if they'd been trussed up in duffel coats and sheepskin gloves; a tippy-toed lightness of being, an arching of the spine.

However, on this dusty Provençal afternoon, the girls had afforded decency a cursory nod by slipping into small print dresses and loose silk skirts for their foray into St Rémy. It seemed only proper. They may pass a cool, dark cathedral nestled into the walls of one of the villages *perchées en route*, and decide to step inside and light a candle. In which case they ought to appear a little less *deshabillé* than usual. Charlotte even went so far as to put on some knickers, but then Charlotte was Catholic.

'I don't know how you can,' Elizabeth groaned as she watched Charlotte struggle with placing first one foot and then the other into the pants.

'I'm always a bit afraid of ants climbing up there anyway.' Charlotte made her excuses and the girls piled into the car; Nathalie driving and the others with limbs slung loosely over one another in the back seat, Elizabeth's thigh over Charlotte's damp knees, on top of Emma's hand.

When they arrived in St Rémy the girls spilled out of the car, easing sticky fabric from their thighs, tugging at the fronts of their dresses to allow a little air in. They each had their own errands to run.

'Meet back here in an hour,' Charlotte said. 'I'm going to the *chocolatier*.'

Charlotte had once been given a box of Monsieur Gérard's chocolates for Christmas. She was particularly looking forward to sinking her teeth into another of the truffle centres. Charlotte wandered the narrow streets, seeking out the rich waft of chocolate, but could smell only cypress and dust. Then, as she was about to give up her search for Monsieur Gérard and make do with a seat at a roadside café, she spotted the tidy little shop front: Gérard's Chocolat.

She pushed open the door and a bell sounded through the shop.

'*Bonjour.*' The man behind the counter didn't look up. He was placing row after row of square chocolates behind the glass display: almond and hazelnut, pistachio, his dark head lowered in concentration.

'*Bonjour, Monsieur.*' Charlotte quietly closed the door behind her and sighed as the cool air lifted the hairs on her arms into thousands of tiny goosebumps. *Monsieur* looked up and as he did so, the strap of Charlotte's dress slid down her shoulder. Whether it was a spontaneous reaction to the proximity of so much chocolate, or simply her subconscious desire to expose her burning flesh to as much cool air as possible, she wasn't sure. But she hastily lifted the strap back up and settled it back on to her slightly pink, freckled shoulder.

'What would you like?' M. Gérard noted the errant dress-strap, but with impeccable French disdain chose not to be roused.

'*Je voudrais deux framboise, s'il vous plaît.*' She pointed to the two dark chocolate squares and Monsieur duly deposited them into a box.

'*Et trois cassis. Et puis deux violettes,*' she said, cleverly remembering that it was veeo-lay.

'*Violet,*' *Monsieur* corrected her. Charlotte raised an eyebrow. He looked her in the eye as he dropped *deux violettes* into the box.

'*Vio-let,*' Charlotte practised, her tongue glancing the back of her teeth as she said it.

'*Très bien.*' He smiled ever so slightly and picked a chocolate from the cabinet. '*Pour toi,*' he said and held it out to her. Charlotte was about to retrieve it with her hand when she realised that this was not his intention. Not wanting to seem ungrateful, she allowed him to place it between her lips. His fingers lingered a moment longer than was necessary and then he stood back and watched her intently as she bit into it.

'*Cerise,*' he pointed out. Charlotte nodded. Indeed it was, and the *cerise* oozed out, coating her tongue and spilling down her throat. She smiled a polite thank-you.

'*Praline,*' he informed her as he took the next neat little square between his fingers. Charlotte noted that he was very proud of his handiwork.

'You make them all yourself?' she asked. He nodded and pursed his lips, waiting for her to shut up so he could slide another miniature work of art into her perfectly pink mouth.

'*Merci.*' Charlotte opened her lips eagerly. For chocolates were not the only delicious thing about *Monsieur*. She noticed now, as he held out his hand, that he had the long, tapering fingers of a craftsman and the soft skin of a man who spent his days pummelling butter and cream, and pulling the stalks off cherries. As he slipped the pale milk praline into her mouth, he deftly turned the sign behind the door to *Fermé*. For a moment Charlotte was shocked. Then she noticed that her dress was absolutely delighted. It had slid once more along her arm and she was now revealing the upper corner of her left nipple. This time *Monsieur* was not disdainful. He led her by the hand into his kitchen. The shimmering metallic work surface glinted and half-mixed bowls of chocolate and caramel littered the room.

'*Ici*.' He pushed Charlotte towards the worktop and eased the other strap of her dress down, revealing tiny, nut-brown nipples. Charlotte wrapped her hands around his back as she felt the rough cloth of his apron against her breasts. He lifted her up on to the stainless-steel table and she gasped as the cold, hard surface pressed against the back of her sunburnt thighs.

As he began to unzip the back of her dress Charlotte noticed a bowl of whipped cream beside her. Even as a child she had never been able to resist licking a bowl out. She dipped a finger into the thick white foam and was about to lick it off when *Monsieur* took hold of her wrist. He looked first at the cream and then at her eager lips. He took the finger and placed it in her mouth, watching as she first licked off the cream, then closed her lips around her finger and sucked it clean.

'*Ah, bon*,' he murmured as he began to ease her dress down her firm, golden body. Days in the sun and afternoons of rosé and olives had left Charlotte's breasts and stomach curving voluptuously, and caused her thighs to join together at the very top a little more closely than usual.

Even *Monsieur*, with his careful taste, was delighted by the girl on his work top. *Très, très bien*, he thought to himself as he eased her thighs apart with hands usually reserved for shaping perfect little chocolates. Charlotte watched as he buried his face between her legs. She let her shoes drop to the floor and rested a hand in his thick, wavy hair as he delighted her almost as much as the bitter dark chocolate she was licking from a nearby wooden spoon.

'*Et maintenant . . .* ' *Monsieur* lifted his expectant face to Charlotte's. Her mouth was smeared in chocolate like a five-year-old's. She laughed and nodded,

'*D'accord*.' Charlotte hopped off the worktop and kissed *Monsieur Le Chocolatier* first on the lips with her messy, sweet mouth, then all down his body, pausing for a sharp little bite on his nipple and then a long, lazy lick all the way down to his waist. As she eased off his trousers, Charlotte smiled and wondered how much heaven a girl could take. Chocolate and *Monsieur*. He was indeed very French and very proud. Almost as eagerly as she had devoured the chocolates, Charlotte set about enjoying his smooth, golden cock.

In fact she was paying it such great attention she barely noticed him easing her from him by her hair. He pulled her head towards his and kissed her with force as he thrust his cock inside her. Charlotte closed her eyes and gasped in surprise and pleasure. She was glad now that she hadn't stayed by the pool that afternoon.

PULP FICTION

Nick Campion

*C*alifornia – land of the golden-armed girls. Golden thighs, too, and cleavages. Golden bodies – golden as a Yukon Potato Gold crisp, soft as a pot of pre-baked garlic cloves, tanned as a rotisserie chicken. I first fell in lust with the supermarkets here. Their aisles multiplied like porn-site home page links, always promising more. I could barely contain myself, but until now I'd always been disappointed at their fare.

Whenever I get the grub home, it all tastes like pulp; it always does. You buy this magnificently prepared stuff: marinated dry steak, free-range chicken breasts stuffed with fresh cranberries and corn, live Maine lobsters. You get the $25 bottle of local wine. And it all tastes like pulp. It makes hungry where most it should satisfy. Even the water tastes like pulp and doesn't quench my thirst. I realise the air is pulpy too. I've been here for two months, alone, going what the Yanks call 'stir crazy'. And I can't get anything from the supermarket any more.

So, inanely, I try to pick up a cashier – all frothy peroxide hair and silicone valleys and summits. 'How are we today?' She's got a Colgate halo around her porcelain teeth. Ting! 'That depends,' I say in a quiet, but assured fashion, trying to sound like Michael Caine but coming on more like Terry Thomas, gap-toothed and yellow-fanged.

'You're English!' she cries, delighted. I nod in an embarrassed, Hugh-Grant-sort-of-way. Then she calls everyone over and they all look at me, expecting some Noël Coward witticism. I'm faced with five golden-limbed beauties: 'So, what are you all doing this evening, girls?'

'Isn't he cute! You have a great day, now.' And she's on to the next in line, a reptilian creature who's probably a Nazi war criminal by the way he scowls at me. I'm already outside, in the sunshine, sweating and feeling foolish. I leer at two schoolgirls in brilliantly short skirts. They smile and wave back. All

I've got in my bag is a pile of pulp. I need to kiss a pair of those cinnamon lips and stroke a pair of those golden breasts just to remind myself I might be alive. So I call up the local escort agency.

Within half an hour the phone rings: 'Hi, I'm Brandi. I'm twenty-three-years-old, five' eight", 34B, slim. I work out. Shall I come over to see you?' She's there in another ten minutes. I open the door to a golden superbabe with gigantic hair, wearing two small strips of leather over her tits and crotch. 'How are we today?' she says. She's got a Colgate halo around her porcelain teeth. Ting!

'That depends,' I say, in a quiet but assured fashion, still trying to sound like Michael Caine and now coming on like Sid James finding Barbara Windsor in the shower. 'You're English!' she cries, delighted. I nod in this embarrassed fashion I've become unaccountably accomplished at affecting. But she's very professional. She takes the money straight away, asks where the bedroom is, and sits on the edge of the bed, removing her shoes. She talks incessantly, the sort of chat you get when you have your hair cut: 'Where are you from? . . . Here for long? . . . What do you do? . . . Do you like it here? . . . Isn't it wonderful here? . . . Gee, what a great place you've got . . . Can you turn up the heating?' By now she's down to her black lace bra and silver knickers, and gets into bed; she's left me standing.

I'm amazed she's so beautiful. Golden breasts with pips like cherry stones. And though she won't let me kiss her cinnamon lips, her body's like a tight cross between old mahogany and the latest toffee ice cream (hard and soft in all the right ways) and the only place she isn't tanned is between her arse-cheeks, as I eventually discover. I fuck her the usual three ways. And all this takes the best part of an hour as she's constantly rolling condoms on and off me and applying lube like mayonnaise on to a hotdog.

At one point her curiosity gets the better of her and she suddenly says, 'What do you call it in England – your thingy?'

'I call it my thingy.' So that ends that conversation. The rest of the time it is: 'Don't mess up my hair . . . Are you sure the heating's on? . . . Where did you say you were from? . . . What does your girlfriend do? . . . Did you remember mother's day? . . . ' She sucks me for a bit (which at least shuts her up) and I get to thinking about how, despite all the immaculate gloss, she still feels like the food, sort of pulpy.

'You lasted a long time,' she says, with a hint of reproach as she pulls on her iridescent knickers, prinks her hair and wraps her tempered body back up in its leather. And then she's out the door: 'You have a great day, now.'

Next time I go to the supermarket I don't feel like buying anything I bought there before; indeed I'm feeling somewhat sickly at all the pulp I've had to eat up in my time here. That is, until I see a girl at the deli counter. She pulls on her latex gloves as gently and surely as Brandi pulled those condoms on to me. And then she squirts lube (sorry, mayo) all over a thingy (sorry, sausage) . . . and then she sees me staring at her.

'How are we today?' she says. She's got a Colgate halo around her porcelain teeth. Ting! I mumble something inaudible.

'You have a great day, now.'

'Er, yeah, I guess I will.' The supermarket aisles stretch before me, suddenly packed with wild temptations. Well, if pulp is all I've got, I'd better get stuck in.

THE BREAKFAST

Alan Jenkins

That day, I filled the house with fruit,
with strawberries that shame the root,
their red hearts filled to bursting, and
with grapes, each one a swollen gland;
with melons pumped to ripeness, with
the peaches that are grown in myth –
plump and downy, blushing tints –
with mango, guava, kumquat, quince:

with food for love to breakfast on,
the juice-filled flesh, the skins that shone
like health; the tones of still-lifes by
some Dutch or Spanish master. I
heaped up this little Golden Age
for you to wake to, built a stage
on which we'd act our amorous parts
with strawberries, those redder hearts,

with melons, those fantastic breasts,
with grapes and mangoes and the rest;
you'd nibble cherries, bedhead-strung,
while I feasted with my tongue –
a couple from Fellini's kitsch
Satyricon, the bedroom rich
in sunlit colours and the scents
of fruits and flowers, deep, intense.

For with those fruits I'd also bought
a dozen lilies – afterthought,
except I knew this much: that you,
no matter how the garden grew,
loved whatever blossomed there
and lent its fragrance to the air –
so was subconsciously impelled
to buy the gorgeous, fluted, belled,

white- and waxy-petalled bunch.
Fruit would be our breakfast; lunch
would be more fruit, washed down with wine;
and we'd so twist and intertwine,
the bedroom would become a bower
and every passing sunlit hour
spent there, a bacchanal, baroque
and bronzed, a scene from *vieux Maroc*.

But in the restaurant that night
we quarrelled. Loss of appetite
drove our maddened voices on,
drink lent them venom. Gone
in a blazing instant, chair upturned,
you looked back once, and that look burned
its way into me – hot green knife,
lasering the source of life!

I moped my way back to the house
and all the time played cat-and-mouse
with my own thoughts. The stairs. The door.
And something touched the open sore
my mind had now become – the fruit!
The bowls of it, the senseless, brute
new fact that it would go to waste
with you not here, to eat, to taste!

I couldn't stand to see it there,
to see each black grape ooze and stare
its accusation at me, each
pineapple, kumquat, plum and peach
grow over-ripe and rot. What use
those bleeding hearts, when all their juice
would pour itself out over no one's
mouth, what use those glowing suns

of mangoes, when there was no skin
to see their glow reflected in?
No more could I have thrown away
the feast I'd planned for us all day
– a pointless end, unplanned, unsought –
than I could cauterise my thought
of what a desert I had sown
in all that plenty . . . So, alone

in Barcelona for a week
I'd haunt the *barri gòtic*
where you had lived two lonely years
and shed my solitary tears
in streets so full of you, I felt
you walking everywhere, and smelt
in every vaulted tapas bar
The strange amalgam that you are –

the sweet, the pungent and the salt.
Was I, I ask you now, at fault
to sense in the cathedral's hush
your whispered *Yes*, your lovely flush
spreading as I stroked you? Was
I far beyond the pale because
I wanted you so much, I'd pause
before Picasso's minotaurs,

their huge balls taut, their massive cocks
like keys unlocking all the locks
in gaping, thick-thighed girls, and stare
as if I saw *you* lying there,
welcoming the hot intrusion?
If I saw, in my confusion,
Dalí's elongated globes
of female flesh, from arse to lobes,

as versions of the parts I missed,
distended by the onanist's
grim fantasy – by mine as well,
since I was in a wanker's hell –
grotesquely stretched, like space, like time
itself, tormented by this crime
against love's natural law? No end
to long white nights without a friend . . .

And so I left for Paris, where
we'd clasped hands in the freezing air
and sat like breathing statues in
the Luxembourg, and watched the skin
grow darker on our *café-crèmes*
among the butches and the fems
in Le Sélect, and gorged on love
and all the arty gossip of

the lunchtime ghosts in La Coupole;
but this time I could not be whole
or hungry, and each night I'd wake
and feel a sharp familiar ache
to have you there before I died –
to turn you over, slip inside
and fuck you, half asleep; to feel
you feeding on me, while my meal

was what I savoured from behind,
the flesh, the pulp, the juice, the rind –
before I died one flophouse night,
oozing sour sweat, drink and fright,
staring into darkness, raw
and red-eyed, hating what I saw;
alone with shapes made by my shame
in pillows where I groaned your name.

By day the galleries I'd haunt –
shambling, spectral, shy and gaunt,
myself another kind of ghost –
showed me what I needed most:
Matisse's *houris*, Bonnard's Marthe
who glowed serenely in her bath
and, most of all, great Rodin's nudes –
the woman, *here* in all her moods

and manias, her ancient power
and beauty, offered for an hour,
a lifetime, to those lucky men
she chooses, then claimed back again
to please herself alone, her friends.
But none of these could make amends
for what I'd lost or thrown away,
while André Breton, Hemingway,

Apollinaire and Gertrude Stein
all whispered of what had been mine.
Their voices told at every turn
the home truths that I had to learn:
I'd lost the thread, the plot, the way,
my *luxe*, my *calme*, my *volupté*;
I'd lost the object of my gaze,
the magnet of my nights, my days.

And Paris was, by day, by night
a monument to appetite,
to everything we crave, from sex
to food, from art to discothèques;
market-streets where stalls spilled fruit
in front of me; here, *en route*
from room to adult cinema,
a woman splayed across a car;

there, to advertise a watch,
a pouting face, a swelling crotch;
shop-windows stuffed with bras and pants
(the simulacra of romance),
with toys and leather, whips and creams
to smooth the passage of our dreams . . .
The films themselves dug deep in dirt.
I'd sit transfixed and tug and spurt

and sob to think I'd sunk so low.
How could I stay? How could I go
back home to what was waiting there,
the sweet corruption, foetid air,
the poisoned, seeping world I'd made?
I festered, shivering, afraid –
not of blackened flowers, not mould,
but the much blacker tale they told:

of stupid anger, mindless haste,
of happiness that goes to waste.
I took the London train, to find
the fruit was mush. As was my mind.
One thought wormed its way out: to mend
what I had broken, make an end
of breakfasts without you. Sit, eat
with me these first-fruits, bitter-sweet.

FAST FOOD

Christine Pountney

When I was just sixteen years old, I went to San Francisco on a school trip. To the boys in my class I was sexless. I was too tall, too gangly. My breasts were too firm, too high, and my hips were too much like their own. For all their bravado and sexual boasting, they were unsophisticated and lacked imagination. They required the cumbersome trappings of obvious sexual characteristics to arouse their desire and preferred the Greek girls, with their hairy forearms suggesting advanced pubic growth, and the physical handicap of fully developed, oversized breasts.

Sexless as I may have seemed to my peers, I had already attracted the attention of various older men, and I knew with the instinct of a vixen when the scent was up and a man was snared. I liked the attention I received from older men, and I assumed the coy and sullen persona that my teenage years allowed. But above all, I assumed a passive, yet provocative sexual role. I wore my school kilt as short as I could get away with, without actually getting expelled, and let my tie hang as loose and indolent as my morals.

It was a glaringly bright day, and we were taking a walking tour of San Francisco's vast and labyrinthine China Town. I was dawdling at a stall with an exotic array of sea creatures, fish eyes and large, phallic molluscs. Entranced by the purple tentacles of a squid, I stood there, fingering its tiny little suction cups. When I finally looked up, I realised that my class had moved on and that I was alone.

I didn't mind; in fact, I felt exhilarated and relinquished myself to the muscular movement of the sidewalk throng. I let the crowd nudge me forward, brush past me, stroke me anonymously and urge me down a side street; the smell of jasmine and rice filling my nostrils; the shrill cry of hawkers and the cawing of seagulls overhead colluding to heighten my sense of disorientation. I looked up past the sharp edges of the buildings at the liquid blue sky and let the sun fizzle on my retina.

Temporarily blinded, my eyes watering, I collided with a woman running down the street. She knocked me sideways into a bunch of garbage cans at the edge of an alleyway. I scrambled to my feet and, groping my way along the walls, I retreated from the din of the market. When my vision cleared, I saw that I was at a dead end and that in front of me was a door, slightly ajar.

A blue light seemed to beckon me inside. I entered a hallway and the door closed quietly behind me.

At the end of the corridor was a curtain of blue glass beads, from behind which quavered the stretched elastic tones of oriental music. I brushed the beads aside and stepped into a smoky, windowless room. It was, in fact, a sushi restaurant and was filled with Japanese businessmen in immaculate dark suits, with white starched shirts and silver ties that shimmered as if they were made of fish scales. They were seated in clusters, huddled around a wide *kaiten* that snaked its way slowly around the room. There was very little conversation, just the clicking of chopsticks like cockroaches scuttling across chrome.

Slowly, the men turned to look at me standing there, my hair tousled, my lips slightly parted, my breath quickening at finding myself suddenly the centre of attention. The air was cooler than outside and I could feel goose-bumps rising on the sensitive skin behind my knees and spreading up the length of my thighs, sending little shock waves of pleasure across my hips and buttocks.

When all the men had stopped eating and were looking at me, I heard a harsh whisper like a command and a beautiful young man came over, gave me a quick bow and then, placing his hand gingerly on the small of my back, ushered me forward. There was more whispering and suddenly the room exploded like a stock market as the men began to argue between themselves. It was as if they

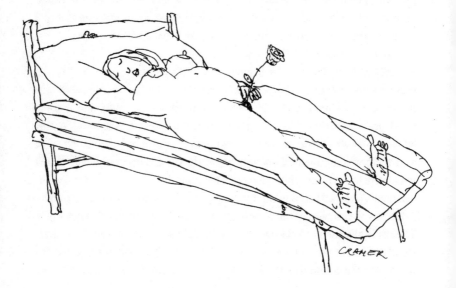

were heckling over a slave. I looked at the man who was standing beside me and he seemed defiant. He was stomping his feet and yelling something in Japanese. Eventually, the chef, an old man wearing a white *kapogi*, came out from behind a counter and raised his hands. The businessmen obediently surrendered to his seniority and the room fell silent again.

The old man bowed to me, then said, in clipped English for my benefit, 'She too young. No touch. Only look.'

There was some dissent among the men, which the old man quelled with another command barked in the staccato rhythm of his dialect. The young man with the delicate features then turned to me and, holding up his hands in a gesture suggesting he wouldn't lay a hand on me, deftly removed my school tie and then my shirt without once touching my skin. There was a murmur of approval among the men. He handed my tie and shirt to another man, who folded them neatly and placed them to one side.

All eyes were upon me and I felt an overpowering sexual fire light up inside my body. My groin began to ache as the blood rushed to my vulva. The old man clapped his hands and the nice young man sat down and another man came forward. He was shorter than the last one and plump. He was breathing rapidly and little beads of sweat stood out on his upper lip. He looked at me and I thought he was going to grab me. I wanted him to! Instead, he gave me a short, sharp bow, walked around behind me and undid my kilt. He didn't let it fall to the floor, but drew it down slowly and carefully. I could feel his breath on my legs as he held it in place while I lifted my feet and stepped out. He took my skirt back to his table and also folded it neatly. He never once touched me.

Another man came forward and, kneeling in front of me so close I could feel the static coming off the hairs on his head, he removed my shoes and socks. He too bowed quickly, then sat down. I stood there exposed, with only the air to caress my naked skin. I squared my shoulders and stood there in my white cotton panties and white lace bra, a hundred eyes burning on my adolescent body, driving me crazy with desire. I wanted to be touched. I felt as if there was a growing hollow in my body and I wanted it filled, but the men were quiet, admiring their captive; and like a deer caught in the headlights of a car, I couldn't move.

It was the old man who came forward again, this time with a large knife. The blade glistened and flashed blue in the light from the paper lanterns. He stood in front of me and, with several deft flicks of his knife, he denuded me. My underwear fell to the floor in little pieces like cherry blossom. It took all the strength I had not to reach out and place the old man's hands on my breasts, but I didn't dare displease him. He clapped his hands again and barked an order and a large man came over and got down on all fours. He pointed to the conveyor belt. He wanted me to use the man's back as a step and get on to the *kaiten*, along with the sushi.

There was sushi all around me, *tekkamaki* rolls on ebony *saras*, and wooden *getas* with two or three pieces of *sashimi*; lying side by side like praying Muslims. I pushed the dishes aside, but couldn't avoid squishing a few pieces underneath my body. When I had reclined on the conveyor belt and was slowly gliding like Cleopatra on her burnished throne around the room, the old man shouted, 'He who overcome desire grow strong! Now eat!' and all the businessmen obediently resumed the clicking of chopsticks. With dizzying efficiency, they selected dish after dish from the moving conveyor belt and began lifting succulent bits of grey mullet dipped in soya sauce into their hungry mouths. The men seemed intent on ignoring me and the air was charged with disciplined restraint, with a desperate stifling of desire.

I rolled over on to my stomach and tried to catch their gaze. I rolled on to my back. I lay on my side and smothered my breasts with the palms of my hands. Some of the men looked askance, some fidgeted, one began to choke on his *miso* soup. I saw the beautiful young man shoot a glance at the chef as if to challenge him, but most of them simply refused to look at me and stared at their plates. I was approaching the counter where the old man was preparing his perfectly wrought edible works of art and, as I passed him, I picked up a handful of *sushi* rolls wrapped in seaweed and placed them on my belly. I lay back and felt around me and picked up a cool slice of red snapper. I placed it on my nipple. I didn't dare move. I lay there, slowly drifting around the room and waited until, finally, with the speed of a frog's tongue, a pair of chopsticks darted out and the slippery fish was plucked, with a little pinch, from my nipple.

I gasped with pleasure and placed another piece of fish where the last one had been. It was immediately removed. I began frantically covering my body with more *sashimi*. I placed them on my breasts, my belly and my pubic mound. I rolled over and got on all fours and placed a piece of sushi snug between my buttocks. I felt the little flick of a pair of chopsticks before it was plucked out.

I rolled on to my back and lifted my legs until my knees were level with my chest and placed a piece of *tamango* in the silk cup of my vagina. I pulled my knees apart and it sunk deeper into my cunt and I felt a faint suction when it was removed. I tucked a piece of *temaki* firmly between the swollen folds of my labia and suddenly all hell broke loose. Men started jumping up, knocking their chairs over. The beautiful young man scrambled on to the conveyor belt to my delight, while the old man tried desperately to impose some order and control by yelling over and over again, 'She too young. No touch! No touch!'

The young man got on all fours between my legs. I could feel his hot breath on my skin. His tie slipped out of his jacket and caressed my thighs. I panted breathlessly, 'Touch me! Touch me!' and pulled my legs even further apart with my hands. A kind of suspended hush fell over the other men as they waited to see what would happen. I could hear the old man repeating his mantra in a whisper, 'She too young. No touch. No touch.' The young man bent ever so slowly forward and took the wet glistening morsel of *temaki* between his teeth and slowly sucked it out of my cunt. My hand immediately shot out and found another piece of sushi. In fact, the men were providing them now and there was no end to the raw fish that appeared at my fingertips.

Then another man jumped on to the conveyor belt. He too got on all fours and sucked a piece of sushi up, along and off the tip of my clitoris. 'Touch me,' I kept whimpering in unison with the old man's 'No touch, no touch.' The businessmen were hopping on and off the conveyor belt, tussling and wrestling each other to the floor. And amidst all of this commotion I lay there, unviolable, untouched except for the sucking and popping out of bits of fish, until finally the men fell into a rhythm, lining up like schoolboys to feed off me. Kneeling before me as if before the Buddha to bend, kiss, bite and suck until I began to convulse with pleasure. So hot was my orgasm that when it had passed, I lay shivering with exhaustion, while the men lay sprawled around the room, glutted and satiated by our mutual feast.

And then, as swiftly as I was swept up in their Epicurean ritual, I was lifted down, presented with my clothes and ushered back through the curtain of blue glass beads into a bright San Francisco alley.

FRUITS DE MER

Lizzie Speller

Afterwards, I asked myself why I never thought it strange that a young woman should go swimming by herself in an English sea on a winter's day. It was the police who concentrated my mind on that detail. I have had so much time to reflect on it now, but I can only say that it seemed, or rather she seemed, entirely natural as she walked from the waves. The water, pewter grey behind her, its further horizon indistinct against a wet sky; the fall and cry of gulls; and there she was, between fractured breakers, emerging from the salt-milk foam, not at all like Aphrodite. She was dark-haired and lean, and her skin was bluish, and not just from cold. Her feet were abraded by the rocks, and filaments of seaweed like fine leather thongs were caught around her ankles. She was all of a piece with the sea and the day and she stumbled as the water fell away from her.

She had quite wide shoulders, small, high breasts – yes, that was one of the first things I noticed – and she made no attempt to cover them (or anything else) when she saw me standing on the rocks, about to descend. It was a tiny bay, which I had come to regard as my own. Only when the tide was at its lowest, could I make the precarious climb over the headland and have this tiny space of new, tight, rippled sand to myself; a skim of foam on the surface of small pools and the caves dripping into the retreating water.

Why did I not ask her what had become of her clothes? Well, all I can say now is that it seemed to me that she accounted for herself. I assumed a farther bay, currents, fatigue, fear, resignation and then divine intervention; and here she was, wrapped in my oilskin, a red scarf incongruously over her hair, limping beside me. My boots were much too large for her and their movement against her grazes caused her more pain than going barefoot. We made slow progress, but in my rented two-room cottage she was safe. No, there was no one she should contact. Anyway I had no phone, and yes, she would like a hot bath; yes, she was a little hungry.

And now you ask, Did she speak English? Yes, of course she did. Did she seem foreign? I don't know. *I don't know.* She talked little. It didn't seem important. How long had I been alone? How long since I last saw my neighbours? It was winter. I was there to work. Solitude was the point. And no, I didn't resent her intrusion.

She was silent in the bathroom. She left behind her a cave of steam where moisture rolled down the walls and mirror, and a sediment of grit and tiny fragments of shell in the bath.

What did she wear? In truth, she never really dressed in any conventional sense. That first day I remember she wore all the towels round her legs and my thickest jumper. Only when she moved, which she seldom did, did I notice that she was naked from the hem of my jumper to the first fold of towel half-way down her thighs. She seemed unselfconscious. Her hair there was dense and the light so poor, I could see nothing more. Yes, I looked. You would have looked too.

I made her tea in a green mug, which she held to her chest but scarcely touched. And I gave her potted shrimps, which she savoured, pinching buttery chunks between finger and thumb, and brown bread, which she rejected.

The next day it was stormy. We stayed by the fire: indeed, she had slept there. I had offered her my bed, but she preferred to pull a blanket and my jacket over her. When I came down in the morning, she was there, her head resting on her arms, her hair in limp strands across her white skin. Sometime in the night she had banked up the fire. She had thrown off her covers in her sleep and I gazed down at the pallor of her thighs, then knelt down beside her. She smelt salty and fishy, and of scorched wool, and when she opened her eyes she seemed not all surprised to find me there, looking.

She had crabsticks for breakfast and I made Cornish rarebit for lunch. She picked off the anchovies, licked the cheese like a cat and left the rest. For dinner we ate by candlelight: mussels steaming in a liquor of shallots and white wine. She never offered to assist me. She didn't read, she had no interest in music. Upstairs I listened quietly, fearfully, to the radio for reports of missing women.

She ate gulls' eggs I had found on the cliffs and sardines sizzling from the pan, which she lifted by the tails and lowered into her mouth, wincing at the hot fat. She would eat no meat or dairy produce, and she ignored her wine. She played with the driftwood and pebbles I had left along the hearth; and when I looked up from my page, there she was, teasing out the knots out of her hair, turning towards the catchment window into darkness.

At some point (was it hours or days later?), the wind and rain were displaced by uncertain patches of aquamarine sky in white cloud. She did not want to accompany me to the village. Her feet, she indicated, still hurt and although the cuts were healing, the bruising looked worse. Besides, there were no shoes for her. I bought fish and lemons and a child's shell necklace.

That proved a mistake, for the shopkeeper asked me if I had visitors, and I denied it. No, it wasn't quite the truth, but I meant well. You must believe me.

And then, not long after that, I came down one morning and she was at the door, a dark shadow surrounded by light, looking out to sea. She was naked and her hair was damp. She didn't hear me, I think, as I moved behind her. Yet, when I reached out to touch her, she turned, passively, and I pulled her towards me. Of course, I couldn't feel her against me through the thickness of my clothes, but I could smell her. My hands cupped her cool flesh and I could hear, not her breathing, but my own, reflected back from the hollow of her neck. And my tongue was in the curves of her ear and then between her cool lips, and then in the slipperiness of her mouth. My fingertips felt the planes of her shoulder blades, and counted the vertebrae under her thin skin, which retained the slight stickiness of the sea.

I don't think she pushed me away, but when she moved through the doorway and across the coarse grass, I followed. The tide was way, way out, the sun hazy and without warmth. There was only intermittent wind and anyway she didn't seem to feel it. She looked back at me and smiled; it was the first time I saw her smile, and the last time.

On the shore, I sat by the cliff and she came to me. I prized off cockles and she drank them from the shells. I touched her sore feet, the cuts reopened by the rocks. I lifted a foot and licked it, kissed it. I ran my fingers through her dry dark hai;, I held it behind her neck, pulled her mouth up to mine, and pushed her back on to the wet sand. I sunk her into it, and kneaded her skin. But I was not as gentle as I should have been. My hands, rough with sand, were too eager to explore, too desperate to know her. I pushed my fingers into her mouth and opened her, felt her sharp teeth with my fingertips. I kissed her, grinding her head back, tasting fish and salt, forcing my tongue into her, feeling her tongue retreat, running my own inside her lips, digging into the sand beneath her to pull her to me.

Throughout all this she uttered not a word, not a gasp. She looked not at but through me. I grew madder; I needed a reaction. I took her small dark nipple between my teeth and bit hard, then bit again on the veined skin of her breast and, when I withdrew, there was my mark. I tore off my clothes. The cold caught my skin and a thousand tiny hairs bristled. I pushed her shoulders down.

And then as my thumbs bruised her hipbones, aroused by her lack of response, and so hard that I had to have her, I passed my hand down her belly and her skin became more rough. And there was . . . not nothing, not horror, but something both known and strange. Where I felt for the shadows I had glimpsed as she moved about my house, where I felt for accepting folds of flesh, there was instead, all wetness, all curve. I looked down. She was iridescent in the March light. There was the plane of her stomach, then little bumps like goose-pimples, then darker, rougher plaques. And then she was fish.

What followed does me no credit. But, oh, the sight of her pale face, her breasts, her narrow waist and then that great tail! Living flesh covered in scales like sequins; quicksilver, petrol blue, graphite, all turning desire into madness. I fell on her, pinned her down, moved insistently against her. Behind me the sea was starting to crawl up the beach. The tide had turned.

I did not – I could not – possess her, but the rhythm of my movements against her unfamiliar body – muscular, lubricated, glistening – was unimaginably more than a simple act of penetration. Her nipples were hard, her mouth a little open, her eyes half-closed and I began, at last, to hear her as she took fast and shallow breaths. She moved now, awkward and helpless, as the water swirled around my feet. It lapped our bodies, lifted her hair and let it drop again. As I came, she cried out and grasped me to her.

And then the waves were coming in fast, the gulls rising from the rocks. You have to believe me, she was limp but conscious, and when she opened her eyes she gazed out to sea. She did not want to come back with me across the shore. I braced myself and lifted her but she was heavy, the weight and slipperiness of that tail made it impossible to move more than a few paces. She turned her head into my shoulder, her arm across my body. I looked down at her. She was a wonder, a gift, the most beautiful creature I had ever seen. I walked into the waves, trying to keep my balance, and I let her go.

I was lucky to outrun the sea. I returned home, drenched and numb. No, again, I did not think to tell anybody because there was nothing to tell. She came from the sea and she returned to the sea. Possibly the body you showed me yesterday was her – she was much changed. Yes, I understand about the bite marks. Yes, I understand she was already dead by the time the boat severed her torso from her . . . lower body. No, I cannot explain why the post-mortem showed that she had not drowned, but was asphyxiated.

Please let me go. I must go back to the sea.

PART 12

Daisy Chain

TRIO

Bel Mooney

*E*lizabeth likes to go places alone, for then she can indulge her pastime: watching people. Making up stories, eavesdropping, sometimes talking, but never giving anything away about herself. On buses, trains, planes, ferries; in cafés, restaurants and bars she will watch and listen, glad to be no longer young, when the world is a threat and the eyes of men appraise.

This place is for watching. Filling up now with the buzz of serious listeners drawn to hear the Abdullah Ibrahim trio. There will be no talking when the music begins. Behind the bar is a sign which bears just four capital letters, 'STFU' – a cryptogram the regulars know means 'Shut the fuck up!' Sometimes, at Christmas perhaps, or for a stag night, there is a party which does not understand the rules of the place – noisy people who pay to talk over music, their voices rising in combat with saxophone or piano until the people around hiss their disapproval. What kind of people would come to drown Andy Sheppard, when you can blab all evening in a pub? Elizabeth's 'Shhhh' is as contemptuous and assertive as anybody's. She is not interested in watching the red-faced young office workers on an outing, leaning across the table, flirting, smoking all the more as the bottles empty, waving their hands – yet imagining that by being here they are 'cool'. They are a collective entity, she thinks, marching to the same tune like an amateur brass band, and therefore uninteresting.

Jazz is a collection of individual stories.

'Excuse me – are these seats taken?'

The man is in his late forties, and American. The broad blue braces are not necessary to hold up well-cut chinos; he raises a hand to his moustache to draw attention to its glossy statement. Elizabeth reads him, down to his loafers. 'No – go ahead. Please.'

She allows the transatlantic nuance to creep in, and smiles. Her wave at the three empty chairs at the small, round table is proprietorial as she picks up her glass of Chardonnay and sips.

The man swivels the chair almost opposite Elizabeth's, pulling it slightly to the right and turning it round completely, so it faces the stage. He gestures to his companion to sit, then takes the chair on Elizabeth's right, adjusting it slightly, so that he too faces the stage, almost behind the woman. There is a precision to these movements which pleases Elizabeth. Like her, this man likes to arrange things so that they may be taken seriously.

'Nice place.'

'Yes, it is.' She pauses. 'I come here quite a lot.'

His eyes flicker for a second to the fourth chair at their table, then back to Elizabeth's face, his eyebrow raising a fraction. She makes a pretence of gazing away to where a waiter has dropped an ashtray with a clatter, and frowns. Let him wonder, she thinks. Let him be curious that I choose to come here, like this. Let him look at my smooth cap of still-dark hair, and my black trouser suit with the pink shirt, and wonder why I am alone.

'Hi, I'm Ria.'

His companion has swivelled to face them, resting her hands on the back of her chair. She is in her early thirties – or else wearing very well, Elizabeth adds to herself with a spurt of jealousy. Her dark reddish-brown hair twists in tendrils around her broad face, and forms sinuous curls down on her neck. When she gazes about the room, her profile undulates like dunes. There is a sheen each side of her nose, and her teeth glitter in the low light. When she stretches her arm to push up the sleeves of her blue velvet top, silver and Navaho turquoise weigh heavy on her wrists and fingers. Elizabeth imagines that through the heady perfume (Dioressence, surely?) she can smell the flesh of this woman, oily and salty as the Atlantic.

'I'm Carter,' he smiles, thrusting out a hand, 'Carter Johnson.'

Forced to introduce herself, Elizabeth wonders somewhat sourly why so many Americans call their children by surnames instead of Christian names. Carter Johnson or Johnson Carter . . . What is the difference? But her frisson of irritation is not about his name. The point is, he knows her name now, and so does Ria. Elizabeth feels unsettled, but is saved from further conversation by the club manager mounting the stage and raising a hand. A reverent hush descends. 'Ladies and gentlemen, welcome! And tonight we welcome you specially because it is a night of peace, since jazz is a universal music . . . And it is a great honour to welcome our South African brothers, and our Islamic brothers, whose music is the music of peace – I am, of course, talking about the music of . . . Abdullah Ibrahim!'

Elizabeth joins the loud applause. There are a few enthusiastic yelps from behind her as the musicians walk across the stage, the star in white robes, his double bass player and percussionist in jeans. Ibrahim barely glances at the audience; he seats himself at the piano, stark against its blackness, and rests his hands briefly on the top as if in prayer. There is a moment's silence, into which Elizabeth feels herself falling. She herself is the instrument, waiting to be played. The air trembles with anticipation. The shared breath of the crowd is a sigh. 'Ah.'

The music begins, soft at first, the whisper of a brush across drumskin, the stroke of fingers on gut. Elizabeth closes her eyes, waiting for the piano, visualising, within the warm red behind her eyes, the dark fingers poised over ivory. The first note comes, so cool it is barely audible, as if the musician is holding back, not giving, not yet. Elizabeth thinks it wise not to give; the borders around her life are wide. She knows that others talk about her at work, not liking her but marvelling at her reserve, and wondering about her private life. Let them, she says to herself in defiance once again. This is her music, slipping around her like a breath, restrained and distant, barely acknowledging the hushed listeners and watchers. The darkness behind her eyes is blue-black. She lets her own sigh of contentment slip into the air and leans back in her chair, tilting her head slightly to the ceiling where the notes hang, chilly and aloof as angels.

Elizabeth opens her eyes at last, allowing herself to see the source. Just then a young man glides to the front, kneels, and takes a photograph. The aficionados draw breath at this affront, and Ibrahim stares down, the break in his playing imperceptible.

'You're disturbing us, man,' he says.

Ria glances over her shoulder at Carter, without a smile, then turns her head back to the front. But Elizabeth saw, and is puzzled by the complicity of that glance. Did the faint upward roll of her eyes indicate irritation, and if so with whom? Ria gleams with knowledge – but of what? And the curve of her cheek is more tantalising now, soft and round as a buttock, and downed in soft hair. Elizabeth stares at the woman's head, disconcerted by this break in her habitual concentration. She resents it and wishes this couple had not chosen to share her table.

The music continues unbroken until the interval, but something is wrong. When at last the trio leave the stage, to reverential applause, and the room is filled with light, Ria and Carter whirl round towards her with an energy that tears the air, making her flinch from their urge towards communication.

'Well . . .' says Carter.

'My Gahd,' smiles Ria.

Now Carter lays a hand briefly on Elizabeth's arm. 'I could see you were really into that,' he said, 'Am I right, Elizabeth?'

'I love Ibrahim's work,' she replies coolly.

Ria's mouth turns downwards, and she wrinkles her nose, knowing perhaps that the charming grimace makes her look even younger.

'Yeah, but . . . '

'But what?' Elizabeth asks, almost indignant.

'It's . . . kinda bloodless, isn't it?' the woman says.

'So cool it freezes its own ass,' laughs the man.

'Not like real jazz – you know?' Ria adds.

Elizabeth frowns. 'I don't honestly think it's possible to use a phrase like "real jazz",' she protests, feeling at the same time how English she sounds, how chilly, how frigid. It is their fault. These people have made her feel like this, with their very speech – rolling around the air in which she sits and bringing the vertiginous depths of the Canyon, the damp, fetid heat of the Florida Keys.

'I guess I mean Chicago, and New Orleans,' says Ria.

'And the blues,' says Carter.

'Stuff with real soul,' says Ria.

'Yeah, kinda . . . blood, guts and passion, you know?' says Carter, raising a finger to stroke his moustache.

Elizabeth does not know. All her shutters close against these words. Her mouth twists as she leans back in her chair and says dismissively, 'Not my kind of thing, I'm afraid.'

The American offers to fetch her another glass of wine, but she refuses. Carter rises, and reaches to touch Ria's arm, saying he will get two beers. Elizabeth stares at Ria. Ria looks back, merry with her secrets. The two women fall silent until he returns – not before time, as the trio is about to walk on stage again. The hubbub dies to sacred silence once again, and Elizabeth is relieved. She came for the music, not for conversation.

Piano, double bass and drums make their patterns, and Elizabeth leans forward a fraction in her chair to concentrate, as usual. This is serious. The trio speaks to her spirit.

But in front, Carter reaches out and starts to stroke Ria's ear, his touch, her pulse, and the rhythms all one. The woman settles back a little, leaning into the caress which travels down her neck, his hand moving over her skin like a merchant stroking velvet or silk. Elizabeth is helpless: mesmerised by the to-and-fro, to-and-fro. It is as if she has entered a black room, one spot only illuminated, and the sound of skin on skin replaces the music – the subterranean beat of blood adding a new percussion.

The man's hand traces the curves of neck and cheek like a life artist's charcoal, dwelling on one spot for a while, then moving on, fingertips exploring the little nubs of bone. Briefly, Ria glances back, brightening the air with a smile of promise, before allowing the dark lashes to bat back down on her cheek for a second. As if in answer, he drops his hand to her back, stroking, exploring, kneading. Then round to the side, where the curve of her breast is visible beneath her arm, to touch, and weigh – cupping with gentle fingers. His other hand begins on her neck again.

Elizabeth's mouth is parched. For a second her hand is with his hand, feeling that soft weight in the fingers, the juiciness of almost-rotting peaches, so easy to bruise, so easy . . . And now, unable to bear it, she switches her gaze to the two golden beers, craving that wetness on her lips, the rolling of liquid the tongue, the relief of swallowing.

Ah . . .

But there is no hope for it. She has said no, and remains imprisoned in the desert she has chosen – forced to sit watching as Carter touches Ria's pliant waist and buttocks, and his fingertips walk her spine. And time and the music stop.

And Elizabeth knows she will watch these hands moving over their instrument until the music is finished. But not finished. It will not be over then. For within her mind she will hear him turn to her and say, 'Are you coming?' Then she will follow them from the club and walk with them to the hotel, laugh with them as the elevator door closes and they are free to embrace. Elizabeth closes her eyes.

'Have you done this before?' asks Carter. 'No, never,' Elizabeth says, hoping they do not see her fear. As the lift rattles skywards, Ria leans against her briefly, so that the heady cocktail of Dioressence, oil and salt curdles in Elizabeth's stomach. 'Mmm, I hope not,' she whispers, 'because it's more fun when at least one of the trio is a virgin.'

Again they laugh, and Elizabeth joins in, not knowing why, since any joke must be on her – the afraid, the unknowing. But these two have such white teeth, their eyes gleam, and their laughter draws her deep into the redness of throats. What choice does she have?

Now they are at the door of the room – 609 – and Carter is fumbling with the key. Ria stands there, staring at Elizabeth as if she wonders what she is doing there. Then her tongue wets the outline of her full lips, making them shine.

'Do you always watch things?' Ria asks.

'Always.' Elizabeth replies.

'Good,' Ria whispers, 'because I like to be watched.'

The door is open. Carter allows his hand to rest briefly on her shoulder as he stands back to let her pass. But once there, Elizabeth is forgotten. They waste no time. Elizabeth sees them fold together, clothes littering the floor, hands and tongues penetrating here . . . and here . . . and here . . . as she stands there, hands by her side, like a marionette whose puppet-master has been distracted by a passing dream.

'Come and help me undress her,' Carter says, laying Ria on the bed.

Obedient as ever, Elizabeth is moving over towards them. She is helping him peel off Ria's clothes – to reveal brown skin so silky-sleek it is barely tolerable to see, and sepia nipples so huge she has to avert her gaze. And now Ria's arms are reaching for her, as Carter starts to undress her too, and she sloughs her safe clothes like a skin, as the woman's red tongue flutters in her mouth. A smell of oil and salt. A slick of spit at the corner of her mouth. And now his fingers are moving and penetrating, while Ria rolls over and above her, to tantalise her mouth with fruit, so sweet . . . and now it is impossible to tell whose touch is where, whose taste and smell is everywhere, whose hair this is, and where . . . For there never was any need for talking, Elizabeth thinks, as she is sucked down, drowning in salt water – not when the trio is playing. Not when the rhythms are working so perfectly, now together, now separate, now two, now all three . . . At last, Elizabeth knows, it is time for her to learn to shut the fuck up, stuffed with sweet flesh at last until she is full. Now.

Ah . . .

Abdullah Ibrahim's hands rose from the keyboard in a final gesture, then came to rest in his lap, on the pure white robe. It was over. The crowd broke the tension with a roar.

Elizabeth blinked, shuddered, then joined in the applause, clapping with her usual English restraint while nodding her head sagely, as if to tell other aficionados that she had heard something new and approved of it very much. But now it was over, and there was no choice but to go home as usual, lock the door behind, and turn to face whatever sterile ghosts lurked in that neat apartment which defined her.

'Did you think the second set was better?' Elizabeth asked Carter as he rose quickly, pulling out the chair for his woman as if Elizabeth was not there. 'Sure,' he said, 'it was just fine.'

Ria turned to face her, and smiled. 'I still prefer something with sweat to it,' she said, 'You know – the kinda music you hear here.' She rubbed a hand in gentle circular movements over her own stomach.

'I think I know what you mean,' said Elizabeth faintly.

Carter and Ria looked at each other, then back at her. Did they see the pleading in her eyes? Did they see?

They smiled at each other, and exchanged a nod. Then Ria stepped around the table, and leant forward so that her breasts brushed Elizabeth's arm with the weight Carter had appraised, long ago, when the trio was playing. Elizabeth felt the woman's breath in her ear, and smelt the saline dampness of her flesh, beneath leather, velvet and silver.

Ah . . .

And – 'Come on, Elizabeth,' whispered Ria. 'You're coming back with us.'

DADA

Toby Litt

*I*t is 1976. Brighton, the Grand Hotel. An as-yet-unfamous pop group from Sweden has just won the Europrism Singing Contest. They are called DaDa (pronounced as if referring to a lickle baby's daddykins rather than a dubious European art movement of the early twentieth century). The song with which they have triumphed is called 'Stalingrad'. It likens the joyous terror of knowingly beginning an abusive relationship to the encirclement by Wehrmacht forces of the Russian city of Stalingrad. The chorus goes: 'Stalingrad! / You beat my sister up really bad. / Stalingrad! / I never knew you were such a cad. / Stalingrad! / Meet me tonight at the helipad. / Stalingrad! / I want some more of what sissie had.'

After the awards ceremony, DaDa retire to one of their two matching penthouse suites at the Grand Hotel.

The members of the band are two foxy chicks, A1 and A2, and two horny guys, B1 and B2.

A1 is wearing a blue chiffon jump suit trimmed with yak fur, knee-length suede boots and a knitted Peruvian menstruation hat, with symbolic ear-flaps (i.e., whatever you say, I won't fucking listen).

A2 is dressed in a more fireside-porno look: *crème-caramel*-coloured silk blouse under an I-read-books-sometimes cardigan, fitted-by-a-gynaecologist, spray-on blue jeans and Scholl-but-sexy clogs.

A1 has long blonde Aryan hair; A2 has a tight chestnut perm.

As for the guys, B1 looks like he is seeking political asylum from the Glitter Band; whereas B2 is sporting the latest designer-Serf outfit (complete with encrusted faecal traces) by international Swedish designer Sprog Max Borgstern.

B1 and B2 both have big bushy beards.

A1 and B1 have been married for three years but manage with effort to combine being recovering alcoholics with being on the rocks.

A2 and B2 are an item: Lot 69 in the Stockholm I'll-Be-Your-Sex-Slave-For-The-Long-Winter-Months Auction, September 1975.

Unbeknownst to B1, A1 is having an affair with B2. A2 is fully aware of what's going on – in fact, she encourages it, because it allows her to pursue her illicit flinglet with B1. A1, of course, is completely ignorant of A2's affair with her beloved husband.

That is the situation as they burst triumphantly back into the second of their two direly decorated hotel rooms. The wallpaper is a Touch-Me TM velvety effect, just, in a way, as Austria mimicked Germany during the inter-war (1918 to 1939) period.

B1 turns on the headboard radio and a Stiltonesque-Bontempi-organ and Electro-zither track begins to play, in C minor.

B2 strokes the dimmer-switch with practised forefinger (he has one of these, a dimmer-switch, not a forefinger – urrh, you silly dur-brain! – amongst the myriad gidgets and gizmos in his batch-pad back in Stockholm).

A1 says, 'I feels so hot and am really turned on by the winning we have done of Europrism, no?'

A2 replies, 'God, here below I am such of a wet pussy, you know . . . I drip and I am horny, so I want taking hard and now, baby.'

(Being Swedish, DaDa talk like a porn movie all the time, of course, yah? Until now, however, they have never acted in a porno way, too.)

B2 says, 'As you say, the idea of all those pretty girlies from all over the Europe, just with the hots for me, it makes me hard in the pants like a stick of the famous Brighton rock, but much more wide.'

B1 replies, 'You are correct in that I feel as long and rigid as the pier penetrating the womanish sea that I am seeing outside this very window here.'

A1 says to B1, 'I cannot wait for privacy in a room of one's own. Take me here and now, in a rough manner, from behind.'

As she speaks, however, A1 winks at B2; B2, pretending to smoulder at A2, but actually directing his linguistic lust back at A1, says, 'My hot-rod of throb will in the very next moment be riding down your sticky-Tarmacked highway of desire.'

B1 rips off his sheepskin jerkin and begins to unlace his mediaevo-flies. At which point, A2 looks at designated fuck B2 and says, 'All this bad horniness is making me of the very same persuasion. I am here for you to take me wherever we want to go.'

With this declaration, A2 flings her cardigan across the room. It lands on the textured mini-bar, knocking over the six assembled bottles of Babycham. (One of which is suspiciously empty. Oh, no! Could someone else be in the room, hiding somewhere?)

B1 continues to struggle with his immensely complex crotch-fastening arrangements. A2 finds it equally hard to remove her the-world's-your-speculum blue jeans. By contrast, A1 pulls the ripcord on her jump suit and 'has it off' in a mere demi-hemi-semi-trice.

And B2, once the sparkly shoulderpads are ditched, nudifies himself with utter celerity.

As she has very little else to do, A1 kneels down and starts to find out just how sugary sweet B1's stick of Brighton rock really is.

Oh, no! A divorce could be in the offing.

But the sight of their co-band members getting down on it merely inspires A2 and B1 to redouble their efforts of fashion escapology.

'I am to you a microphone,' groans B2 to A1. 'Show me the technique you are having.'

Finally, B1 says, 'Have you a pair of scissors in your possession?'

A2 replies, 'Good, Batman.' Her handbag is very handy, and soon she is snipping her way through his twenty leather-look pant tighteners. They ping and they pung, and soon his Palace Pier is being lapped by the incoming tides of A2's saliva.

But more (and other) is to come.

A2 reaches across and, in a post-Global-telecast frenzy of Sapphic lust, tweaks A1's bright red nipple.

'The fans,' she says, 'they are wanting us to be do-be-do-be-doing this to each other for the longest day.'

A1 groans and, removing B2's lurve-microphone from her imminently million-selling larynx, says, 'I am a waterfall of wanting this dream to come true. Let me "visit with your close family".'

With which rare Swedish lesbo-idiom, A1 muff-dives across the room like a Furby on heat. (If you'll excuse the anachronism.)

In her delight at being so pleasured, A2 releases B1's schlong from its dental clamp.

The massive Euro-penis strafes the room with heavy threat, like a Sherman tank about to liberate Paris.

He puts his hands on his lithe hips and says to song-writing chum B2, 'How about you and me, melodic big boy?'

Big-beefy-beardy B2 needs no further RSVP. He is suckety-sucking before you can say Roger Wilco John Thomas.

All of top Swedish pop band DaDa are now naked as the day they last sauna-ed together. (Wednesday.)

Gay fellatio and dykey cunnilingus last for a long while.

Then A1 says, 'Now give it to me up where the sun ain't gonna shine any more.'

B1 and B2 look at each other confusedly. In order to do this, B2 has to make a small centre parting in the Afro-bush of B1's pubic hair. Neither of them knows which of them A1 meant. All they are sure of is that A2 wasn't the addressee.

So, how do you solve this tricksy problemo?

Well, surely, by pulling themselves apart and then by pulling apart A1's pert bum-cheeks.

'I'm to die for it,' she says. 'I ache like a tooth.'

The Swedish are a polite people.

'After you,' says B2.

'No,' says B1. 'After you.'

Eventually their prevarication annoys A2 into taking action. She turns her soon-to-be equally unit-shifting shitter ceiling-wards and says, 'Last one in's a cissygay-boy.'

And so, B1 slams his schlong into A2 and B2 buries his hatchet in A1.

Swedish ugghs and mnnns sound much like English ones.

The ex-backing-singer nymphettes, side by side on the chocolate counterpane, ride the hard cocks of what will, in twenty years, be widely acknowledged as the greatest song-writing partnership since Lennon and McCartney.

Hands reach out from one coupling to touch the humping humps of the other.

Now the shit really hits the fan, who has been hiding half under the bed all this time. (After celebrating the band's success by quaffing a bottle of their Babycham – Aha!)

She is 16, a virgin, but very obviously up for it: viz. she is wearing an ultra-clingy DaDa T-shirt and a pair of hot pants that would make even the Turin Shroud's eyes water.

She can no longer remain anonymous.

The squits of superstar bum juice in her flaxen hair are just too much for this little fuck-kitten's neurons to process.

She crawls out on hands and knees, much to the poptabulous quartet's surprise and delight.

Her yellow-butterflied bunches swing as she says, 'Make me depraved like you guys.'

The fan's pert titties jiggle beneath the DaDa logo like two heads giving blow-jobs. B1 and B2 immediately pull their un-Trojan stallions out of their particular siege situations.

The fan seizes her opportunity, in both hands.

Her cutesy-girl clothes are ripped from her soft English flesh. And, pretty damn soon, A1 and A2 are collaborating in holding her spread-eagled on the floor while B1 and B2 unite in de-hymening her Limey love-passage.

'Your songs mean so much to me,' the fan yelps. 'They helped me get over my break-up with Derek.'

With their free hands, A1 and A2 begin to twist her beehive-shaped, honey-sweet nipples.

'Ow,' she says. 'That hurts in an unexpectedly nice way.'

'Hold her in a still position down,' A1 demands. 'While I fetch the equipment.'

A2 sits her fanny on the fan's face.

'Tongue my wet parts,' she says. 'That's an order corporal. If you don't, we won't be doing no Christmas Message on your stupid Fan Club flexidisc this year.'

B1 and B2 are banging into the fan like the rhythm section on 'Nympho Hippo, Hunky Monkey', which is to be the follow-up single to 'Stalingrad'.

('Nympho Hippo, Hunky Monkey' concerns the attempts of a grossly overweight Norwegian girl to seduce a particularly well-hung orang-utan in Oslo Zoo, one dark and windy night.)

A1 returns from the bedside table with her King Dong KlassiK vibrator – twelve inches of throbbing battery-powered silicone.

'Let me coming through,' she says.

Miraculously, B1 and B2 part – like the Polish populace in 1939 for the invading German Panzer tanks.

The fan faces the black fucksimile of a porn god.

'Pierce me like an ear,' she shrieks. Clever B1 and B2 are soon giving her a taste of the wonders of stereo, stud-style.

A2 is feeling left out of all the fun, and so she fetches her own unmatronly orgasmatron – it's a 'Holmes', and pretty soon it's installed in front of a roaring fire, having a bit of crumpet, up her own personal Baker Street. 'Aaaagh,' A2 shrieks, like an out-of-sync disco violin.

At this moment, both B1 and B2 have an idea for a follow-up single to 'Nympho Hippo, Hunky Monkey'. It will be called 'What's Yours Is Mine (and What's Mine is Yours)'. The subject of the dead-cert gold-disc song will be the transfer of the *herpes simplex* virus from a Belgian child prostitute to a senior member of the Royal Family of Luxembourg and thence, by stages, in each succeeding verse, to an English butler, a Spanish opera singer and finally – in a delicious irony – the child prostitute's own grandmother. The chorus will go: 'It's cold, it's sore / It's really rather raw / From poor-oh whore-oh / to Euro bore-oh / from Tea-at-four-oh / to Toreador-oh / to At-Death's-Door-oh! / What's yours is mine / (and what's mine is yours) / Oh!'

The thought of creating such a musico-masterpiece makes B1 and B2 simultaneously ejaculate in such an extravagantly creamy fashion that the shagpile carpet of the penthouse suite of the Grand Hotel, Brighton, will need a shampoo and set before the room is once again fit for human habitation. But the fan-gangbang night has many more hours and many, many more pervy permutations to get through before Dawn spreads her rosy cunt-lips. (Dawn being, of course, the chambermaid.)

THE ROOM

Tim Parks

*T*his afternoon she didn't go straight to the room. Instead, she mooched for half an hour, first in a music shop, then looking through posters in a place that mainly sold bric-à-brac for tourists. She imagined the posters on the wall opposite her bed, each one changing the colour and flavour of her life. Then she imagined buying one for the room. Apparently this was a strange thought, for she stood there frowning at a boldly painted naïve image of man, woman and child against a postmodern backdrop. What sense would there be in hanging this in the room?

And she decided not to buy fruit today. Today would be different. Perhaps this was what had been disturbing her. Sameness. Or, more specifically, lack of progress. Looking at her watch, seeing she was going to be late, she very deliberately did not quicken her pace. And this perhaps was a far greater change than anything that might be worked by the purchase of a poster or the non-purchase of fruit.

Life. Walking past dreary boarding houses in Earls Court, this young woman was very beautiful, though she herself did not believe so. Her camellia-coloured skin had the faintest soft freckling below wide, plum-dark eyes. She walked too quickly in flat shoes and loose, casual clothes, hiding everything, one among so many on these pavements. Essentially she was a happy person.

Arriving at the famous 69 (trust him to remark on its appropriateness), she let herself in, discreetly obeying all the rules they had established: a light, but not hurried pace along threadbare carpeting; softly down the stairs with the creak where they turned; almost silent insertion of the key.

She opened an old brown London door on to the familiar stale smell.

The room. It was untidy, for today was Monday and the others always left it like that. There was the bed to be made up, a bit of clearing away to be done. These were tasks she would normally tackle brightly, lowering shabby drape curtains over the legs of passers-by, lighting the spots, finding music on the radio. Today she swung her shoulder bag on to an armchair that no charity shop would accept and lay down on the bare mattress. The mattress, in sharp contrast to everything else, was new. Sweet Dreams was called. Nobody, so far as she knew, had ever slept on it.

And how odd that today of all days, with her feeling the way she did, he was late. She remembered a recent conversation. Since he taught statistics, since she had studied with him, it was not unusual for them to talk about chance, probability, coincidence, though usually in jest. ('Assuming a man comes once in every bout of lovemaking and a woman twice, and given a mean copulative frequency of the population as a whole – pensioners, infants and war-wounded included – of once a month, what is the probability that the total number of achieved, non-masturbatory orgasms, of a randomly selected sample, will, etc. etc.' They used to laugh about this kind of thing.).

But it must have been last week when he had said quite seriously that he had noticed that when he was feeling different sometimes, different things happened; a curiously inarticulate proposition, coming from him, as she had swiftly, joyfully pointed out, as he had freely acknowledged, and yet he honestly had noticed it, as if there were such a thing as premonition after all. But not in the classic sense. More a sort of extraordinary subterranean process by which one's feelings were already attuned to an eventuality before it happened. So intriguing if one could think of a way of analysing it statistically: frequency, circumstances. Yet he himself could hardly offer one concrete example. Something was going on, but it was so elusive.

Lying on the superior sprung surface manufactured by Sweet Dreams Ltd, the only significant investment in this shabbily furnished room, Alice observed that she was not crying, nor especially sad. Yet by that curious process he had spoken of, she realised that she was already prepared for what would happen. She knew they would not make love today. Nor ever, ever again perhaps. Those terrible words.

Then she was just thinking of where she, Alice Norton, had come from, where she might be going to and what place this room might have in her life between those two distant points, when the scratching of a key in the door appeared to belie her melancholy. He was here. Immediately she was on her feet, pulling the clean bedlinen out of the bag by the dresser. Bustle, bustle. Spread the sheets, pull on the pillow slips, mix a drink perhaps, if the others had left any. They would only have an hour or so at max. Glasses. Those bastards hadn't even washed the glasses.

'Sorry,' a woman's voice spoke behind her.

She turned in shock. For heaven's sake, could this be the wife?

The woman by the door was older, a shade thick about the middle, but very fashionably dressed in skirt, silk blouse, a light jacket around her shoulders. Her face was at once authoritative and friendly, the skin only faintly tired about the cheeks, the corners of the mouth.

'I'm sorry,' she repeated with a full, strong voice. 'I really didn't mean to disturb. Just that I left my watch here, I think. I'd hate to lose it.'

They looked at each other. Alice understood and relaxed.

She must be Jonathan's friend's woman, the other couple who used the room. She smiled broadly, almost burst out laughing, the release from tension generating a sense of hilarity; naughty children getting away with things. So when the other woman had found her watch on the floor by the bed, she suggested: 'Why don't you stay and have a cup of tea till he gets here? It's so odd actually seeing you after all this time. You must be Christine, right?'

Smiling, somewhat wryly, the woman agreed. They sat at the table with its sticky wooden surface below light filtering through the curtains; it was early afternoon.

'Oh, by the way,' Alice began, 'can I make a complaint? You never clean up properly. I mean, the dishes and crumbs on the carpet and stuff. Even the loo is dirty sometimes.'

The woman was straightforward, unembarrassed: 'I'm sorry. You're right. Jack tells his wife he's playing football, so he only has a couple of hours, and if I stayed on behind I'd have to get the tube and bus home, and there's my boy waiting for me. We always mean to clean up,' she added, 'but Jack's so impulsive. We end up making love right to the last minute. We only have the once a week, you know.'

'Jonathan's incredibly orderly,' Alice said. 'He always says we should leave it tidy for you.'

For a moment both women, one old enough to be the other's mother, laughed. The afternoon ticked by in this small, quiet run-down room in

London which two lovers had rented to pleasure their mistresses.

Alice looked at her watch: 'He's disgustingly late, he's never been late before.' She laughed again. 'We should really get them to put a phone in here. Perhaps with an answering machine, you know, to leave messages.' Then, barely pausing and only realising the truth of her words as she spoke them, this beautiful young woman said: 'Though I was meaning to tell him it was over today.' No sooner was it out than she felt that dazed surprise that comes with the realisation of the glaringly obvious. So this was what had been on her mind.

'What? Why?'

'Oh, I don't know.' Alice stood up and ploughed a hand into the jet-black hair he raved about so much. 'It's become such a ritual. OK, he loves me so much, he really does, and we make love so well, it's not like with anyone else. But in the end, there's his wife, there's his children. If it was just her, he says he'd leave. But not the kids. I've seen him with them. We went out for the day once with his boy. He'll never leave them. They're so lovely.'

Sipping her tea, the older woman asked, 'How old are you?'

'Twenty-one.'

'And Jonathan?'

'Thirty-four.'

'Like Jack.' She smiled. 'I'm forty-one.' Then merely added, 'I wonder if he'll be able to afford to keep the room on his own if you two drop out. Perhaps we'll have to sort out some other arrangement.' For a few moments neither spoke, apparently stilled by the dustiness of this small, sad space, usually so alive for both of them with the intensities of erotic pleasure.

Straight-backed, dignified, a definite air of careful preservation about her, Christine sipped her tea. Alice paced about the room. Then the girl said, 'Oh shit,' and plumped herself down on the edge of the Sweet Dreams mattress. 'At the beginning it was so wonderful. We even went to Paris . . . And of course I half believed then something might come of it. You know how you do. Just that now it's such a ritual. We come here. We mix a drink, put the radio on. We make love, gloriously. We smoke, we eat grapes or kiwis . . . ' She paused, considering. 'Well, I get my degree next month and that's it. I'll break it off. Start a new life.'

To hear her speak, she gave the impression of talking to one who didn't believe her. But the older woman nodded her comprehension: 'I've never met him, but Jack told me something about him, that he'd leave home and live with you, but for the kids.' She shrugged her shoulders in an expression that told the younger woman, '*C'est la vie*.' It wasn't perhaps quite the sort of older-sisterly comfort Alice had been expecting, and now she asked almost abrasively, 'And Jack?'

'What?'

'Is he planning to leave his wife?'

'Good heavens, no.'

'So he has children too.'

'No, he doesn't actually. The wife wants kids, but it seems they haven't been able to have them.'

'So he could leave her tomorrow if he wanted! He has no excuse at all!'

'I suppose he feels sorry for her. If he left her now she'd be forty with no kids, nothing.'

'But feeling sorry for someone's hardly a good reason for staying with them, is it?'

'No, but probably he's not that unhappy with her or the whole arrangement anyway.' She laughed quite cheerfully: 'He always says: "Inertia will pull me through in the end."'

Still chuckling, this older woman, whom Alice now found time to notice was heavily though tastefully made up, began to hunt for and eventually found a packet of cigarettes in her handbag.

'But you, wouldn't you be better off with someone who could give you everything?'

'Oh, he has a fine line in dirty talk. I like that. He's good company. He knows how to give me what I want.'

'But that's an awful thing to say.'

Her tea finished, the mature woman held up a hand, then ducked a little out of habit to light her cigarette. She tossed her hair back with simple, stylish self-assurance. 'Sweetheart, I was actually married for fifteen years. I have a twelve-year-old son. We had affairs, but we never split up. I don't know why. It wasn't just Joey, my boy. More a feeling that, well, that life went that way, that that was the direction. You know?' And now she added, as if inconsequentially, 'A couple of years later he died in a car crash.'

'I'm sorry.'

'Oh, you don't have to be. All I'm saying is that one learns, I suppose, to separate passion, sex, from the mainstream of life.'

Taking this in, Alice said intelligently, 'I think that's awfully sad.'

'Well, maybe at first.'

Alice stood up again and went to look in a foggy mirror, which showed her full-length and tomboyish in jeans and yellow T-shirt. Her movements as she swayed there, then swung away on one heel, were so much those of a girl doing some sport, rather than a woman who knows how to wear clothes and hold her body. Which curiously made her seem vulnerable in her very vitality.

With sudden fervour, she said, 'Well, I don't accept it. I won't. I'm going to tell him, either he leaves his wife or it's over.'

'You're not of an age to accept it.'

'I hate it,' Alice snapped, raising her voice, 'when people try to circumvent any proper argument by simply saying I'm too young. It's terrible.'

'It is terrible,' the other equally agreed with one raised eyebrow.

'Anyway,' Alice tried to explain. 'He'll understand. He's idealistic too. I mean, he suffers this separation of his love life from his family life, coming here to this squalid little shit-hole to fuck, never being able to go out together in company.' The girl hesitated. Emotion had brought quite bright spots of colour to her cheeks. 'All I'm saying is, he understands perfectly well that the situation's not ideal. He'd never ask me to accept it permanently.'

For reply, the older woman pulled a mirror from her handbag and scrutinised her face as one who is preparing to leave.

'Whereas this Jack of yours is just in it for fun and fucks, I gather.'

But this deliberate provocation drew only a broad smile that the mature woman exchanged with herself in her compact.

'Oh, I'm sorry,' Alice said. 'What a stupid little girl I'm being.'

'Not at all. You're perfectly right. We're in it for sex, fun, excitement, to relieve the boredom. What's the fuss? Neither of us really wants to change anything, I shouldn't imagine. And if this Jonathan's got any sense,' she added, 'nor would he.'

'Well, I think that's awful. It's dishonest. To others and to yourself.'

The older woman put her mirror back in her bag and began to edge out from behind the table, dusting cigarette ash from her jacket sleeve. And again Alice had that impression of careful, cosmetic preservation. 'Dishonest,' she repeated, almost in tears now. 'I mean, there must be happy marriages, relationships that contain everything.'

After a moment's pause, straightening her jacket, the older woman looked up and said, 'Yes. There must be. That would be the best thing.'

'Well, I think Jonathan and I could do it. I really do. And that's why I'm going to tell him it's over. To force him into action. One thing or the other.'

There was a challenge in Alice's voice. Checking her watch, Christine said, 'The only advice I'd give you, love, is that if you really want to go where you think you do, I wouldn't start from where you are now. That's all.

To which the younger woman came back with a student's sharpness, 'I don't care how rough the ground is, you can always draw a line between two geographical coordinates.' But then quite suddenly she burst into tears.

The other woman came over to sit by her side, though without touching her. She asked, 'Do you love him, then?'

The girl moaned, 'All day every day.'

'And he tells you he loves you?'

'But he does, I know he does.'

'That's not exactly the point.' And then she said, 'Look, if he was supposed to be here an hour ago, he's obviously not coming now. Why don't we nip out together and grab a sandwich or an ice-cream or something. Cheer you up. Then I'll have to get back to work.' When the girl went on crying, this fashionable, carefully dressed, middle-aged woman put a hand on her back and caressed her lightly. Speaking softly, she said, 'London's teeming with rooms like this, you know, teeming, but they're never really part of anybody's home, are they? Come on. That's the way to see it.'

'No! No! No!' the girl suddenly shrieked. 'I won't!'

The older woman was clearly shocked by the wild energy of this refusal, for she immediately jumped up and backwards, as if scorched.

'Oh, I'm sorry,' Alice said, calming as suddenly as she had lost control a moment before. 'I don't know what's come over me today. I'll just wash my face a minute, then I'd love to come out with you.'

She got up and padded to the tiny bathroom where they had often joked that you could perfectly well shower sitting on the loo if you wanted; and so at last she found his note.

Taped to the mirror. Obviously he had supposed she would, as always, make straight for the bathroom to prepare herself, not imagining that her mood might mysteriously have attuned itself to this event beforehand in the very way he had himself observed. She had not gone to the bathroom because she had known there would be no sex today. And she had told herself she was fed up with sameness because in some remote part of herself she had known things would never be the same again. The note said:

Dearest, my dearest Alice. I know this is no way to announce things. I do know. It's cowardly. It's mean. But I can't face telling you in person. I would simply burst out in howls and sobs. I love you so dearly. Our times together have been so precious. But I feel constantly pulled in two directions, the object of some vicious tug-of-war. God knows we've talked about it often enough, and as you yourself suggested once, seeing you makes it impossible for me to act normally at home and be a good husband and father. At the same time I know now that I will never have the courage to leave my family for you and am plagued with guilt at the thought that I am wasting your life, your marvellous capacity for love and tenderness.

Oh, Alice, my beauty, my dark eyes, my endless little giggler, I think of you so constantly, of your extraordinary capacity to be cheerful and make others so. I think of how happy, how light-hearted, I have always been with you, and the idea that all this must end is torture.

Please, please remember me with affection.

Your truly loving,

Jonathan.

With turning on the taps then to wash her face, Alice did not hear the sound of the room's main door opening, but, catching just the vaguest tremble when it slammed shut on its spring as it always would, she imagined that the older woman must have decided to leave alone. So, with towel in hand, she slipped quickly out of the bathroom to catch up with her, not wanting to be left without company at this unhappy moment; and was thus able to cover her face in a moment with the red cloth to hide the inevitable shock when she saw what she saw.

'Jack,' the woman who called herself Christine beamed. 'Jack. This is Alice, Jonathan's girl.' There he was.

And in an extraordinary act of generosity, or perhaps contempt, and anyway with that apparent gaiety he had always most appreciated in her, and most misunderstood, she managed to ask, appearing from her towel and even offering a hand, 'Oh, have you forgotten something too? What a day!'

'My diary,' he invented, as promptly as he must often have been obliged to with his wife. 'Is this a page from it?' The paper was in her hand.

But his eyes were imploring. What? Forgiveness? Or more? Clearly his only reason for arriving like this must have been to revoke the contents of that note. He had changed his mind.

'I'll leave the field to you then,' she said very practically, 'since Jonathan's obviously not coming.' For indeed, the other woman was at this moment kicking off her high heels as she rapidly made up the bed. He stared at her, but nothing more. Almost expressionless. She felt his eyes follow her out.

And emerging a few moments later into a grey afternoon light, walking by the curtains drawn over their pleasure (so dusty from this side), finding the note still crumpled in her hand, it occurred to Alice very lucidly that perhaps he had been entirely sincere in what he said there. Why not? She was worth so much more than the older woman; she had so much further to go. Let them keep their squalid room.

PART 13

Past Pleasures

PILGRIMAGE TO PAPHOS

Christopher Hart

*T*he deer leans towards me, little more than a fawn, almond-eyed, foreleg tentatively outstretched, a delicate hoof beside my foot, its soft, moist muzzle cupped in the palm of my hand. (The tameness of these deer, sacred to Apollo Hylates, never fails to amaze and delight me.) In the distance, through the last few pines and the shimmering pine-laden air, I can just make out, with my old and rheumy eyes, the temple of Paphian Aphrodite, and the slumbering sea beyond.

Needles crunch underfoot. More pilgrims are coming down through the woods behind us. My fawn's ears flick back and forth alternately, she turns her head away from me, and then abruptly she trots off. I am alone. Where is the boy?

I find him bathing naked in a pool fed by springs from the hills, from high Olympus and Tripylos. He says nothing, clambers out, droplets of cold mountain water on his smooth, hairless chest, rubs himself dry with his himation, and slings it around his waist. I toss a coin into the pond and make a wish – for youth or love, or immortal life or some such folly.

Emerging from the woods, we see streams of pilgrims on the road below leading into the town, on foot or on mule, from Magna Graecia and Lydia, Phrygia and Crete, Egypt, Libya, Nubia . . . Devotees all of the Goddess of Love and, some poets say, the oldest of the Fates. Beyond the town as we approach, we can see the rocky islands out to sea, inhabited only by seabirds wheeling and crying in the summer air. Over the last rise and there is Paphos, flat white rooftops hurting white under the sun. My boy claps his hands and leaps at my side. I cannot resist a smile.

The best rooms in the town are all taken, and even the cheapest are beyond the means of a peripatetic philosopher and his pupil. We lay out our blankets in the almond orchards behind the great temple. Last year's almond shells in the grass beneath our blankets, brown and sun-dried, crackle when we lie down. New almonds ripen on the trees. Autumn is coming.

It is three days until the Aphrodisia. It is very hot. The cicadas are shrilling. We drink and dispute in the tavern, under a cool trellis-arbour of trailing vines. A Syrian dancing-girl, her hair caught up in a fillet, sways her quivering flanks to the castanets' rattle, half-drunk, lascivious, wanton eyes sleepy and half-closed, her hands on her hips and then on my boy's shoulders. 'What thanks will cold ashes give?' she sings. It is sweet to lie in the shade, and reap the scarlet lips of a pretty girl.

I lie under the stars, see the trail of Perseus to the north-east over the dark Troödos mountains, and that most beautiful star of summer, Vega in Lyra, and Arcturus slowly falling towards dawn. My head is heavy with wine, but I sleep little. Before daybreak my boy returns and slips under the blanket beside me. His flesh is cool but his heart is beating like a startled fawn's. I kiss him. 'Your skin,' I murmur. 'Sandalwood, cinnamon, nard . . . You smell of Syria.' He smiles, his teeth gleaming white and wolfish in the darkness.

In the morning we walk into the town and I lecture him along the way about the Goddess. He is sullen and adolescent, does not listen, kicks a peach stone along the road, walks ahead of me on long, coltish legs, squints out to the far horizon of the sea. I strike him a vehement blow across his back with my stick. He swings round, blinking with pain. I reprimand him for paying no attention to my words. He turns away again, but not with impudence. He speaks like a man. 'What is there to learn from you?' he sneers. 'What do you know of Aphrodite? I can learn all I need to know of her between a woman's thighs.'

I run at him – lumber rather – to strike him again, but he skips away and mocks me. 'Old men should chase old men,' he yells, 'not young boys! You'll never catch us!' He flicks up his himation and bares his arse at me, and then runs on into town.

I do not see him again that day.

(The manners of the young these days! It was not like that when I was a boy.)

In the gardens of the temple of Aphrodite I couple with a sacred prostitute, who performs her duties with manifest pride, laying aside her elaborate head-dress first with great reverence. I pay her her due and thank her courteously.

In the town I hire a local guide, but I should have saved my money. All Cretans are liars – and all Cypriots too. This charlatan kindly informs me that the temples of Paphos were all built by Dedalus himself; that Hercules was born here (showing me the very house); and that only thirty years since, a great sea-monster arose out of the waves and devoured a dozen virgins on the beach.

In the tavern I learn of the Hierodouli, a slaves' festival for the Goddess, which took place only a few days before our arrival. The slaves build huts of myrtle branches in which they make offerings to wax models of the Goddess, and implore fertility. Garlanded with flowers and praying without ceasing, they often enter into trances, having ecstatic visions of far-off lands, or holding conversations with their own ancestors of many years ago, when they were free.

The Aphrodisia begins on the sea-front, where the Goddess herself first stepped ashore out of the foam.

A priestess anoints the great stone statue with oil and then the virgins wash naked in the waves, emerging dripping with saltwater, pert and glowing, each reborn as a young Aphrodite Anadyomene herself. They approach the statue of the Goddess and dance around her, a dance formal and restrained, bending to kiss and caress it, the dancing and touching being their initiation into the mysteries of seduction and the sensual life.

The priestess then signals the end of the dance, and with it, the coming of autumn, of fruitfulness and then the darkening days and the cold end of the year. The virgins disperse into the crowd to choose for themselves their first lovers, their first act of love being both an initiation and an offering to the Goddess. After this there are more sacrifices and auguries, incense and prayers, singing and dancing and love feasts and poetry, and wheatcakes and honey and wine, scenes of riot and delight in the gardens and groves of the great temple.

Amid such scenes I glimpse my boy, seated naked on a wall, a young girl standing facing him, clasped between his bare legs, kissing him ardently. He looks up suddenly and sees me. His eyes are green and blank, and pitiless as the sea. The girl turns and looks in my direction too. He cups her face in his hands and leans down and kisses her again. I turn and walk away, and after nightfall return to the orchard to sleep, like Sappho, alone.

Long into the night, when the moon and the Pleiades have set and the night is at its darkest, I feel him creep under my blanket. I say nothing – sulking, I admit it. Recognising my mood, he slithers down and begins to pleasure me, to tickle and kiss and caress me, arousing me against my will, and I ache with desire. I do not look down. I gaze at the stars overhead, unmoving, sigh a little – wheeze, perhaps. Then I notice, standing to one side, watching us – my boy. I throw back the blanket and look down.

It is the girl, his girl. Her mouth is soft on me, feather-light, a trail of hot kisses across my skin, a lizard over a sun-warm wall, her tongue a dance of lizard flicks, and then more greedily devouring me. I lose a year in age with every kiss, grow young again, hot-blooded and heedless. I reach down and cup her head in my hands, my fingers twining in her hair. She looks up at me, smiles, then rises up, her slim boyish silhouette against the starry night, and very quickly, pragmatically, she straddles me and drives me inside her with a little gasp, so warm and tight. She leans forward and whispers in my ear, her loosened hair tickling my face. 'Not bad – for an old man!'

And there I lie – the indignity of it! Stretched underneath a woman, a slip of a girl, I in the supine position of a slave, while she bucks and rides me like an old mule, whispering teasing endearments in my ear!

I turn my head and there is my boy, squatting beside us now like a little satyr, the girl's slim hand snaking out and reaching around his satyrical phallus, her face still turned to me, smiling down on me, knowingly, riding me triumphantly. And my boy watching us, his eyes gleaming, so pleased with this gift he has brought me, his hands reaching out in turn to caress the girl as she makes love to me, his fingertips trickling over her buttocks, over my own hands that hold her there, over her breasts and her damp thighs, while I lie back and laugh, a happy old slave of Aphrodite, Goddess of Love and oldest and most powerful and irresistible of the Fates, straddled by a Paphian girl whose name I never even knew.

NOTHING NEW IN BONDAGE

Russell Hoban

*M*nemosyne, mother of the Muses, trundling her trolley through my head, dispenses, like tea and digestive biscuits, images, sounds, smells and flavours. Flashes of Manhattan forty years ago and more: sunlight and shadows, moving ladders of time under the Third Avenue El, where the ghost of Kong, free of his chains, roars in silence. Or the smell of frying from the all-night beacon of the White tower with its gleaming coffee urn tended by a tall and priestly short-order cook steeped in the silence of the small hours. Or rain falling on the tar-paper roof of the news-stand on the south-east corner of Third Avenue and 14th Street.

On that corner, up a flight of stairs, was the archival establishment of Irving (or was it Irwin?) Klaw. Mnemosyne isn't as certain of anything as she used to be, but in her way she's erotic – by her very nature erotic, calling up from long ago the fires of youth, the juices of life, the sunlight and the shadows and the moving ladders of time. How did I find Irving or Irwin Klaw? I was an illustrator back then and I needed reference material for a Wells Fargo stagecoach with a six-horse team. Or it might have been a Spencer carbine and the uniform of the trooper firing it.

There was nothing useful in the picture collection of the New York Public Library at Fifth Avenue and 42nd Street, although Truth Beareth Away the Victory, I think it says on the pediment. Bryant Park is behind it, overlooked by the building from the roof of which Gene Hackman aimed ultra-sensitive microphones at the strolling plotters below him in *The Conversation*. Pigeons in the summer sun. Girls in their summer dresses. Long, long ago. No, not Bryant Park, some other park or plaza on the West Coast – San Francisco? Where was I? Nothing useful, so the librarian referred me to Irwin or Irving Klaw's collection of movie stills.

Do all stairs of a certain kind smell of urine? I'm not sure. Maybe this essence can be bought to lend an air of authenticity. Did Irwin or Irving Klaw's stairs smell that way? Mnemosyne, though stripped to suspender belt and stockings, shakes her head; she can't say.

Never mind. Movie stills might have been at the front of the Klaw archive but there was still more to it. I have in mind a long counter with heavy albums on it secured by chains. The handmaidens who served the customers wore long grey smocks (later I wondered if they might be naked under them). While I was sorting through my movie stills there came up the stairs a man in a dirty mac who bore himself like Irate Citizen, or, as you might say, Disgusted of Tunbridge Wells.

'Can I help you?' said one of the possibly-naked-under-her-smock handmaidens.

'Bondage,' said Irate Citizen in a Mr Hyde voice.

'Here they are,' said the handmaiden, indicating two of the chained albums.

Irate Citizen rattled the chains and rapidly riffled the pages of the albums, then made a little irate sound, 'Pfeh.' Would he write to *The Times*? 'I've seen all of these,' he said hoarsely. Did he raise his walking stick? Did he trample a child? Sorry, I'm going all astray here. The sight of Mnemosyne in nothing but suspender belt and black stockings has unsettled me. I hate it when I have to mentally dress her. Because she's old like me.

'Isn't there anything else?' said Irate Citizen. Hoarsely.

'That's all we've got,' said the handmaiden. 'There's nothing new in bondage.'

Did I look into those chained albums? For God's sake, Mnemosyne, put some clothes on and tell me, because I can't recall what I did.

Lolling in a greasy kimono, her hair in curlers, a bottle of gin in her hand, Mnemosyne shakes her head: she can't do any more for me than she's already done.

ROSES OF HELIOGABALUS

Lizzie Speller

*E*ven now that I am an old woman, I cannot bear the smell of roses. Up here on my son's estates in the cool of the Alban Hills, there are flowers in profusion, vines, ripeness, but no roses. He is a good boy. We have never mentioned it, but he knows there must never be roses.

Sometimes, early on, a stranger might arrive with a posy and my nose was so sensitive that I could immediately inhale that sweetness and feel again the seduction of death and desire and then, almost immediately, other unspeakable odours of sweat and vomit and bodily waste.

And such a person, seeing my great age (I was born in the reign of the great African Emperor, Septimius Severus) might ask, tentatively, 'Were you there?' And their eyes shine a little because they too are not immune to the allure of the rose and they want to feel my story. But why should I gratify them? Usually, I reply sharply, 'Oh I was there, but what is extraordinary is that I am HERE. Before you. Still here.' And they breathe a little faster, but they learn nothing.

And yet it is hard to imagine how it seemed then. Look at the stern soldier who is our Caesar now. A man's man. A military man's military man. Not to be confused with that young, long-dead prince who brought a beautiful horror into our lives. There had been battles. There were always battles then, but for us they never made much difference. They were fought on bleak, barbaric frontiers, where nobody but soldiers would wish to go and all we saw of them were the victorious processions of generals climbing triumphantly to the Capitol and handsome legionaries and their spoils, and chained, miserable slaves.

But this time it was a new Emperor who came to us. Some had seen his portrait, but for most of us it was a day of excitement; he was rumoured to be very young and very beautiful, and a priest of an unknown religious sect, which worshipped a stone that fell from the sky. So we girls of good family were seated along the way with the boys and their tutors below. And the crowd was beginning to get restless; it was a hot, still day, when slaves ran in, spreading gold dust, turning the processional way into a magical ribbon of light. And then, very slowly, our new Emperor could be seen, walking backwards, reverently, behind a dray on which, drawn by six milk-white horses and decked in gems, was a huge, shiny black stone and that was our new Emperor's God.

And it was hard not to look at the God, but the boy Emperor was almost as beautiful. He was dressed in what seemed to be tissue, opaque folds of shimmering cloth. Even at a little distance, we could see he had been painted like a woman with rose-pink and white cheeks, and blue shadow round his eyes, and those eyes darkened with eastern kohl. And some of the boys sniggered, but not very loud because who knew what were the appetites of such a God? Or of the Emperor?

But our families liked us to be at court. For the girls there was a little matter of placing a wife in the Emperor's way, and, for young courtiers, Heliogabalus's palace was the most exciting place to be. By now the God and the Emperor were one; a sort of holy duality. No more soldiers and bureaucrats, but performers, dancers, youths and athletes. And the jokes. Well, Heliogabalus seemed to think they were serious, but for us it was a time of luxury and fun, and beauty and outrageousness, and seeing our elders fret about un-Roman-ness. And if the gilded youth at the time appeared a little odd or unfathomable, we put it down to his exotic origins and various misunderstandings about the role of the Priest of the Great Black Stone.

And from his part of the Empire he brought some wonders. Silk in every imaginable colour, soft as skin. And the roses, of course. Not that we didn't have roses before, but they were tidy, bright, clear-coloured things, growing just a foot or so towards the sun, scarcely smelling of anything but freshness. But Heliogabalus brought roses that were distant relatives of ours. Some were as black as obsidian, some so soft a pink you could believe them made of flesh; one was angry magenta, another fiery orange with a pink heart and tiny stamens. There were tight secret buds and jagged-edge petals crammed into hairy sepals, stalks that were covered in fine thorns like the legs of a poisonous insect and glorious waxy, full-leafed white roses which climbed and climbed – swathing the austere stones of our palace with a perfume so heady they say it could be smelt at the foot of the Palatine.

We bathed in decoctions of roses, we ate crystallised petals, we wove them into our hair, we dried the most aromatic and filled our cushions with them.

And in the God's temple there were the finest wines, spices and scents that made you feel first sick and dizzy, then enfolded and then lost. Syrian dancing girls swirled and sang in a strange tongue to formless music. But in the midst of the beauty there was horror and it started right there with the God. Behind the attar of roses and the myrrh and the burnt oil was a decaying sweetness that was not floral, but darker and set the heart racing with atavistic memory. Around the God's altar it was sticky and black, tarry with the blood of unknown victims. My cousin, coming one night to worship, plunged her hands into the bowl of rose heads by the sanctuary doors and felt a cold, moist something that was not floral, something that was human, that had been human, such an intimate part that she was found unconscious on the steps. And monkeys gibbered in the darkness of the building.

Heliogabalus himself danced, or rather he swayed, made little movements of delight or distaste. Some of the young men copied him and became his favourites and seemed to be neither men nor women, but beautiful painted creatures. Circling Heliogabalus in his gilt hairnets, watching while he played the harlot, slipping from behind bead and jewel curtains to sell himself.

And although Heliogabalus married and took women to his bed, scandalising our elders by raping a Vestal, it was rumoured that as he thrust into them, brought them to pleasure, he watched coldly, sometimes taking notes of their response, sometimes muttering to himself.

And then he declared he was to marry Astarte, the silvery Goddess of the Syrians. But for pleasure incarnate he took men as husbands and, my brother, alas an intimate, told me he used his knowledge of women's sexual pleasure to mimic it in the arms of a man. So entranced was he by assuming the form of a woman that he had the surgeons remove his male organ and make instead a welcome place for his lovers to enter him. He even encouraged his lovers to catch him in some transgression and beat him for it.

His agents scoured the land to look for men of exceptional endowment but it was at the games that he first saw the athlete Hierocles. Well, we all saw him when, in the heat of the moment and with considerable forethought, the fighter's loincloth was torn from his body. For a moment there was silence, but for the distant growling of caged beasts. Hierocles had something of a reputation and when he arrived at the palace the Emperor had him stripped and, finding him equal to anything that had gone before, fell into his arms. But jealousy is a nasty thing and into Hierocles's late-night draught a rival had placed an anaphrodisiac which softened and unmanned the golden boy. Heliogabalus was distant and dreaming and lost, I now know, to decadence.

But he was not stupid and his advisers told him to draw away from the dreadful compulsions and companions that were making the Senate and army restless. So he devised a summer's feast in marble arcades next to the fountains and pools of the Summer Palace. He and his companions lay on the couches on the highest tier, we others dined on cushions in the deep well of the building. There were caged birds singing and silver fish, as I recall, in the water beyond. We were all young. We were all drinking wine. Some were fondling each other, others had legs entwined. My brother had slipped my breast out of my robe. A couple passed sugared petals from mouth to mouth. And there were magnificent dishes of rich and unknown foods but the smell was so strong, the perfume of roses so heavy, that it stifled the appetite, so that when he cried, 'Eat, eat,' we could only play at feasting.

And the ceiling above us was swathed with silk; gauzy, white, weighted with myriad rose petals, whose pinkness we could just glimpse and whose crushed stain seeped through the fine fabric.

And then, then. A black slave stepped to each corner and loosed mighty gold ropes and the petals started to fall, and for one moment it seemed like heaven and then it became hell. They fell so fast and so abundantly and they stuck clammily to the skin, and the vapour was so overwhelming that at first it was more terrible than the petals, blush, peach, nacre, indigo, bronze, scarlet. And because we were drowsed by grapes and by arousal, and by warm proximity and the benign nature of roses, there was very little struggle. My brother fell from me, his mouth open and full of sweetness, he tried to wipe petals from his nostrils but was gone. My sister screamed briefly as she saw her fate, but was suffocated immediately. Her legs twitched against mine and then she was reduced to odour as her body emptied.

Above the sea, hands rose, fingers splayed in agony, folded and sank. There were muffled thuds beneath the bowl of petals as vessels fell or someone *in extremis* upturned a couch. I was on the edge. I choked, vomited petals and mucus. And then someone – a slave? a friend? – pulled me clear, behind a pillar. It was just in time. Heliogabalus looked at his work, smiled slightly, walked away and minions stepped forward and started stabbing pikes into the mass of petals, which turned red and brown, but remained silent.

And they are gone, and I am here, and out there beyond the hills the roses still grow, and women crush them on their bodies for their scent.

PART 14

Treats in Store

THE JOY OF PORN

Matt Thorne

W hat is it about you and women and porn?' a female friend asked me the other day. We'd been out at a party and three women had come up to me to talk about their favourite magazines, movies and web-sites. I couldn't really answer her question, except to suggest it might be the *Sex, Lies and Videotape* effect. Show enough interest in whatever gets people off, and they'll be more than happy to share their secrets.

Not that porn is even that much of a secret these days. And I have to say I think that's a good thing. At first it seemed really disturbing to see those counters at the bottom of a web-site: You are the 112,345th visitor to this site. What an odd thought. But then, as I heard more and more people talking about what they liked, I realised how it was probably a good thing. Get rid of the guilt, and a lot of bad stuff goes with it (misogyny, double standards, the whore/Madonna complex – although if that's what you're into, don't let me stop you). Pornography is becoming increasingly less of a male preserve, and this can only be a good thing. It doesn't mean that porn has to clean up or become politically correct or any of those other terrible things that quickly turns the erotic unerotic. But the idea that we might start talking to each other about what we find sexy can only be a step forward.

This is one of the things I like best about Vicky and Charlie's film reviews. They look at porn from a detached, amused perspective, but they're not afraid to talk about which scenes turn them on. This is something that is almost always forgotten about in conversations about pornography: it's potentially always a two-way thing (not to mention the huge commercial success of gay porn). And as porn becomes more mainstream and increasingly talented directors (such as Andrew Blake, whose movie *Wet* is reviewed here) get involved, it will become something entirely different from most detractors' primitive view of what constitutes pornography.

Another often-forgotten fact about porn is that everyone looks at it differently. There's no reason why pornography should be any less interesting than any other genre or medium. I have a slightly disturbing male friend who watches it for the bored look in the actors' and actresses' eyes: for some reason what gets him off most is the idea that the people participating in it might be composing their shopping lists while being filmed having sex. Lots of women I know are connoisseurs of the tacky furnishings that often crop up. But the most exciting thing is that you never know exactly what effect this sort of stuff is going to have. For every occasion a film or photographed scenario seems boring or stupid, there's another time when an image or scene cuts right to the core, unearthing fantasies or desires you'd forgotten or perhaps never realized you felt.

For me, pornography is all about promise. I cannot help seeing it on an aesthetic rather than a political level, as once these picture are taken or these movies made, it stops being about bodies and starts being about more information. That might not sound that sexy, but my point is, looking at porn is an extension of our overwhelming desire to discover what's hidden in ourselves or others. What interests me is not what goes on in the photographer's studio or on the film set, but the mental baggage that people bring with them when they see these images.

It's a safe way of feeling a sexual connection beyond a relationship, and tapping into the fantasyland that we all have in our heads but most of us can't always indulge in. It's to do with that disconnection and disassociation that makes De Sade amazing to read but also impossible to live out. Few of us want to star in porn films, but almost everyone likes the possibility of doing just that. Good porn, like good films or good literature, allows us the chance to live other lives, and let loose the id. That alone seems more than enough reason for it to exist.

VIDEO: JOLLY ROGERING

Vicky and Charlie

This is the cleanest, straightest skin flick we have ever seen. It is the Tim Henman of hardcore porn. If Henman himself were going to appear in a porn film, butt-fucking Cliff Richard while Gloria Hunniford looked on, it would be this one. It's that clean.

Which is not to say that it doesn't feature anal sex, rimming and lesbian double-dildo action. It just features them cleanly. You could eat your dinner off those dildoes.

The story unfolds on a big yacht. On board are two married couples (they swing and screw), a bunch of fun-loving gals (they lick and suck), a Brazilian band (they twiddle and jig), a successful English businessman (he shouts 'Here's to this year's Whitley & Smythe sales figures!' before buggering his elated secretaries) and international porn star Jenna Jameson. Some Latino pirates swarm on deck, fuck Jenna, fall overboard and the film ends.

On paper, writer-director and star Brad Armstrong must have thought he had a winning formula. But he hadn't done the maths. Porn plus pirates does not necessarily equal a sexy film. Though it's an easy mistake to make, and one that Charlie would almost certainly have made, given a DV camera and a selection of randy Mexicans.

All porn directors understand the following equation: porn = A + B, where A is the camera and B is the sexual act.

However, the erotic in porn = (A + B) x C, where C is any one of the following: plot, character, motivation, psychological depth, creative imagination. This might include piracy.

Armstrong clearly wanted one hell of a lot of C. He hired a big boat, costumes, guns and a cast of thirty. Most porn films use seven or eight actors at most, with a couple of extras for the crowd scenes (i.e. the gangbangs). Having got his hands on a big yacht, he decided not to restrict himself to a sex cruise, but to branch out into a sex cruise which is hijacked by devious drug-running pirates with a grudge against the Second Officer.

Unfortunately, in all his fervour for costume and plot, he left no space in his script for character or motive. (Kevin Costner made the same mistake with Robin Hood, *Prince of Thieves*, and he didn't even manage to get his cock sucked. He must have felt a right fool. He certainly looks like one. Particularly when he gets off the boat at Dover and says, 'We'll be in Nottingham by nightfall.' You wouldn't even manage that on British Rail, matey. Now fuck off back to Hollywood.)

That is why *Dangerous Tides* is so oddly clean. Full marks to the director for having Jenna Jameson fuck one of the pirates in an attempt to get his gun. But Armstrong squanders the erotic potential by making it a straight, decorous, even tender fuck. Where is Jenna's shame and horror at submitting to the grubby villain? Where is his rough, unforgiving aggression as he rips off her bikini pants and slams himself inside?

Instead, we see him engage in loving oral foreplay, while she gasps with pleasure and strokes his hair. She gets more attention from this Romeo than your average happily married housewife gets from her devoted husband in a year.

Even in his concern for gripping narrative, Brad Armstrong gets confused. In his head, it is a startling plot twist to have Captain Nelson called away to the engine room just as he is about to enter Jenna, so she has to shag Second Officer Thompson instead. To us though, it's just Jenna fucking one anonymous porn actor rather than another. It would be a twist if Captain Nelson returned in the middle and started buggering his lieutenant, and it would also be a bit more dirty and exciting. But no; Nelson stays in the engine room while Jenna and Thompson have a nice clean one-on-one.

We feel sure that Henman, Hunniford and Sir Cliff would also approve of the film's moral stance towards illegal drug use. As the vengeful pirates demand to know where Second Officer Thompson is, they shout, 'He is a drug-runner! He corrupts your children and pollutes your streets!', which makes it absolutely fine for Jenna immediately to grass up her recent lover. Never mind that your average American would say that Jenna Jameson herself 'corrupts your children and pollutes your streets'. There is no solidarity of the immoral here.

So . . . drugs are bad; bikinis are good; tits are huge and plastic; baddies fall into the sea; the narrative is creaky; the blonde girl saves the day; and it's all presented with an over-produced soft-rock soundtrack and slo-mo cutaways to a sun-dappled ocean. Take away the actual fucking, and you've got a half-decent episode of *Baywatch*. And, like *Baywatch*, it's a lot less sexy than it pretends to be.

VIDEO: WET

Vicky and Charlie

*T*he box said *The Devil in Miss Jones*. Vicky was delighted at the idea of seeing this fabled porn classic. Charlie hoped it might in fact be an X-rated re-working of *Rising Damp*, recounting the sexploits of a horny Frances de la Tour. Of course, it was neither. Porn is all about the unattainable – and the mendacious video sleeve is just the first step. You think you've got your hands on *Deep Throat*; in fact, you've got *Fat Housewives Go Lesbo 9*. In German. With subtitles in Dutch. But by the time you realise this, you're sitting at home with your cock out and can't be bothered to complain. It's not like being served the wrong wine. In that situation, you simply pop your cock back into your trousers and summon the wine waiter.

So today we fell for it again; we expected Miss Jones and got *Wet. Wet* is not just wet, it's sopping. It makes *Waterworld* look like *Lawrence of Arabia*. Swimming pools, showers, seas, saliva, hoses, bottles of wine, buckets of milk . . . the liquid doesn't stop.

Wet is all about beautiful women getting wet. It's actually rather classy. The women look like supermodels (no plastic tits, no badly bleached hair) and they lie around in genuinely opulent hallways pouring wine on to each other's cunts – all shot on well-lit film to the sound of Manhattan piano-bar music courtesy of composer Raoul Valve. (Why does everybody on a porn film crew have to have a porn name?)

The costumes are pretty. The scenery is nice. It looks like *The Bold and the Beautiful* in porn form. It's the absolute opposite end of the porn spectrum to the cheap VT work of the Bogas Brothers, in which the brothers look like seedy sex pests and the girls look like crack whores. In fact, they are seedy sex pests and crack whores.

In *Wet*, handsome, silent men in dinner jackets pay sexual service to stunning women in perfect make-up. You half expect to see Gwyneth Paltrow gliding across in the background, frigging herself softly as she goes.

There is very little dialogue, and a great deal of slo-mo fingering. It's dreamlike. And one of its most dreamlike qualities is that there is no climax. The women are in a constant, prolonged state of sexual arousal. But they don't come. They're just wet. All the time. They don't 'become' wet and they don't 'stop' being wet. They lick and kiss and suck and play, and tell us, 'I'm always ready for pleasure', and they slip in and out of showers and pools and get even wetter.

The traditional porn structure is build-up, build-up, orgasm; build-up, build-up, orgasm – supposedly mirroring the experience of the viewer. But here, they start aroused, they stay aroused and they end aroused. Even as the film finishes, with Dahlia Gray's snatch being towelled dry by Anita Blond, the towelling becomes masturbating and she gets wet all over again. Not that she was ever dry in the first place.

This is a very sexy film. But it isn't the kind you slip into the VCR for a quick five-minute wank when your husband has nipped to the shops. (Deconstruction fans note: we originally wrote 'wife' in that sentence, but a short shouted debate led to an amendment. As we write, Charlie is still muttering, 'It should be partner!')

You wouldn't have a favourite scene in *Wet* which gets you off every time; no obvious bit where the butler spunks in the housemaid's face. It's all the same: rather delightful, calming, well-lit, well-groomed, sexy wetness. It would be the ideal thing to play in the background of a wife-swapping ('Partner-swapping!' shouts Charlie) party in Kensington.

Or just as a talking point at a bridge game. You wouldn't need to rush off and lock yourself in the bathroom, but it would put you in a sexy mood – and encourage everyone to over-bid, which always makes for a better game.

Vicky would like to go on record as saying that this is a skin flick of which she whole-heartedly approves. Dahlia (the star and associate producer) is stunning and (as far as the medium allows) utterly undegraded. She looks like the sort of porn star who would hang out with Prince at A-list parties and be considered exciting and glamourous for the way she makes her living.

The camera is pleasantly voyeuristic without being intrusive. If Vicky could be in porn films, this is the kind of porn film she'd like to be in. It looks like fun. But so far, she's only been offered *Lots More Luv Chunks 5* and her agent advised against it.

Charlie would like to go one record as saying that he liked it, but he'd still rather have seen *The Devil in Miss Jones*. Fortunately, he's heard that Frances de la Tour is currently playing Cleopatra naked at The Barbican. So if he needs a wank, he knows where to go.

VIDEO: DIRTY DREAMER 3

Vicky and Charlie

We all know the great closing lines of film history. 'This could be the beginning of a beautiful friendship.' 'Oh well, tomorrow is another day.' 'Nobody's perfect.'

And, of course: 'You fucked my ass good, Daddy.'

We admit that the last of these is perhaps not as well known as the others. But it deserves to be. For all you film buffs who want to quote it at dinner parties, this is the last line of *Head Rush*, the third in the Dirty Dreamer series from Dazed Entertainment. It is only when we hear these words, gently murmured by a grateful, yet exhausted stepmother, that we realise quite what a journey we have travelled since she first walked into the room and uttered the words, 'Hullo, and how's my favourite little stepdaughter?'

The journey is, like all the great film journeys, one of self-discovery. At the beginning of the scene, stepmom is a stern disciplinarian. She does not take kindly to finding that her naughty stepdaughter has a secret drawer full of dildoes. Like any responsible moral guardian, she sees only one appropriate course of action: bend the errant teenager over her knee, pull up her skirt and give her a good firm spanking until her bum goes pink.

A lesser parent might have left it at that. Not so our redoubtable stepmom. She snatches up the offending prosthetics and puts them right where they belong: up the tyke's cunt. That'll teach her.

'You've been a very bad girl,' warns stepmom, expertly sliding a vibrator up the young scamp's arse and dispensing a few corrective slaps to her clitoris. Nobody could say these were unmerited.

As a final slap lands on the squirming teenage quim, the protesting girl cries, 'You can't do this! I'm at college now!' This is a turning point.

Stepmom has cunningly brought home to the girl that she's an adult now and should be treated as such. Had stepmom continued to administer the clitoral spanking (as Charlie was advising from the sofa), she would

have been no sort of parent.

With age comes responsibility, and both parties must acknowledge this. In a symbolic gesture representing the girl's maturity, stepmom ritually hands over the largest of the dildoes. Understanding immediately the significance of the moment, the girl shoulders the burden of responsibility, straps on the plastic cock, and fucks her stepmother till the older woman is squealing like a litter of piglets.

And so the younger girl's journey is complete. But that still leaves stepmom with a prosthetic dick up her arse and some lessons to learn. Potent in her new-found authority, the girl informs her surrogate parent 'I'm gonna fuck you like Daddy never could.' When the ensuing fuck is finished, stepmom leans up, kisses her charge and murmurs softly: 'You fucked my ass good, Daddy.' Her mothering task is done; her little fledgling has learnt to fly.

Ah, but here's the rub. Well, there have been several rubs, but here's the crucial one. The dildo action is, as in all the best children's stories, just a dream. It's stepmom's fantasy. All she's really doing is sitting on the tumble-drier whacking off. And the closest she comes to good parenting in 'reality' is wistfully sniffing her stepdaughter's pants. What a rubbish mum.

The motif of the Dirty Dreamer series is that all the sex scenes are dream sequences. There are four other scenarios in *Head Rush* besides stepmom. A dazed boxer fantasises about butt-fucking two eager fight fans. A lady chauffeur enjoys a reverie in which she is double-penetrated by two clients, while a hooker sucks her tits. A postman bangs his head on a step, passes out and dreams that a topless householder is guzzling on his schlong. And a bored secretary has a vision of whipping her pants down, clambering on a desk and shoving her buttocks in the boss's face for him to eagerly spread and rim.

We don't understand the necessity for the dream device. What happens in all these dreams is that people have kinky sex. But this is porn. They'd be having kinky sex anyway. Porn is already a fantasy where you can get butt-fucked, arse-licked, cunt-spanked and face-spunked as often as you want, and you don't have to bang your head on a step to get it.

Not so real life. When Charlie is getting his arse licked and his dick sucked by a couple of eager blondes, he soon realises that he must be asleep. When Vicky notices that she's being double-penetrated by a couple of hairy gangsters in the back of a limo, they're likely to be joined by her dead grandma and Princess Margaret in the front seat, singing show tunes.

In porn, stepmothers are allowed to shove dildoes up their stepdaughters' bums. That's the joy of porn. So, discovering that stepmom is merely wanking on a washing machine is something of a disappointment.

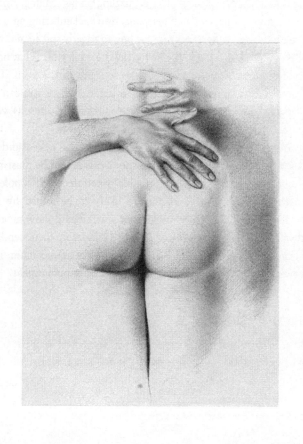

PICTURE CREDITS

Illustrations by the following artists appear on the pages listed: Steven Appleby (pp.151, 208); John Cramer (pp.11, 78, 154, 172); Don Grant (p.146); Monica Guevara (pp.108, 116–17, 158, 202); Michael Heath (p.107); Damien Hirst (p.126); David Holland (pp.12, 41, 73, 180, 187); Byron Humphrey (pp.28, 66, 129); Boris Johnson (p.134); Sylvie Jones (p.220-21); Tim Major (pp.4, 48); Tom Poulton (p.213); Martin Rowson (pp.52, 93, 164); Lynn Paula Russell (pp.3, 223); Mike Tingle (p.30); Vania Zouravliov (pp.45, 122); Henrietta Webb (p.119).

Our thanks to Julian Murphy for permission to reproduce his illustration *Web* as an endpaper (from *The Illustrated Art of Julian Murphy*, The Erotic Print Society).